SLOW BURN

ANDY HAYES MYSTERIES

by Andrew Welsh-Huggins

Fourth Down and Out

Slow Burn

Capitol Punishment (forthcoming)

SLOW BURN

AN ANDY HAYES MYSTERY

ANDREW WELSH-HUGGINS

SWALLOW PRESS
OHIO UNIVERSITY PRESS
ATHENS

Swallow Press
An imprint of Ohio University Press, Athens, Ohio 45701
ohioswallow.com

To obtain permission to quote, reprint, or otherwise reproduce or distribute
material from Swallow Press / Ohio University Press publications, please contact
our rights and permissions department at (740) 593-1154 or (740) 593-4536 (fax).

Printed in the United States of America
Swallow Press / Ohio University Press books are printed on acid-free paper ∞ ™

25 24 23 22 21 20 19 18 17 16 15   5 4 3 2 1

Library of Congress Cataloging-in-Publication Data

Welsh-Huggins, Andrew.
 Slow burn : an Andy Hayes mystery / by Andrew Welsh-Huggins.
    pages ; cm
 ISBN 978-0-8040-1160-0 (hc : alk. paper) — ISBN 978-0-8040-4064-8 (pdf)
 1. Private investigators—Ohio—Fiction. 2. Ex-football players—Fiction. 3.
Columbus (Ohio)—Fiction. I. Title.
 PS3623.E4824S58 2015
 813'.6—dc23
                          2015000890

My late in-laws, Pat and Tom Welsh, always had
books in their hands. Pat loved mysteries, while
Tom's thing was nonfiction, usually history or
geography. Sometimes they found a title they agreed
on and read aloud to one another. As readers, but
more importantly, as a second set of parents, they
always supported this writer. I wish they could have
met Andy Hayes, but their spirits are in these pages.
This book is dedicated to them.

What is reconstructed has a lot to do with what was destroyed. The shallower and smaller the wound, the simpler the process and the more quickly it is accomplished. The deeper and larger the wound, the more likely it is to require surgical intervention.

—Barbara Ravage, *Burn Unit:*
Saving Lives after the Flames

Wretched man, what becomes of me now, at last?

—Odysseus, in Homer's *Odyssey*

Prologue

Collapsed, knees buckled, hands on the ground, I had a dim memory of striking a similar pose decades ago, more than once, brought low on the playing field. I felt a lot lower now. Behind us, pops and snaps intensified as the fire began to spread. Both of us stank of smoke. I could hear sirens, but far off. I tried not to look at what was left of the man in the next yard over, the pant of his moans like someone laughing as he's being strangled. I tried not to think about the other man, the one collapsed on the porch steps. I knew I should try to stand up. I was just so tired, and I hurt so much.

Lying on the grass in front of me, Helen said something, indistinct.

"It's OK," I said. But was it, after everything that had happened?

I looked around me. People were emerging onto porches on either side of the house, roused by the commotion. I saw a young man on his cell phone in the next yard over. Next to him another young man—all students in this neighborhood— staring at the flames visible through the windows of the house. Behind him stood a couple, boy and girl, clutching each other, him in T-shirt and shorts, her wrapped in a scarlet-and-gray quilted Ohio State comforter.

"Water?" I said.

The spectators looked at each other. No one moved. I meant the stuff from a bottle, not a hydrant, but it didn't really matter. We were alive, and help was on its way.

"I called 911," offered the boy on the cell phone.

Helen spoke again, her voice low and raspy. I caught a single word: "Upstairs."

I gulped air, trying to expunge the acrid stink from my nostrils and mouth and throat. I fought off fogginess. I thought about what had led me to the house a few minutes earlier, or more to the point, what had nearly kept me from coming at all. I looked again at Helen, assuring myself she was OK.

Someone handed me a bottle of pop. I splashed some into my mouth, swirled it and spat. I lifted Helen's head and tried to give her a sip. She pushed it away and started to cry.

I sat back in the grass in what passed for a yard in that part of Columbus and tried to think. There was going to be a lot of explaining to do when authorities arrived, and I wasn't quite sure where to start. I turned and looked at the house and the flames inside and shook my head. We had been lucky. Very lucky.

I caught the word again, from Helen, through her sobs. *"Upstairs."*

"What about it?" I asked.

"Lori," she said, struggling to get up. "She's upstairs. Came home after all."

I looked at the house, saw the flames in the living room, the smoke pouring from open windows. Listened for the sirens, definitely close, but still a few blocks off. Thought about the speed at which fire sweeps through buildings. Four minutes from ignition to flashover—isn't that what they said? I took another breath, tried to stand up, swayed, nearly collapsed, swore, then tried again, and a third time, until I was up.

I glanced around, mind working slowly, too slowly, then settled on the girl wrapped in the comforter. It would have to do. I limped toward her, grabbed a corner and pulled. She gave a shriek as it fell away. As I turned and stumbled toward the burning house, I caught a glimpse of her sprinting in the opposite direction wearing exactly the same amount of clothes she'd had on the day she was born.

"Sorry," I mumbled, wrapping the blanket around my shoulders and head.

I made it up the concrete porch stairs, glanced briefly at the man lying to the side, out of harm's way for now, pushed open the door, and barged back into the maelstrom. Smoke alarms were screeching, the front hall was filled with smoke, and the flames had gone straight up the stairs to the second floor, pulled like fire up a chimney, blocking that approach.

"Lori!" I called.

No answer.

I stepped farther in, into the living room to the left. It was an old house, with building materials less apt to burn quickly, but filled with polypropylene-infused furniture and appliances and clothes, perfect fuel for modern fires. A draw, but a deadly one. Even in the few minutes since the blaze had begun, the flames had grown immeasurably. I didn't have much time left. I had to get upstairs.

What was the lawyer's expression for me? Indefatigable asshole? Time to prove it once more.

Except this time, I thought, as I crouched to avoid the cloud of heated gas and smoke rapidly forming overhead, my stick-to-it-iveness might be fatal.

1

"SAY THAT AGAIN?"

"You heard me correctly," the woman said.

It had all begun three weeks earlier on a Thursday morning, nearing mid-April. Anne and I were working our way north along the Olentangy River exercise trail. She was looking smart in black shorts and a green jogging top, with her mane of red hair wrestled into a bouncing ponytail as she ran at a comfortable training pace for the upcoming Discovering Columbus Half Marathon. I was riding beside her on my twelve-year-old mountain bike, trying to look smart in a pair of faded gray workout shorts and an Otterbein College sweatshirt with at least two holes in it, admiring the fact she was training for a half marathon. The day was going well. Only one person had apparently recognized me, a woman riding a beater bike in the opposite direction, and her insult, "*Shameful*," was so quiet and she was past us so quickly I was pretty sure Anne hadn't heard.

"What are you thinking?" she said as we negotiated the downhill by Third Avenue and were rewarded with the sight of a heron wading in shoals not twenty feet away.

"What a beautiful day," I said.

"Anything else?"

"What a beautiful day to be working out with my favorite college professor?"

"Better," she said.

"Only better?"

"It's like I tell my students. You're not trying hard enough."

"What a beautiful day to be thinking impure thoughts about my favorite college professor, with clouds overhead like shredded cotton balls?"

"I'd go with torn skeins of fresh-washed wool," she said. "But not bad."

Anne did her long runs with a group of girlfriends on Saturdays, which had led me to privately dub our Thursday outings the "lunkhead" run, since I knew next to nothing about training for a half marathon and the only way I could keep up with her was on a bike. I tried not to let the fact that she was free on a Thursday morning because her classes didn't begin until later bother me, given that I was free on a Thursday morning because I was, well, between jobs.

Which is why, when the opening notes of "Small Town" by John Mellencamp sounded from my fanny pack, I didn't hesitate to reach down and extract the cell phone. Between jobs was between jobs.

"Mr. Hayes?"

"Yes."

"You're the private detective?"

"That's right."

"My name is Dorothy Custer. I'd like to talk about hiring you."

"I'd like that too," I said. "For what?"

"My grandson."

"What about him?"
"I need help clearing his name."
"What did he do?"
"He's in prison for murdering three people."
"Say that again?"

2

DOROTHY CUSTER LIVED IN A BEIGE DUTCH Colonial off North Broadway in Clintonville, an old city neighborhood north of campus so comfortable and also so occasionally full of itself it had threatened secession from Columbus proper more than once. Her house had a slightly sloping lawn, a two-car garage, and a redbud tree in the front yard that was just beginning to glow with color.

"Thank you for coming," she said when she opened the door a few hours after her call. She wore tan slacks, a cream blouse, and a thin brown sweater. Her earrings were silver and tasteful and hinted at wealth without shouting it. Hair, short and white. Reading glasses around her neck. I put her in her midseventies.

She led me into her living room, where a carafe of coffee along with cups, cream, and sugar awaited us on a glass-topped table.

"You're Frank Custer's widow," I said after I'd seated myself in a chair opposite the table.

"That's right."

"I'm a fan," I explained. "*Old Hickory and Young America.* One of my favorite books. I put it together after you called."

"You're a detective, of course."

"Didn't take much detecting. You're in the acknowledgments."

She smiled. "Touché."

Old Hickory and Young America: Andrew Jackson and the Bloody Battle for a New Presidency. A best-selling biography a few years back by Dorothy's husband, an Ohio State history professor. Among other things, he had explored Jackson's somewhat complicated relationship with his children, including two adopted Indian sons and several wards, in deep psychological detail. As the father of two sons, neither of whom is in my custody, I'd paid more than the usual attention.

"Optioned for a movie, if I'm not mistaken?" I said.

"Optioned being the right word. It's a slow process."

"Hope it happens," I said. "Great book."

"Thank you," she said, a little stiffly. "That would have pleased Frank. He was an admirer of yours. At least, before your difficulties."

"That's true of a lot of people in town."

"People make mistakes," she said. "I tried to tell him that."

"I'm sorry I didn't make the connection when you called," I said. "About Frank."

"No apology needed. The world's full of Custers."

"Any relation to George?"

"Distantly, in fact. Enough of a family curiosity to inspire a career as a history professor. Though not of Native American history." A smile. Old joke, no doubt. "Cream or sugar?"

"Black," I said.

When I'd been served, I said, "You mentioned your grandson on the phone."

"Yes," she said. "Aaron."

"Aaron Custer."

"You're familiar with him."

"Yes."

"Tell me what you know."

I sat back in the chair and sipped the coffee.

I said, "He set fire to an off-campus house eighteen months ago. Three people died, and a fourth, a boy, I think, was badly injured."

"A girl, actually. Helen Chen. I hear she's back on campus finally. Thank God. Go on."

"There'd been a party at the house earlier in the evening. One of the students' birthdays."

She nodded. "Matt Cummings."

"Aaron showed up, drunk, unwelcome, and was eventually kicked out."

"That's correct."

"As he left, he shouted something at people on the porch. Something threatening."

"He said, 'I'll fucking kill you fucking bastards if it's the last fucking thing I ever do,'" Dorothy said, as matter-of-factly as if she were reading potluck items off a church bulletin.

"OK, then," I said. "He came back a few hours later, middle of the night, with a milk jug of gasoline and a lighter. Both found on the lawn. There was a usable print on the lighter, which led police to Aaron, since he'd been arrested before."

"Correct again."

"Arrested for setting a fire, in fact."

"Yes."

"There was also security camera footage from a gas station on High Street showing him filling the jug earlier that night. Between the time he left the party and the time of the fire."

"Yes."

"He was found nearby, badly injured."

"That's right. Someone had beaten him up."

"Like he'd gotten in a fight afterward," I said.

"The conclusion was he got in a fight as he ran away. Or was mugged. Or maybe was chased down by someone who supposedly saw him light the fire."

"Odd coincidence."

"The street where the fire happened is on the edge of a pretty tough neighborhood."

"They never found out what happened."

"No."

"He confessed almost immediately, after he recovered," I said.

"That's right."

"Between the video, the threat, the fingerprint, and his own criminal history, it was an ironclad case."

Dorothy nodded.

I said, "He was headed to trial, but pleaded guilty at the last minute. To avoid the death penalty."

"Almost."

"Meaning?"

"Officially, he pleaded guilty at the last minute. Unofficially, he wanted to plead guilty all along."

"Why?"

"He was certain he did it. Still is."

"But if he's certain . . . ," I said.

"He's certain because he has no memory of that night. Confronted with the evidence, he drew the same conclusion any rational person would."

"No memory?"

"He's an alcoholic, on top of all his other problems. Like his father, my son, I might add. Like his father *was*. You're familiar with blackout drinking?"

"Yes," I said. "I am."

"Between being dead drunk that night and the beating he took, it's a complete blank."

"He's assuming he did it."

"That's right."

I said, "I never understood why prosecutors went for the plea. Given the evidence."

"Pressure from the families to end it quickly. Can you blame them? The trauma of reliving everything. The certainty of endless appeals since it was a capital case. I don't know if 'satisfied' is the right word, but they were willing to accept life with no chance of parole."

"Which is what he got."

"Yes."

"Where's he housed?"

"Mansfield Correctional."

"All well and good," I said. "So why am I here?"

"Because of Eddie Miller," Dorothy said. "And a baseball cap."

3

SHE LIFTED A THICK MANILA FOLDER OFF
the coffee table, opened it, and handed me the sheet of
paper on top. It was a photocopy of a short Associated Press
article printed off the Internet. "Ohio prison inmate hangs
self with sheet," the headline said. The story was only a few
paragraphs. The subject was the man she'd just mentioned.
He'd been found in his cell a week earlier. At Mansfield, I
noted. Two months into a fifteen-year sentence for bank
robbery.

"OK," I said, handing her back the paper.

"Miller arrived at Mansfield about a month ago," Dorothy
said. "After he'd been processed. Aaron explained that part to
me. It's not like in the movies, where you just go to prison.
There are evaluations first."

"That's right," I said.

After a moment, she said, "Of course you would know
that. I'm sorry."

"Don't worry," I said. "A lot of it actually is like the movies."

"Well," she said, flustered.

"Please continue," I said, flashing back to several of the least favorite months of my life.

She said, "Lots of inmates know Aaron, or know who he is, because of the fire. Such a prominent case. But Miller was different."

"How?"

"He sought Aaron out right away. Wanted to talk to him."

"About what?"

"He told Aaron there was a witness that night, someone nobody knew about. Someone who could vouch for the fact that Aaron didn't do it."

"Who?"

"He wouldn't say. Said he knew somebody who knew somebody who'd seen what really happened. He wanted money for the name."

"How much?"

"Fifty thousand dollars."

"Lot of money."

"Indeed."

"For thirdhand information," I said.

"That's where the baseball cap comes in," she said. "It was an antique, from the Columbus Red Birds. An old minor league team in town, back in the forties and fifties."

"I've heard of them," I said. "Before the Columbus Jets."

"The hat belonged to Frank. Aaron inherited it when he died. It was the one thing he asked for after the funeral."

"When was that?"

"Four years ago. Frank was in a car accident. He was terribly injured. He lingered for several months. He died at home, where we'd been caring for him."

"We?"

"Mike, our son. Aaron's father. But mainly the home health aides."

"I see."

"Aaron and Frank were close," she said. "They used to go to Clippers games when Aaron was younger." The city's current minor league team, successor to the Red Birds and Jets.

"Frank had his own nickname for Aaron," Dorothy said. "*Boss.* Called him that from the day he was born. *'Hey, boss.'* Aaron used to run up to him. *'Hey, Grandpa. The boss is here.'* "

I nodded. "So he had the cap."

"That's right. And the point is, he was wearing it that night. After he came back to the house with the gasoline. At least that's what Miller said. Said the witness had seen Aaron wearing the cap. It was Miller's way of proving his information was legitimate."

"The witness saw Aaron at the house with the gasoline? Doesn't that just clinch it?"

"Miller told Aaron the witness saw him get cold feet at the last second. But that somebody else was there, and that person set the fire."

"Does Aaron remember wearing the cap?"

She shook her head. "But the fact Miller knew about the cap got his attention. Our attention. How could he know that otherwise?"

"Where was Miller from?" I said.

"Columbus."

"Could he have seen Aaron wearing it somehow? Before he went in?"

"I don't think so," she said. "Aaron hadn't worn it in a while."

"Miller have a motive for this mystery arsonist? Why he supposedly set a fire that killed three people?"

"Not that I know of."

I thought of something else. "Wouldn't everyone else at the party also have seen the cap?"

"He didn't wear it there. He put it on afterward. Or at least, that's what he surmises." She paused. "He only wore it on special occasions."

"Like burning down a house."

"Like thinking about burning down a house," Dorothy said. "What made Miller think Aaron had that kind of money?"

"Aaron has a big mouth and a rich grandmother."

Of course. *Old Hickory and Young America.*

I said, "What did Miller propose doing with fifty thousand dollars in prison?"

"He didn't say. Just told Aaron that was the deal."

"When did you find out about this?"

"About three weeks ago. I had driven up for a visit. Aaron didn't want to put anything in writing or say it on the phone."

"Smart."

"After that, I contacted Aaron's attorney. The one who handled his plea."

"What'd he say?"

"She. She wouldn't touch it. She said the same thing you did, that thirdhand was worse than no information at all. And even if the tip was usable, which she says it's not, the payment made it a nonstarter. She called it borderline extortion."

"What'd she say about the cap?"

"That it was intriguing, but inconclusive. Plus, it meant someone had positively identified Aaron at the scene of the fire. Clinched it, like you said."

"Who's the lawyer?"

"Karen Feinberg."

"I know her. She's good. If she won't try to reopen it . . ."

"Then Aaron's spending the rest of his life in prison," Dorothy said.

I didn't respond. I leaned back, taking another sip of coffee. Thought of what else I knew about the case. The street where it happened, Orton Avenue, was lined with off-campus rentals, many of them century-old brick houses that had once been single-family residences but were now chopped up into five or more bedroom-sized apartments apiece. Cash cows for landlords sopping up the gravy from Ohio State students. They were pits, a lot of them, though not necessarily firetraps, since it would be a foolhardy rental company that risked its investment literally going up in smoke. That hadn't stopped a civil lawsuit against the company that owned the house, alleging that more working smoke alarms could have saved lives.

I said, "Pretty suspicious that Miller committed suicide right after telling Aaron about the witness."

"Obviously."

"Have you talked to Aaron since?"

"Not in person. There's a prison e-mail system you can use. Faster than letters. We traded a few messages. He says Miller had gotten some bad news earlier in the day. Something about his sister."

"People do commit suicide," I said. "Especially in prison. Especially after getting bad news."

"Yes, they do," she said. "That's what makes this even harder."

"In what way?"

"Aaron's father, Mike. Frank's and my son," she said. "He also committed suicide."

I sat quiet for a moment, feeling stupid. I should have known this.

"When?" I said.

"Just a few weeks before Frank died. He turned the car on in the garage and rolled down the window."

"I'm sorry."

"I hate that response. But thank you anyway."

"What happened," I said. "If I may ask?"

"He'd hit rock bottom. His latest business had gone under. A food truck he started with a friend. 'Olen-Tangy Tots.' Variations on tater tots—tots with barbecue sauce, salsa, cheese."

"Clever," I said. The Olentangy River—the Old and Dingy—ran through the heart of Columbus and bordered Clintonville on the west. The same river Anne and I had been exercising next to a few hours earlier.

"Not clever enough to keep him from losing everything. Mike never had a head for the business side, and his partner was skimming from the till. And all this as he and Molly, Aaron's mother, were divorcing. And the drinking. He killed himself the day after the bank took the truck."

"And this was right before your husband died?"

"That's right."

"So Aaron lost his father and grandfather back to back."

"Yes."

"Why did Aaron's parents split up?"

"It's complicated," Dorothy said.

I nodded and decided to leave it at that. I was familiar with complicated divorces.

I said, "Aaron's problems began after that?"

"That's right. Drugs, alcohol, running with the wrong crowd. Hard to blame him, in hindsight."

"The fires? They started then too?"

"Yes."

"Houses?"

She shook her head. "Dumpsters, woodpiles, that sort of thing."

"Classic cry for help."

"You could call it that."

"He was arrested."

"He set a fire near campus. Trash bin in Pearl Alley. Police saw him running from the scene. He wasn't quite eighteen, so he ended up with court-ordered counseling and a year's probation."

"Did it help?"

"He pulled himself together, got his GED, and started taking classes at Columbus State. Talked about transferring to OSU."

"But."

"The drinking got worse. He dropped out of school. Started setting fires again." She paused. "Then came Orton Avenue. You know the rest."

I sat back in my chair. Looked at the wall of bookshelves behind her, crowded with thick volumes. I said, "So what would you like me to do?"

"This Eddie Miller," she said. "His suicide doesn't change the fact there's a witness who could exonerate Aaron."

"If he exists."

"If," she acknowledged.

"And if he does, you'd like me to find him."

"That's right."

"Aaron willing to talk to me?"

"Of course," she said. "Just keep in mind he doesn't re-member anything about that night."

"Aaron's mother."

"Molly."

"She know about Eddie Miller?"

"Aaron told her."

"She's on board with this assignment?"

"As far as I know. But just to be clear, this is not a family job, if I may put it that way. You'd be working for me."

"I would have expected her to be here today," I said. "Talk-ing about this."

"Molly keeps her own counsel," Dorothy said. "She knows I called you."

"It's a bit of a wild goose chase," I said.

"I'm aware of that."

"Miller's suicide suggests he wasn't entirely stable. Which suggests he might have been trying to scam Aaron."

"I'm aware of that too," she said. "Frankly, that's true whether he killed himself or not. The whole thing sounds fan-tastic, and you could be excused for chalking it up to the des-perate fantasies of an old woman. Except for one thing."

I thought for a moment. "The cap," I said.

"That's right," Dorothy said. "Without the Columbus Red Birds cap, we're not having this conversation."

I didn't respond. I'd had clients before with desperate fantasies. Dorothy wasn't even close. She seemed to know what she was asking, up to and including her insistence on being the one calling the shots. I wouldn't have a problem taking her money, especially since, by the looks of her well-appointed home, there was no shortage of it. It was more the nature of the job itself. Reopening the Orton Avenue fire would not be easy. The only thing people in Columbus had wanted more than Aaron's hide nailed to the wall of the criminal justice system was closure; shutting the book on a horrible episode that was the nightmare of every parent who'd ever sent a kid to college. My sniffing around would be the rough equivalent of informing the people in Sandy Hook that the shooter who'd killed twenty first-graders hadn't acted alone after all. That the whole morass of pain and agony had to be revisited. Again.

Which in a way made my decision to take the job easy enough.

When you have as many detractors as I do, what's a few thousand more?

4

DESPITE MY DECISION, I WAS MORE THAN
a little troubled as I walked out of Dorothy Custer's house.
The jobs I get rarely come neatly wrapped with bows on top.
But this was like an empty box with a blank card inside. Aaron
Custer had all the hallmarks of a troubled kid who made a
tragic decision. The fact that Karen Feinberg had declined to
reopen the case spoke volumes. The business with the Red
Birds cap was intriguing but hardly airtight. The late Eddie
Miller could have easily elicited a description of the cap somehow, then turned it around on Aaron to make him believe he
was innocent. Dime-store psychics did it all the time. Why not
conniving inmates?

I got in my Honda Odyssey and backed out carefully
onto North Broadway. I turned east, drove up to Indianola,
and went left at the light. Two minutes later I was parking in Indianola Plaza, and a minute after that was walking
into Weiland's Market. I grabbed a grocery cart, asked an
employee for directions, then a moment later scooped up
three containers of Weiland's Own Smoked Rainbow Trout

Spread, a favorite of Anne's. I picked up packages of the store's original brats and cheddar brats and more spreads, and spent a little time ogling the fresh fish lying on ice under the watchful eye of a full-sized model of a swordfish hanging overhead. I perused the meat, and in particular a special on pork roasts, but restrained myself. Getting soft in my old age. I completed my trip with two jars of Frog Ranch salsa made down in Athens, two bags of Crimson Cup coffee, and a couple bottles of red wine.

As I loaded the groceries into the back of the van, I reflected on the fact I had just spent three or four times what I should have, since my real object had been just the spread. Truthfully, the night Anne brought it, I had liked it OK at best. But the purchase was less about the product itself than trying to do something nice for her. I had not been in the habit of doing nice things for the women I'd been with in the past, unless you counted spending money I didn't have on drinks and expensive meals in exchange for nights at their houses, where more times than not I didn't behave well and left the toilet seat up to boot. It was going to be different with Anne.

At least that's what I had told myself every day for the last four and a half months.

I AWOKE EARLY THE next morning, frisky with the knowledge I had a job, however fleeting Aaron's case turned out to be. I'd fallen asleep reading *World War Z*, a zombie apocalypse novel I'd picked up for the same reason I'd purchased the smoked trout spread: to connect with Anne, who was teaching the book in her science fiction class at Columbus State Community College. The things we do for love, considering my tastes run more to biographies like Frank Custer's book about Jackson. I placed the novel on the night stand, sat up, thumped Hopalong, lying beside me with an expectant twitch to his nose, then got out of bed.

A few minutes later, shaved and waking up after my first cup of coffee, I led the dog out the back door and waited while he watered a patch of daffodils that had sprung up randomly in the yard this spring. Hopalong had had a debilitating encounter with a shard of glass in the park more than two months ago, and thanks to a secondary infection followed by a cold and blustery March we had not been up to our usual neighborhood walks, let alone jogs. "Hobble-along," the vet dubbed him with a smile. She thought he'd be up to speed in another couple weeks. She hadn't commented on my own need to start exercising again, though I could have sworn at our last appointment I caught her frowning at the hint of a spare tire the winter's inactivity had won me. I looked guiltily at my running shoes when Hopalong came back inside. Then I looked at the time and made a solemn promise to go out in the afternoon instead.

I was settled at my kitchen table with my laptop, looking up stories about the Orton Avenue fire, when Roy called.

"What are you doing tomorrow night?" he demanded.

"Polishing cutlery," I said. "The dishwasher keeps leaving little specks."

"Why I eat off plastic. Lucy and I are going on an expedition. Care to join us?"

"Where?"

"Downtown bike trail. North of the railroad tracks, east of the moon. Kind of hard to describe."

"You're going at night?"

"We've had trouble finding folks this spring. Figured we'd try some one-stop shopping."

I thought about it for a second. "OK if I bring Anne?"

"A date in the woods? How romantic."

"Just a thought."

"She'll have to sign a waiver."

"Guessing she can manage that. If she comes."

"Why wouldn't she?"

"I don't know what she'll think of the idea."

"Haven't you been jogging on the bike trail with her?"

I confessed that I had.

"This is just jogging with drugs and flashlights. Tell her that."

"I'll be sure to do so," I said.

AFTER I HUNG UP I skimmed some of my Internet search results, then started jotting down ideas on a yellow legal pad. Aaron Custer would be one of my first interviews, assuming his grandmother was telling the truth about his willingness to talk. I'd try his mom as well, despite the family tension I'd picked up from Dorothy. I'd pull whatever records were available from the case and talk to the arson squad and the cops, if they'd agree. Which I had my doubts about. Next would come relatives of those killed, the prospect of which didn't thrill me. I could imagine their reaction to hearing what I was up to. And of course, the girl who survived. Helen? Another easy interview.

But the longer I sat and tapped the point of my pen on the yellow lined paper, the more I realized the hardest interview of all had to come first. And I would have done anything, including a full confession of my past sins in front of the marching band entrance on the north side of Ohio Stadium, in exchange for a pass.

But not this time, I thought. Dorothy had handed me the obligation I'd spent years trying to avoid. Time to face the music.

5

JUST BEFORE 5:30 THAT AFTERNOON, WEARING
a blue button-down shirt, a tie so old I couldn't remember which
ex-wife gave it to me, a navy sport coat, and a pair of khakis that
had somehow shrunk a size or two over the winter, I left my
house, walked a few blocks north up Mohawk to Beck, took a
breath, then stepped beneath the lighted glass overhang outside
Lindey's, pulled open the heavy wooden door, and went inside.
I smiled at the inquiring hostess and gestured toward the bar
on the left. Two guys with drinks in their hands took their eyes
off the women they were with long enough for a double take. I
ignored them. I kept my eyes on the object of my pursuit, cur-
rently sitting at the end of the bar next to a brass railing. Where
she sat almost every Friday after work, as I well knew. I began
the long walk in her direction. There had been walls of fire-
breathing three-hundred-pound linemen I'd feared less.

Her back was turned to me as she chatted with a man seated
beside her. As I stopped I realized she hadn't seen me approach,
that there was still time to back out. I thought about it in earnest.
Then I took another breath and tapped her on the shoulder.

As she turned and recognized me, her eyes went wide, just for a moment. My stomach flipped. Those big, beautiful blue eyes. Shock flickered across her face, as palpable as if I'd reached out and slapped her. She blinked twice. Then, just as quickly, the look of surprise disappeared. It was what she did, after all. She reacted to the unexpected with composure. Once upon a time I had done the same thing, only with a football in my hand instead of a microphone. It might have been what brought us together.

Definitely not what drove us apart.

I didn't expect what came next. A real slap, her hand across my cheek, would not have been undeserved. Instead, she smiled and shifted in her chair so her back was to the copper-topped bar and both the man on her left and I were looking at her.

"Speaking of someone I wasn't expecting to see in a thousand years," she said.

"Hello, Suzanne," I said.

"Hello, Andy."

"Mind if I join you?"

"Of course not."

After I pulled up beside her on her right, she leaned back and gestured to her companion. A few years older than me, dark hair flecked with gray, a full face but not fat, blue sport coat and white shirt, no tie. His expression was neutral bordering on hostile. I knew right away he knew who I was.

"Andy, this is Glen Murphy," Suzanne said.

I nodded as I shook his hand. Grip firm but not hardy.

"Glen, this is Andy Hayes. As you probably know, he's the world's biggest asshole."

AS IF ON CUE, the bartender materialized. I ordered a Great Lakes. I looked at Suzanne and after a moment she nodded. She wasn't smiling any more.

"Martini," I said. "Tanqueray, two olives, very, very dirty."

"You remembered," Suzanne said. "How sweet."

I looked at Murphy. "I'm good," he said, after a moment too long.

"Don't be ridiculous," Suzanne said. "He'll have another Lagavulin. But make it a double."

"Excuse me," Murphy said. "I think I'll check on our reservations."

He slid off the stool and without meeting my gaze walked along the bar to the front of the restaurant. I followed his progress, then turned back to Suzanne. She was wearing a French blue sleeveless dress with a hint of cleavage—as much as I knew her station would let her get away with—gold earrings, and a paste pearl necklace that accentuated possibly the world's prettiest neck. Her honey-colored hair looked as perfect as if she'd stepped out of her condo five minutes ago, not spent the day traipsing around Columbus with a videographer in tow.

"You look great," I offered.

"You fucking turd," she said. "What are you doing here?"

It was a good question. And there was no going back now. Not after a double of Lagavulin I knew I was paying for.

"I need a favor."

"A favor?"

"That's right."

"You've got to be kidding me."

"Afraid not," I said.

"What kind of favor?"

"Aaron Custer," I said.

"What about him."

"I need some information about his case."

"He killed three innocent college kids and almost crippled a fourth. What else is there to know?"

"I was hoping I could pick your brain. Ask you some questions."

27

"Why?"

I told her about my assignment.

"And you want to talk to me why?"

"Because you owned the story."

"Goddamn right I did. But how would you know that?"

"I kept up on the coverage."

"You watched my reports."

I nodded.

"And that's supposed to impress me?"

"You always own your stories," I continued. "The heroin pieces you've been doing. All the overdoses. The Mexican connection. It's good stuff."

"Suck up all you want. It doesn't change anything."

"Why I figured I'd come to you first," I persisted. "You know the most."

"Really? No other reason?"

For just a moment her blue eyes had gotten shiny. She turned away. When she swiveled back her eyes were dry and she looked furious. A few years ago, Suzanne had continued broadcasting live without breaking a sweat as gunfire broke out at the Poindexter Village public housing complex on the near east side. She was not used to losing control.

"*Of all the gin joints in all the towns in all the world,*" she said.

I said nothing.

Our drinks arrived. The bartender looked for Murphy. I jerked my thumb toward the entrance, where Murphy had taken a seat at the far end of the bar. I laid two twenties and a ten down on the counter and shook my head when he asked if I needed change.

"A witness," Suzanne said a moment later. "Someone who saw what happened."

"What the grandmother says."

"You believe her?"

"For now."

"Because she's paying you."

"How this works."

"Why don't you call Kevin Harding at the *Dispatch?* Isn't he your special friend? I recall seeing him every time I turned around on that story."

"Kevin's a good source," I said. "But that's the point."

"What is?"

"You saw him every time you turned around. Because you got places first. Talked to people first. Got the documents first. And I believe you've got an Emmy and a Murrow to prove it."

That earned me a twitch and possibly a fractional diminishing of her anger.

But then she said, "Of course, if the grandmother's story is true, then I didn't own the story. I got it totally wrong."

"You owned the aftermath and the families and the plea deal and the lawsuit and everything. This doesn't change any of that."

"The fact Custer might be innocent doesn't change anything? Have you traded down from Black Label to crack cocaine? It changes *everything.*"

"Might be innocent. I'm not saying he is."

"Which didn't stop you from taking the job."

"You stop reporting every story that seems like a long shot?"

"Go to hell," she said.

"I'm in the same boat. I don't know right from wrong on this one. So I came to the one person who knows the most about the case in the city."

"I'm tempted to say that's about as sincere a statement as Charles Manson bringing flowers to Sharon Tate's gravesite."

"I deserved that," I said. "But I'm still asking. It's all I can do."

"Fire department knows as much as I do," she said. "Cops too."

"Bullshit," I said. "They turned on the TV to find out what they needed to know. Just like everybody else."

Suzanne reached out and took a sip of her martini. I followed suit with my beer.

She said, "You remember the last time we were together?"

"I do."

"You have anything to say to me?"

"I don't."

"No apology?"

"Would it matter?"

"Probably not."

We left it at that. Sipped our drinks. Out of the corner of my eye I could see Murphy at the other end of the bar watching us.

Suzanne said, "So you just walk in here after all this time and ask for the stupidest goddamn favor possible and don't apologize or even attempt to deal with the past. Is that it?"

"That's about right," I said. "I wish I could say something meaningful. Wish I could do something that would set things straight. But I know how I was and I know how it is. So all I can do is tell my pale ale here, and anybody else who might be listening, that I'm not quite the person I used to be, though I remember him well. And my semi-new self doesn't know any other way to manage things but head on."

"What a pretty speech."

"With the benefit of being true."

"I didn't date for three years after you. Did you know that?"

I studied my beer.

"When I tried again I was damaged goods. 'Didn't you used to go out with Woody Hayes?'"

I kept studying.

"Glen's the first man who's stayed with me longer than a month. Though whether I've got another hour left with him is debatable, thanks to you."

"He seems nice," I lied. "What's he do?"

"Businessman."

"What kind of business?"

"The kind that makes money."

"Just asking."

"Oil and gas. Satisfied?"

"Fracking?"

"The old-fashioned kind. Still plenty of money in it. Even in Ohio."

"Drill, baby, drill," I said, then immediately regretted it.

"Asshole," she said.

"Sorry. That was unwarranted."

"So thanks to you," she continued, "I'm still dating at thirty-five when all my girlfriends are married and half have kids."

I looked up the bar at Murphy, then went back to my beer. I knew she was lying about her age, and she knew I knew it, and somehow it broke the tension just a bit.

"I'm sorry you're so angry," I said.

"I'm angry because you're such a shit."

"A recovering shit."

"Like that makes a difference."

"Some people think so."

She guessed right away. "You're seeing someone," she said.

"Starting to see someone."

"Isn't that nice."

"Thank you."

"I'm thinking 'Senior Zumba Instructor,'" she said. The title emphasized with air quotes. "Blonde with a rack?"

Like you should talk, I thought, but kept my mouth shut for a change. "She's a college professor. Our age."

"Our age," she said. "Nice touch. So what's the catch? Is she married?"

"Widowed."

This gave her pause, as I knew it would.

31

I took a drink of my beer. I said, quietly, "Can we get back to my favor?"

"Not yet," she said. "I'm just starting to enjoy myself. Do you have any nicknames for her, like you did with me? Let's see—is she more 'fat cow' or 'dumb cunt'?"

I shut my eyes. I'd known starting out this was probably a bad idea. It was dawning on me I hadn't anticipated just how bad.

I opened my eyes, looked up the bar. Took in the tall cabinet of wine bottles across from where Murphy sat.

I said, "We both know you're the expert on this story. We also know I didn't behave like a knight in shining armor when we were together." She guffawed, and not nicely. I continued: "And we also know there's nothing I can do to make up for the past short of giving you the exclusive while I commit hara-kiri live on TV. So why don't you just tell me the level of fawning you need and I'll provide it and then maybe we could reach an accord and I could get on with my questions."

"Hara-kiri," she said. "I like the sound of that."

I waited.

"What's in it for me?"

"I don't know. What do you want?"

"I want the exclusive story, obviously. If there is one, which I doubt."

"I can't promise that."

"Then fuck you."

"I can't promise an exclusive because I have to talk to a lot of people. And I can't promise they won't talk."

"That's a piss-poor offer."

"I don't make promises I can't keep. Not anymore."

"Woody Hayes, gentleman?" she snorted.

"Just Andy," I said. "It's Andy Hayes now."

I LEFT HER AND walked up to where Murphy sat, nursing his drink. Ignored the looks I got as I passed. I knew

I exaggerated the likelihood that a lot of people in town recognized me anymore. Memories of a twenty-year-old college football point-shaving scandal faded, even in this city. It was a tinge of paranoia that one of these days I had to get over. But this was different. I knew I was being watched.

I stopped in front of Murphy. He didn't turn to look at me.

"Sorry to interrupt your evening," I said.

"Thanks for the drink," he said after a moment.

"Is it as good as everybody says?"

"What?" he said, sharply.

"The Lagavulin. How is it?"

He relaxed. "It's good," he said. "Very good."

I was turning to go when he said, "Anything I should be worrying about?"

"Excuse me?"

"You and Suzanne. Anything I need to know?"

"Nope," I said. "You're all set."

"That's good. Because I don't need anything screwing this up. Including you."

"There's nothing—"

"Especially you," Murphy said.

6

WALKING HOME DOWN THE BRICK SIDEWALKS
of German Village, I considered the gulf between Suzanne and
me. Considered the irony that Lindey's was so close to my
house, just a few minutes' stroll, yet I hadn't seen Suzanne in
years now—by design. Considered the inadvisability of what
I'd just done. Considered Anne's and my planned movie date
later that night and where my sudden reluctance to keep it
was coming from.

After escorting the wounded Labrador into and out of the
backyard, I cooked three of the Weiland's brats on the small
gas grill I keep on the patio, an optimistic description of a
brick walk the size of a sandbox. While those cooked I boiled
water, added salt, then dumped in a box of pasta. I checked my
phone for updated headlines while I waited. State lawmakers
were debating bills to name a state Indian burial mound, to
honor the recent boys' and girls' state basketball champion-
ship teams, and to approve medical marijuana. Even I could
figure out which of the three was going to die a quick death in
committee. A few minutes later I sank into the couch with my

plate and my copy of *Old Hickory and Young America.* I looked
at the dust jacket and read Custer's biography. Looked at his
picture. He would have cast a long shadow, I thought, thinking of his son. His suicide. Best-selling author, legendary history professor. Ferocious tennis player well into his sixties, I
recalled. Very long shadow indeed. I opened the book, read the
first two chapters. I hadn't been mistaken. Great read.

After dinner I set the dishes in the sink, pulled out my
laptop, took it back to the couch, turned on the Blue Jack-
ets game, set the TV on mute, and started looking up stories
about the fire. I alternated between articles in the *Dispatch,*
which tended to be longer, and Suzanne's written versions for
the Web, which were shorter but usually contained a more telling quote or detail. I printed everything out, which was a lot,
highlighted relevant names, then settled in to learn as much as
I could about the Orton Avenue disaster.

Victim One: Tina Montgomery. Ohio State University junior. Twenty-one years old. From Columbus. Biology major.
Pretty brunette with a strong chin. Apartment house resident.
Found in her upstairs bedroom, cause of death smoke inhalation. Importantly, a friend of Aaron's from high school. Most
importantly, the girl Aaron had been arguing with before he'd
been given the bum's rush.

Victim Two: Matt Cummings. Also an Ohio State junior.
Twenty-two. From Coshocton, a small city in eastern Ohio.
Environmental geology major. Short-cropped dark hair. Traces
of acne, and teeth that could have used braces, but otherwise
a good-looking kid. Resident of the house, found on the floor
just outside his bedroom, also upstairs. It was his birthday the
party had nominally been in honor of. That and the OSU game
earlier that day. Most importantly, the guy who'd tossed Aaron.

Victim Three: Jacob Dunning. Also twenty-two. Also from
Columbus. Biochemistry major. Red hair, freckles, manic grin,
soul patch. Looked to be a good-natured joker. A visitor to the

party but not a resident. Found badly burned downstairs just inside the front door. Cause of death a combination of burns and smoke inhalation.

Survivor: Helen Chen. From Worthington, an old Columbus suburb just north of Clintonville. Another biology major. Pre-med. One of Matt's housemates. Hospitalized for weeks from her injuries, from what I could tell. Severe smoke inhalation. I saw something about a tracheotomy. It appeared she'd never been interviewed, by reporters or investigators. Too badly hurt.

From what I could tell, Suzanne had done reams of interviews with family members and other students who'd been at the party. It was from her I learned that things could have been worse, that six other people also lived in the house but had gone on a last-minute overnight trip to Cleveland to see, of all people, Neil Diamond. Suzanne even managed an interview with Lori Hume, Matt's girlfriend, who hadn't stayed the night because she was getting up early to cheer on a friend at a cross-country meet and wanted to be at her own apartment.

Anne called at 8:00, begging off our movie because Amelia wasn't feeling well. An edge to her voice that I knew full well stemmed from living with her parents, whose home she'd retreated to after the disaster with her husband. She had needed to get out for the night. I tried to console her with the expedition the next evening with Roy and Lucy. Yet when I hung up I realized my own disappointment at not seeing her was tempered with relief. I didn't feel as if I'd been unfaithful to her by seeking out Suzanne. Not much, anyway. But at the same time, it would be a hard one to explain.

I returned to the fire. I found a few more names. Chelsea. Eric. Bill. Genna. Emma. The names blurred. Grieving friends, lucky residents who'd been elsewhere, shocked classmates. The more I read, the more unsettled I became. Watching Suzanne's interviews and going over her stories left me feeling as if the case was more open-and-shut than ever. An emotionally scarred fuckup and convicted arsonist shows up dead drunk at a party where he's not welcome, argues with a girl in front of several witnesses, gets thrown out, and then screams his intention to kill everyone. A couple of hours later he's caught on convenience store security video filling a milk jug with gasoline, and that jug and a lighter with his print on it are found at the scene. The beating afterward strange, but not an indicator of innocence. I thought about Suzanne's accusation at the bar, that I believed Dorothy just enough to take her money.

Before bed I returned to the couch, picked up Frank Custer's book again, intending to reread another chapter or two. Welcome break from zombies. And that's when I noticed the dedication.

For Aaron.

7

AT 9:30 THE NEXT MORNING I WAS DRIVING up High Street through the heart of the campus district. Years earlier, the bar scene on these blocks had been so boisterous that ropes were stretched along the sidewalk to keep drunken students from falling into the road. A redevelopment project a few years back bulldozed the dives into oblivion, and the same stretch was now lined with chain restaurants and retail stores and office space. It was safe and bright and shiny. It also bore about as much resemblance to an authentic collegiate main drag as a new Applebee's to a greasy spoon.

I drove a few blocks farther north and was cheered by the sight of a couple independent pizza places and an actual head shop. After driving around for a little while I found a space at a two-hour meter on Seventeenth Avenue. I parked, walked up to High Street, and opened the door into Buckeye Donuts. It was one of the few times in my life I'd been there when the sun was actually up. I glanced at the painting on the wall to my right of my sort-of-namesake, former Ohio State football coach Woody Hayes, showing a young Woody and an old

Woody perched together at Ohio Stadium like mythical twin giants. I turned my attention to the girl behind the counter and ordered my usual—four doughnuts, with the fifth one free, all glazed—and added a cup of black coffee. I departed the shop, pulled the first doughnut out of the bag, took a bite, took a sip of coffee, then headed to the scene of the crime.

Orton Avenue was a short street of just a couple of blocks running north-south between Eighteenth and East Wood-ruff Avenues. The area was a maze of one-way streets built in horse-and-buggy days, now lined with cars there was really no room for. I could only imagine the difficulty of getting one fire truck up to a burning house quickly, let alone the several emergency vehicles the blaze had required.

The house where the fire happened sat on the east side of the street and, like all the houses in that neighborhood, was elevated above the sidewalk. You approached by a set of five stairs to the small lawn, and then up another set of stairs to the porch. I looked around. The cars across the street provided one possible place for my mystery witness to hide. A single tree with a sizable trunk grew out of the strip of grass between the street and the sidewalk a little farther down, another option. What caught my eye was a house across the street and catty-corner to the house that burned, where the slope of the lawn had been replaced by a retaining wall, above which grew thick, square ornamental bushes. I crossed the street, went up the stairs of that house, stepped to my right, and crouched down. Possible, I thought, peering through a gap in the leaves. Just possible.

I walked back across the street and returned my attention to the house in question. Red brick, two stories with a peaked roof and an attic. Two large windows upstairs with an attic window above those. Tall, narrow chimney, almost certainly not in use. Porch with a slanted roof supported by three red-brick pillars. The design repeated with minor architectural variations in houses up and down the street, all of them tired-looking and worn, like houses in a documentary about the recession. The only difference being that the other houses' windows weren't covered with plywood, nor did they have a ribbon of ancient yellow crime scene tape fluttering from the black railing along the steps coming up from the sidewalk. I walked up those steps, paused, then walked up to the house and up a couple of the steps to the porch. Here and there black crud still lined the concrete floor. I didn't go any closer. There was no way to get inside even if I'd wanted to. And nothing left to see.

I moved on to doughnut number two and went next door. I stood on the porch taking in a card table and white plastic patio chairs lying on their sides. A bike was visible through the window, parked in the living room. I knocked once, then twice. Then a third time. At last, a sleepy-looking boy in boxer shorts and nothing else answered my summons.

"Yeah," he said, shielding his eyes from the burning 10 a.m. sun.

"Sorry to bother you," I said. "Wondering if you lived here couple years ago. When the house next door burned."

"What?" he said.

"The house, next door," I said, gesturing. "Where the fire was. Three people died. Did you live here then?"

"Sorry," he said. "Do you know what time it is?"

"Yes."

"Pretty early," he said. "You know?"

"Sure," I said. "If you're a barred owl. Late night?"

"Had a party. *Big* party. Haven't been asleep long."

I looked around. I spied two red Solo cups on the lawn and a crumpled bag of chips.

"Inside?"

"What?"

"Was your party inside? Looks pretty undisturbed out here."

"It was *everywhere*," he said, gesturing. Then his face changed: "Are you a cop?"

"No," I said. "Just somebody wondering if you lived here back then."

"No," he said finally. "Was still in the dorms. Heard about it though."

"Good to keep up with the news. Anybody else live here then?"

He didn't say anything. I thought he was mulling the question until I realized he was falling asleep on his feet.

"Son," I said. "Any of your housemates living here then?"

"What?" he said, jerking awake. Then: "No. No one. We all moved in this year. Sure you're not a cop?"

"Positive," I said. "Go back to sleep."

I handed him my card, just in case, and left him standing in the door.

I had similar luck at the house on the other side, except this time a girl answered my knock. She was wearing torn Hello Kitty pajama pants and an Ohio State T-shirt and looked as if she might have gotten an hour more sleep than the first fellow. Like him, she'd only moved in this year. Also like him, she knew about the fire, but not much else. I left my card and walked on. The experience was the same up and down the street, and after three more houses I was about to give up. Finally, at a yellow-brick house near the end of the block, a glimmer of hope from a young woman whom I didn't appear to have dragged out of bed.

"I think this one girl was here then," she said.

"One girl?"

"She's a friend of a friend, sort of," she said.

"Know where she lives?"

"Not exactly."

"Name?"

"Can't remember. Different."

"Different."

"Different kind of name."

"Different how?"

"Just different."

"What did it sound like?" I said.

"Kind of different."

"Never mind."

My card safe in her hand, I went back to the van, retrieved my phone from my coat, finished my doughnuts and coffee while I checked for messages. Calls—none. E-mails—the usual thicket of nonessential messages that constitute my inbox. Reminders from Amazon, alerts from various news outlets I subscribe to, and coupon offers from pet stores.

Text messages. One. From Suzanne Gregory.

Chelsea Fowler. She might be willing to talk. Use my name. Burn me and I'll literally kill you.

A phone number followed a moment later.

Thanks! I texted in return.

I started the van, spent another minute looking for more messages, and was about to pull out when I heard a ping and saw she had replied. In a manner of speaking.

Don't ever contact me again.

8

ROY PULLED UP IN FRONT OF MY HOUSE THAT
night promptly at 7:00 in his old white van, the one that looked
as if it had done more time in Iraq than he had. "Church of the
Holy Apostolic Fire," the sign on the side read.

Anne and I lifted ourselves up off my front steps, walked
over, and got in. Roy was driving, with Lucy in the passenger seat.

"Thank you for the invitation," Anne said.

"Don't thank me until it's over," Roy said.

We drove north out of German Village, cut through downtown, then went west on Spring Street, past the state Bureau
of Workers' Compensation building, under the railroad tracks
by the Arena District, and past North Bank Pavilion along the
river. The downtown skyline glowed behind us. At Souder
Avenue we turned left, then left again into the parking lot at
Confluence Park. Instead of parking, Roy bumped the van
over the curb and drove down the bike path a few hundred feet.

"Is this legal?" I said.

"Engine's too loud," Roy said. "Can't hear you."

We pulled onto a flat patch of grass and unloaded ourselves. Night had fallen, but the sky was clear and the city center lights illuminated our surroundings. Lucy pulled a medical
bag out of the rear, and Roy hoisted a heavy-looking backpack.
I reached into the back and picked up a couple of canvas
folding chairs in red bags labeled "St. Clare."

"Ever been in a homeless camp?" Lucy said to Anne. Roy's
wife, a nurse, was two inches taller than him, hippy but strong-
looking, with short, spiked hair and dark cat's-eye glasses. She'd
traded her usual loose-fitting earth-toned blouse and dangling
earrings for a blue St. Clare's jacket and gold studs.

Anne shook her head.

"Never a good idea to come alone," she said. "They know
Roy and me pretty well."

"Is it dangerous?"

"Not exactly. But they're like anyone else. They don't like
strangers walking into their living room uninvited."

Roy hunted the edge of the woods for a minute with a
flashlight, found the gap he was looking for, then led the way
down a path into the trees. "St. Clare Medical team!" he called
as he walked.

A few moments later we entered a large clearing. Between
Roy's flashlight and the fire in a stone-lined pit I made out a series of tents and crude cabin-like structures scattered through
the trees. A pile of empty green camp-size propane bottles sat at
the edge of the woods, with several bikes next to them and next
to those, three empty shopping carts. A couple people looked up
from the fire, and then, slowly, as Roy announced the presence
of the team, more began to emerge from the tents and shacks
and what seemed like the shadows themselves. To a person they
shook Roy's hand and accepted hugs from Lucy. They looked
askance at Anne and eyed me with downright suspicion.

For the next hour we helped while Roy and Lucy con-
ducted a mini–medical clinic, checking blood pressure, taking

temperatures, treating cuts and scratches, handing out prescriptions and in some cases bottles of pills. Anne drifted off at some point, and a few minutes later I spied her across the camp by the light of the fire talking with a woman holding a baby. I spent most of my time handing Lucy bandages and tubes of salve and helping Roy distribute water bottles.

When we finished we tramped back up the trail, loaded everything back into the van, and then held our breath as Roy drove down and around places I didn't think were covered by any traffic codes, until at last we were back on Souder and headed into downtown. Anne took my hand. I turned to her and saw that her eyes were shining.

"All right back there?" Roy said.

"You sure know how to show a girl a good time," I replied.

A few minutes later we parked the van on High Street in the Short North, and not long after that we were in the Surly Girl Saloon toasting the night's expedition with pints of a local IPA.

"I just can't get over that mom with her baby," Anne said. "She grew up in the suburbs. Had an apartment and a job a year ago."

"Things can change quickly," Lucy said. "We see it all the time."

"Her problem is lack of a safety net," Roy added. "But her mental health is good. It's the ones with issues upstairs that get complicated. They need so much."

"Sam wasn't there," Lucy said. "You notice that?"

"What we're talking about," Roy explained. "Lady who's kind of in and out. On her meds, OK. Off, not so much."

"You think she's all right?" Anne said.

"Probably," Roy said. "She tends to wander. But that's the problem with living on the street. So unpredictable."

Anne said, "What will happen to her? To the lady with the baby."

"She's at the top of the list for housing," Lucy said. "Sort of thing ROOF is there for."

"ROOF?" Anne said.

"Raising Optional Opportunities Foundation," Roy said, eyeing his wife. "Helps with transitional housing. They provide some of the funding for expeditions like this."

"Rings a bell now," Anne said. "One of the people I teach with volunteers at a shelter. He's mentioned it. Don't they do this big fundraiser?"

"Yes," Roy said.

"It sounds like a good thing," Anne said, turning to me. She was obviously moved by the experience of the evening. It was hard to blame her. I'd had the same reaction my first trip with Roy. "We should go to that," she said. "What do you think?"

I looked at Roy. He returned my glance, then studied his beer. Lucy was suddenly fiddling with her phone.

"We could," I said. "We definitely could."

"We should, then."

"We definitely should," I said.

SOMETIME LATER, BACK AT my house, as we lay beside each other in bed, Anne said, "So what's the deal with ROOF? Seemed like I put my foot in it at the bar."

"No deal," I said.

"Come on. What's the big secret?"

"Not so big, I guess."

"What then?"

"Permission to speak candidly."

"Granted."

"It's something I'm not ready to speak candidly about yet."

She hit me with a pillow. "Why not?"

"Because, you know."

"Something bad?"

"Something I'd rather not have come up right now."

"Right now?"

"That's right."

"Right now—with us?"

"Something like that."

"I thought we weren't keeping secrets from each other."

"We aren't," I said. "I just need more time on this one."

"Why?"

"Because."

"Lame answer."

"Guilty as charged."

After a long minute, during which time the only sound came from Hopalong's breathing at the foot of the bed, Anne said, "It's complicated."

"What?"

"This. Us. You and me."

"Complicated," I said. "I suppose. That doesn't have to be a bad thing."

"No," she said. "But it could veer in that direction."

"Unless we keep it from doing that."

"Unless," she said. She rolled away from me, leaned over the side of the bed.

"Everything OK?"

"Texting my mom," she said. "Letting her know I'm going to spend the night." She looked back at me. "If that's all right."

"Of course," I said, relieved. "And it doesn't even sound complicated."

She rolled toward me and took my right hand. And lifted it toward her mouth. And kissed it.

"Don't be so sure," she said. "Things are about to get a lot more complex."

SHE CAME UP BEHIND me, unheard but not unnoticed. Because of her perfume. She had always favored subtle scents, fragrances that pulled you on instead of pushing onto you—one

47

of the many things I appreciated about her. Then she leaned forward and kissed me on the neck, gently, and I murmured, and she kissed me again, and I made another sound, and then she moved a little closer and kissed me on the lips and, well, wow. Then she shifted her head and blew ever so slightly in my ear, and I could feel her breath, warm and inviting, and I made a third sound. And then another sound interrupted, and the dream I'd been having evaporated in a moment and I opened my eyes, heart racing, as I realized John Mellencamp was singing from someplace on my nightstand.

As I detected Anne stirring beside me.

As I realized I'd been dreaming not of her but of Suzanne.

"Andy Hayes," I said, managing to answer before the call went to voice mail. The bedside clock said 6:55 a.m.

"Daddy?"

"Joe?" I said.

"It's *Mike*."

"Mike," I said, sitting up. "You OK?"

"Can you bring my *Redwall* book? I left it there last week."

"*Redwall* book," I said. "Can I bring it?"

"To the hike," he said. "And I think Joe left his shirt there. The Darth Vader one."

"Hike," I said, realizing two seconds too late it was the wrong thing to say.

"We have to *be there* at eight-thirty," Mike said. "You promised. Please don't tell me you forgot."

"I didn't forget," I said.

"Shit," I said, after I'd hung up. "I forgot."

"Everything OK?" Anne said drowsily.

"Boy Scout hike," I said. "Mohican State Park. With Joe and Mike. Vans are leaving from the parking lot at the school at 8:30. Completely forgot. *Shit*."

She propped herself up on an elbow. "How could you forget?" she said.

"Thanks," I said. "Thanks a lot."

"Sorry," she said. "Just a question."

I got up, scrambled to find clothes.

"Can you be ready to go?" I said. "I've got to get moving."

"Sure," she said, curtly, sounding not ready at all.

As I pulled a T-shirt on, I thought of the morning I had planned. Making us breakfast. Strolling up the street, maybe lingering in the Book Loft. Maybe a reprise of our bedtime activities before I had to take her home to Grove City.

Complicated, I thought. No shit, Sherlock.

A few painful minutes later we got into my van, scarcely half a dozen words spoken between us since we'd left the bedroom.

As I started the car, Anne said, "What's that smell?"

"Smell?"

Then I caught a whiff of it too.

"Fuck," I said.

I thought I'd been missing something from Weiland's Market. Figured I'd left a bag at the store. Wouldn't have been the first time. But no, I'd left it in the van. The bag with the smoked trout spread, the gift I'd bought for Anne, the treat I'd picked up trying once in my life to be nice, in the back of the van. For three days.

Which would have summed up the morning all by itself had I not remembered, halfway there, that I'd left Mike's book and Joe's shirt back at the house.

9

I GOT UP THE NEXT MORNING AND WENT through the usual routine. Shave. Throw dog with injured paw in backyard. Tell myself I should go running. Pour second cup of coffee instead.

After breakfast I sat down at the kitchen table and looked up the number for Aaron's mom. Voice mail picked up and I left a message. Her greeting sounded oddly formal, as if she'd typed out the words on a computer then read them aloud. "Hello, this is Mary Custer. I'm not available at the moment . . ." Molly, a nickname, dropped for the formal Mary. Duly noted. Next stop the website for Franklin County Common Pleas Court, where I trolled for details about Eddie Miller. It had gotten a lot easier to access stuff online in recent years, and I was able to find and download his indictment and plea for the bank robbery that had sent him to Mansfield Correctional and into the life of Aaron Custer, however briefly. I noted the name of the defense attorney and assistant prosecutor who had handled his case. I had less luck with the three previous cases against him, which were just old enough to require a trip to the courthouse. I called Karen Feinberg and made arrangements to meet her as long as I was down there.

Next I turned to Chelsea Fowler, the student whose number Suzanne had texted me. I went over my notes. A sophomore at the time of the fire. Business major, from Dayton. She had been at the party for several hours, and had seen Aaron arguing with Tina Montgomery, though she left and went back to her dorm long before the fire. She was an interesting contact for Suzanne to provide. A key witness, but not as key as Helen Chen, the survivor, who I knew I'd have to track down at some point. Or Matt's girlfriend, Lori. An olive branch, but a qualified one? Or was I reading too much into it? Guiltily recalling my dream from the previous morning, I put the thought aside and dialed the number.

"Hello?" she answered after a couple of rings. Young-sounding. Chipper.

I gave her my name, followed by Suzanne's. I explained my mission in vague terms.

"The reporter told you to call me?"

"That's right."

"You want to talk to me about the fire?"

"Just a few questions. Won't take more than fifteen minutes. We can meet anywhere that's convenient for you."

"I don't know," she said. "I told the police everything?"

"Sure," I said. "You were very helpful. Everybody says that. Why I wanted to talk to you. Why Suzanne suggested it."

"You said it won't take long?"

"No time at all."

"All right," she said. "You know where the Union is? I could you meet at, like, four. But not for long."

"The Ohio Union?"

"Yeah. By the statue of Brutus Buckeye. You know where that is?"

"You think maybe Starbucks would be better?" I said.

"Not really. Union works for me. So does that sound good?"
"Sounds good," I lied.

A THIN BLACK MAN and a heavyset white woman
were having a shouting match in front of the Hall of Justice
on South High when I walked over from my parking space
on Mound Street about an hour later and went inside. Franklin County's old ornate courthouse had been demolished
decades earlier, meeting the same fate as so many old but ar-
chitecturally beautiful buildings in the city. Its replacement, a
soaring three-tower complex, was a monument to the magic
of poured concrete on the outside and a testament to controlled chaos inside. In turn, a new environmentally friendly,
heavy-on-the-windows courthouse across the street had replaced the concrete palace a couple of years back, but it had
its own problems, starting with a glass staircase that some
female judges and attorneys complained led to impolitic gap-
ing from people below the stairs looking up. To date, I had
resisted testing this allegation.

Franklin County Municipal Court—"Muni Court"—was
still in the old building, along with numerous administrative
offices. The security line and interior lobbies were crowded
with male and female attorneys in dark suits and distracted
cops and defendants wearing the most unimaginably inap-
propriate T-shirts for a date in court. "Things That Make Me
Hard," read the front of one, worn by a young gentleman in
the metal detector line ahead of me, followed by a list of mind-
boggling possibilities on the back.

"Aaron Custer," Karen Feinberg said when I'd emerged un-
scathed from the gauntlet of wand-waving deputies and joined
her at the small coffee-and-pastry kiosk on the first floor. She
handed me a cup of black and led the way to a bench around
the corner. "You sure know how to pick them."

"I specialize in lost causes," I said. "Just like yourself."

"Always the joker," she said. "Problem is, Aaron's the real thing."

"His grandmother thinks differently."

"His grandmother, with all due respect, is deluded."

"Tell me why you're not taking his appeal."

"There's nothing to appeal. He pleaded guilty."

"His case. You know what I mean."

She sighed. Blew steam off her coffee. She was wearing a navy suit, white blouse, no makeup, and a small nose stud that I happened to know was a real diamond.

She said, "You know how you can tell an addict is lying?"

I shook my head.

"When he moves his lips."

"Who's the joker now?"

"Let's stick with the facts. First off, he pleaded guilty, which means under the law there's nothing to appeal. Second, he's an alcoholic. Third, he's a firebug. Fourth—"

"Eddie Miller?" I interrupted.

"Frequent flier *and* a heroin addict," she said. "In and out of the system his whole life. Like most of my clients. Zero credibility."

"The baseball cap?"

"Colonel Mustard in the parlor with the pruning shears," she said. "Come on, Andy. This isn't TV."

"The cap's real," I protested. "He got it from his grandfather. How could Miller know about that?"

"Maybe Miller saw him wearing it one night when Aaron was out lighting people's trash on fire. Or he knew someone who saw him wearing it. Or Aaron made the whole thing up to con his grandmother. Maybe he and Miller were going to split the money somehow."

I said nothing. I had to concede her points.

"Listen," she said. "I've had plenty of clients who knew they were guilty and wanted to fight the charges tooth and nail. Aaron's the rare bird who knew he was guilty and refused to fight. Tough to defend."

"His grandmother thinks there's hope."

"Deluded. As I said."

"Seemed all there to me."

"She tell you about Aaron's father?"

"His suicide? Yes."

"The divorce?"

"She mentioned it."

"Grandfather's accident?"

"Your point?"

"Aaron is one screwed-up motherfucker. Pardon my Yiddish."

"Screwed-up motherfuckers can't be innocent?"

"Sure they can. And pit bulls are good with children. Except that nine times out of ten, they're not."

"I love it when you play hard to get."

She reached into her briefcase, pulled out a file, handed it to me.

"This is?"

"Guy who killed Kim McDowell."

"And she is?"

"Ever read the paper? The Pendergrass researcher? Killed in her apartment two years ago?"

"Ah," I said. "That Pendergrass researcher."

"Somebody caved her head in during a burglary. Pendergrass folks said it was corporate espionage. She was some kind of scientist there—they were sure she'd been targeted. They were all over the cops. Made it into an international spy thing."

I looked at my watch. "OK," I said.

"They just arrested the student of the year who did it. Guy named Buddy Keeler. He'd been breaking into apartments near hers, off Schrock Road, for weeks. Apparently she surprised him in the act, and—" She slapped the palms of her hands together with a sickening smack.

"Keeler?" I said. "That southern Ohio for 'killer'?"

"So funny. Point is, kid's barely twenty-two, already been in and out of prison and a juvie record a mile long. Spent most of his life before that in foster homes. Mother a prostitute, father a pedophile."

"So he's a screwed-up motherfucker too," I said, handing her back the file.

"Just like Aaron. And back to your comment from before, syllogisms run backward in Muni Court."

"Meaning?"

"Just because someone's a screwed-up motherfucker means they probably *did* do it."

"So you're passing."

"There's lost causes, and then there's the *Titanic* at midnight in the North Atlantic. Yes, I'm passing."

"OK."

"However."

I waited.

"If you find something to change my mind, I'm all ears."

"How Machiavellian of you."

"I have to earn a living, same as you. And Machiavelli."

"Duly noted," I said. "So how's Gabby?"

"Gabby is well, thanks. Still doing probate, still loving it."

"So you defend killers, and she defends the deceased."

"Badda bing. Did you know we're getting married?"

"How domestically tranquil of you. When?"

"Not soon enough, though the invitations we ordered say September."

"Congratulations."

"Thanks. We're pretty happy. My parents too. Gabby's parents, not so much."

"They'll come around," I said.

"I wouldn't be so sure."

"Trust me," I said. "Grandchildren. Works every time."

10

I SAID GOOD-BYE AND WALKED OVER TO THE new courthouse, careful to keep my eyes off the glass stairs, and spent an hour looking up Eddie Miller's priors. Karen was right. Several previous arrests and convictions, almost all drug-related. Prescription painkillers or heroin his poison of choice. No surprise there: the combo was ravaging communities across Ohio, big and small. When the Percocet pills got too expensive, addicts turned to heroin, which was cheap and plentiful. Why Suzanne had started digging into the issue. I called the public defender's office to discover Miller's attorney was on maternity leave. I left a message at the prosecutor's office. I texted Anne in hopes my early morning gaffe the previous day had blown over. No response. I went outside and found a parking ticket on my van. Put it in my pocket. Drove home. Sometimes that's all you can do.

I HAD PLENTY OF time to kill before heading to the Ohio Union to meet Chelsea, a trip I was already dreading. Despite my overblown concerns about being recognized around town, the union was one of the few places in Columbus where the chances soared. I wondered if Suzanne had counted on this when she'd given me Chelsea's number. An olive branch with a thorn on the stem?

I made a list of people I needed to reach. Helen Chen was at the top. Next, families of the victims: Tina Montgomery, Jacob Dunning, and Matt Cummings. I studied their bios a little more. Tina Montgomery had been on the dean's list a couple times. A professor had called Jacob Dunning bright. But Matt was the one who really stood out academically. A few clicks on the Internet brought me to the abstract of a paper he had coauthored on an earthquake in Knox County three years ago. County I grew up in, which piqued my interest. The topic made sense. He was an environmental geology major from eastern Ohio, where thanks to fracking the state's natural gas drilling boom was in full roar. And fracking had been linked to earthquakes. My face reddening, I recalled Suzanne's boyfriend and my boneheaded "Drill, baby, drill" quip. Matt's coauthor was an Ohio State geology professor. I jotted down his information as well.

Despite Matt's academic edge, I was left with the same impression of each victim: good kids, their lives snuffed out too early for no good reason at all. If a motive for their deaths or an alternate suspect was hiding in the digital footprints they'd left behind, I wasn't seeing it.

I took a breath and started placing calls to the family members. I left messages at the numbers for Tina's and Matt's parents and got hung up on by someone at Jacob Dunning's house. I didn't have a number for Helen Chen yet, but figured I'd find that eventually. I went back over my notes. There was a reference in one of Suzanne's stories to fifty or sixty people in the house at one time or another that night. All of them, I supposed, possible witnesses. Or suspects? There was a pizza delivery guy named Rory Ellison. A local guy, D. B. Chambers, on his way to work at McDonald's when he saw the flames and called 911. Two next-door roommates, sisters Kelsey and Karrie Haslett, apparently twins, who thought they heard shouting before the fire started. Ellison was listed, so I called and left a message, but wasn't encouraged by the impersonal electronic recording. Nothing for Chambers, so I did the next best thing and Googled the number for the McDonald's. Someone who answered the phone told me they'd tell him, and then I heard laughter in the background that made me think they might not have been entirely serious. A quick tour of the Ohio State people-finder website failed to turn up the Hasletts, which meant they'd graduated. They weren't listed in Columbus, and their Facebook pages were blocked.

I took a break by calling the state and making a request for the report on Eddie Miller's suicide. Next, I called Mansfield Correctional and got the ball rolling on a visit to Aaron. It was nearly time for lunch by now, and I solved this conundrum with two peanut-butter-and-jelly sandwiches. I looked over my notes while I ate and thumbed through the voluminous clips about Aaron Custer and the fire. I recalled Karen Feinberg's rebuke: "This isn't TV." I knew she had a point. I just didn't want to admit it.

A FEW HOURS LATER I approached the bench inside the Ohio Union where the bronze statue of Ohio State's mascot, Brutus Buckeye, was strategically seated, looking for all the world like a parody of the Headless Horseman with pumpkin firmly in place on his shoulders. I pulled my Columbus Clippers cap down farther over my face, adjusted my sunglasses and waited.

Chelsea Fowler turned out to be a pretty, petite dyed blonde wearing a pink Abercrombie and Fitch sweatshirt, black yoga pants, and too much makeup. She introduced me to Chad, "my boyfriend," a sturdily built fellow with short, sandy hair also wearing an A&F sweatshirt. After strained pleasantries, I convinced them to sidle over to Sloopy's, a diner tucked into one corner of the union, where we sat at a far table. I ordered coffee. They both had pop. I placed two business cards before them. Chelsea's lay unretrieved. Chad picked his up, examined it, then set it down.

"Aaron Custer, innocent?" Chelsea said after our drinks arrived and she'd heard me out. She looked mean when she frowned. "You didn't say anything like that on the phone."

"Allegedly innocent," I said. "It could be nothing. But his grandmother's concerned. You know how grandparents can be."

"Both my grandmas are dead," she said.

"Custer threatened to kill everyone," Chad offered. "Chelsea heard him."

"You heard him arguing with Tina Montgomery," I said, directing the question to Chelsea.

"Yeah," she said.

"What did he say?"

"I already told the police all that? And the reporter? Suzanne?"

"I just want to make sure I have all the facts straight. So if Aaron really *isn't* innocent"—I glanced at Chad—"I have the evidence I need to break the news to his grandmother."

"Fine," she said. "He was saying something like '*The boss is gonna take him out.*' Real slurred like, 'cause he was so drunk."

"The boss?"

"That's right."

I recalled Frank Custer's nickname for Aaron. "*Hey, boss.*" And Aaron's eager adoption of it. "*Hey, Grandpa. The boss is here.*"

"Who was he talking about?"

"What?"

"Him. '*The boss is gonna take him out.*' Who's the him?"

"Jacob Dunning," Chad said.

"Tina knew Jacob?" I said.

"They met at the party," Chelsea said. "They'd been flirting. Aaron knew Jacob somehow, and he was jealous."

"He was jealous of Jacob, for talking to Tina?"

"Yeah," Chelsea said.

"Any idea why?" I said. "Aaron and Tina weren't dating, were they?"

"I don't know," Chelsea said, looking bored. "I just know they were arguing. Aaron didn't like Jacob for some reason."

Fair enough, I thought. I'd had my share of drunken confrontations with guys I'd thought had been talking to girls I thought I'd been dating.

"Are we done?" Chelsea said. "I kind of need to get going."

"Almost," I said. "Who else did Aaron talk to?"

"No idea. It was a big party. I just remember what Aaron was saying. Because he was so drunk. And, I mean, afterward. After the fire and his arrest? It sort of jumped out in my head. You know?"

"How about Jacob? Did Aaron talk to Jacob?"

"I don't know."

"So you remember Aaron arguing with Tina. About Jacob. But you don't know if Aaron ever talked to Jacob himself."

"Yeah. That's what I said."

"I just want to get it straight."

"It's all in the reports and stuff," she said. "Like I said, I told the police all this already."

"Is there anybody else who might have seen Aaron talking to Jacob?"

She shrugged.

"Anybody else you *knew* at the party who might know? Somebody I should talk to."

"I don't know. Lots of people."

"Eric," Chad said.

Chelsea looked at him. "Shut *up*," she said.

"I'm just saying."

"Who's Eric?" I said.

"Just a guy," Chelsea said.

"Eric Jenkins," Chad said. "He was at the party."

"Got a phone number?"

"No," Chelsea said.

"He a student?" I said.

"Yeah," Chad said.

"I have to go now," Chelsea said. She stood up. She looked at Chad. He stood up as well. They hadn't touched their pop.

"Thanks for meeting with me," I said.

"I wish you wouldn't have called me," Chelsea said, and she walked off.

As a trained observer, I couldn't help but notice that Chad's attempt to take her hand as they walked past the Sloopy's cash register was not met with success.

I also observed that Chad, but not Chelsea, had picked up my business card from the table.

11

THERE ARE ONLY A HANDFUL OF FARMS LEFT inside Columbus proper. Mostly a few acres of dairy cows here and there whose owners won't sell. In another year or so one of those farms, tucked into a corner next to the interstate on the west side, was going to disappear, replaced by a new county jail and morgue. Until that happened, the coroner's office was still in Victorian Village, tucked between the university medical center and Battelle Memorial Institute, the Goliath of local research labs to the David of Pendergrass, the employer of the late Kim McDowell. Whose killer Karen Feinberg was now representing. Inside the nondescript brick coroner's office George Huntington seated me at a conference room table, a thick file before me.

"All yours, champ," he said. "Usual warning—it's not pretty."

"Thanks," I said.

"Your case," the coroner's investigator said. "Seems like a stretch. What I know of Custer."

"You may be right."

After he left I glanced at the skeleton some wiseacre had propped behind a podium in a corner of the room, then got to work. Huntington was right about one thing: it wasn't pretty. But not because the morgue photos were any more graphic than others I'd seen. It was the pathos of seeing the bodies of three such promising kids.

Under normal conditions fire is not a selective killer. But it's partial to the young, the old, and in the case of Matt Cummings, the very drunk. His blood alcohol was 0.14. Not the highest I'd ever seen, not by a long shot. But seriously inebriated. Hard to blame him, being his birthday and all. He must have heard or smelled something, because he'd at least made it out of bed. But he hadn't gone much farther than that before collapsing and succumbing to the thick smoke steadily filling the upstairs. The second victim, Tina Montgomery, had a slightly higher level, which meant that, as she was a woman, she was probably much drunker. She was found just outside her upstairs bedroom, overcome, like Matt, by the smoke and fumes.

The puzzle, if you could call it that, was Jacob Dunning. He'd suffered actual burns in addition to smoke inhalation, and was found downstairs, not far from the door. Had he been on the verge of escaping? Had he heard something? Or someone? The Haslett sisters claimed there'd been shouting before the fire. Had Jacob had a fight with the killer? His toxicology turned up alcohol and marijuana, and the combination had obviously taken its toll. It still didn't explain what he was doing downstairs, though.

"OK," I said to George as I walked into his office a few minutes later and placed the file on his desk. "Uncle."

"Tried to warn you," he said. He shifted his considerable weight in his chair and rubbed a neatly trimmed goatee. "Find anything interesting?"

"Not sure." I told him my questions about Jacob.

"Think you've got the bases covered. Burns suggest he might have been downstairs when the gasoline ignited, and got engulfed in flames."

"But the burns didn't kill him."

"Smoke inhalation, like the other two. But they kept him from getting outside, which might have saved him."

"But no way to tell."

"Only person who knows is dead," Huntington said.

"Unless the killer saw what happened."

"You mean Custer?"

"I mean the killer. Whoever it was."

12

"I WAS HOPING TO NEVER SEE YOU AGAIN," Henry Fielding said to me.

"I've missed you as well," I said.

The next day, Tuesday, late morning. Sitting at a table in the café on the second floor of Columbus police headquarters with Fielding, a homicide detective I had the pleasure of meeting the year before. Across from him was Joe Whitestone, the city's lead arson investigator. Both men looked as if they'd rather be anywhere, up to and including home with dysentery, than speaking with me. Though Fielding had agreed to the meeting, we were doing it on his turf. No chummy tête-à-tête at one of the numerous coffee shops within a five-minute walk of headquarters or up near Whitestone's office at the station on North Fourth Street. No, we would do it in a way that every cop in the building could come by for a look at Andy "Woody" Hayes if he or she chose. And to judge by the number of people who lined up for coffee while I sat there, pretty much everyone did. Message received.

"A prison inmate tells Custer he's innocent, then offs himself," Fielding said. "It's original, I'll give you that."

"Points for creativity?" I offered.

"Points for nothing. This is a wild goose chase, except the goose is in prison. Where he belongs."

"Baseball cap?"

"Puts Custer at the scene," Fielding said, as I knew he would.

"New information, though. Wasn't in any of the reports."

"Even assuming it's true, who cares?" Fielding said. "The brand of jeans he was wearing isn't in there either. Doesn't mean he's not 110 percent guilty."

Whitestone cleared his throat. "It's like the drug shit with Dunning."

I turned to him. Whitestone had silver hair and the kind of full, Omar Sharif mustache you don't see much anymore in the age of the goatee. It was hard not to contrast him with Fielding and the detective's hairless, boiled-egg noggin. I knew Fielding's nickname around the shop was Voldemort, and I also knew Fielding knew I knew this, which might have been the one and only advantage I had over him.

"Shit with Dunning," I said.

"Dunning got arrested his sophomore year for possession. Had a whopping three ounces of marijuana in his coat. I'm assuming you already knew that."

"I know he had marijuana in his system when he died."

"Good for you," Whitestone said.

"What's it have to do with him and the fire?" I said. "Probably lots of kids there that night had smoked pot."

"Along the way he admitted he sold a little from time to time. That was enough for wannabe CSI types out there to make him the 'drug dealer.'"

"Three ounces of marijuana is a long way from kingpin status."

"Not in cyberspace, it's not. Plus, his uncle, or more precisely, his mother's sister's husband, is a firefighter."

"Columbus?"

"Cleveland."

"So?"

"So people drew lines between him and some kind of drug deal gone bad, and us ignoring it to protect our own."

"Idea being he was the target."

"Something like that."

"Was he?"

"Yes," Whitestone said. "He was the target of a drunken arsonist named Aaron Custer, just like Matt Cummings and Tina Montgomery and Helen Chen."

"You know what I mean."

"There was no 'drug deal gone bad,'" Fielding said. "Our drug dealers have more on their minds than three ounces of pot."

I thought about Suzanne's recent reports on Channel 7, on the pipeline of black tar heroin coming into town, on rumored cartel connections, on an epidemic of fatal overdoses, more than two a day across the state. I nodded. By comparison, Dunning was small potatoes.

I said, conciliatorily, "So the CSI types aren't swayed by the fact everything points to Custer?"

"Who cares, on Twitter?" Whitestone said. "The same people still think 9/11 was a government conspiracy. And Justin Bieber was framed."

"Any of this make the news?"

Whitestone shook his head. "Suzanne Gregory over at Channel 7 is the only one who even caught onto it, but there was nothing there to report."

Well, well, I thought.

I said, "So what about it?" Directing the question at Whitestone.

"About what?"

"About Aaron Custer."

"You know everything there is to know. Firebug. Threatened to kill everyone. Surveillance video at the gas station. Print on the lighter. Pleaded guilty. Lucky to be alive. Otherwise, case closed."

"Lucky to be alive."

"You heard me."

"I heard you. What's it mean?"

"Means what it means. Leading cause of death among arsonists is the fires they try to set. Lot of times they pour out the gasoline, then wait too long to light it. Vapors build and everything goes up when they light the match, including them. See it all the time. Just our luck the one thing Custer can't get right."

"Vapors," I said.

"That's right. It's called chemistry."

"So firebugs aren't always smart."

"They're smart enough. Lot of times they're the ones that call the fire in. Be the hero."

"OK," I said. "Other than all that, what about him?"

"Case closed," he repeated. "Nothing else to say."

"The beating? Afterward?"

"Kid was a street punk," Fielding said. "Street punk looking for trouble. Shit happens."

"Connected to the fire, maybe?" I said. "Someone from the house? Someone chased him?"

"Who knows? Doesn't matter," Fielding said. "Lot of people say whoever it was should have finished the job."

"How about you? What do you say?"

"I say Aaron Custer was guilty of a fatal arson fire caused by dousing the front of a house with gasoline, then lighting it."

I changed tactics. "Motive?"

"Again—doesn't matter," Fielding said.

"You must have a theory."

"One or two. Starting with, he was a vindictive firebug, and ending with, he was a vindictive firebug."

"He was supposedly arguing with Tina Montgomery about Jacob Dunning."

"That's right."

"But Tina didn't know Jacob. Until that night."

"Right again," Fielding said.

"So why would Custer be mad at Tina over somebody she'd just met?"

"Listen, Woody," Fielding said. "Maybe it's been a while since you were in the dating game. But I've got a hot tip for you. People meet people at parties. They chat. They flirt. Sometimes they trade numbers and go their merry way, and sometimes they sneak into the bathroom and stick their tongues down each other's throats. And sometimes that pisses off other people they've swapped spit with in the past. It's not perfect, but it's life."

"You saying that's what happened with Tina and Jacob? They got it on and Aaron got mad?"

"I'm not saying anything," Fielding said. "Maybe Jacob Dunning had a hard-on for Tina Montgomery, and maybe that explains why he was still there in the middle of the night instead of going back to his place. Or not. It doesn't matter. We know who killed them."

I said, "You're saying Dorothy Custer's wasting her time."

Fielding leaned forward. His jaw had tightened a little. "She's wasting her money. You're wasting her time. And mine."

"Any chance I could look at the files? On Aaron's case?"

"No."

"I could make an open records request."

"Be my guest."

"But be faster if I could just get them."

"Probably."

"So what about it?"

He shook his head. I looked at Whitestone, but all he did was look at Fielding. The records weren't his to give, even if he had them.

69

"Speaking of Suzanne Gregory," Fielding said, out of the blue. "Why don't you ask her? She was all over this case. And you guys go way back, I hear."

"I'll keep that in mind," I said, my voice neutral.

"Just a thought," he said.

13

I HAD OPTIMISTICALLY PUT TWO HOURS
on the Front Street meter before walking into police headquarters. Most of it was left when I walked out. About all I'd
gotten out of the meeting was an appetite. I put two and two
together and walked up to Broad, crossed over, and went into
Danny's Deli. I was early for lunch, and the restaurant was
only partially full. I ordered a corned beef sandwich and iced
tea. While I waited I thought about Jacob Dunning and the
fact Suzanne had known about the marijuana possession but
never reported it. On a lark, after the waitress brought my
drink, I dialed the station.

"Tell her who's calling?" said the young man on the
news desk.

I gave him my name. After a long minute he came back on
the phone, his voice uneasy. "She, ah, isn't available right now."

"What did she say?"

"Like I said, she isn't available."

"Really say, I mean."

He told me.

"Sorry you had to hear that. Tell her it's about Jacob Dunning."

"Dunning?"

"That's right. Just tell her."

After another minute I heard a click on the line, and then her voice.

"I told you not to contact me."

"I'm curious what you know about Dunning and his arrest for marijuana possession."

"You've been talking to Fielding or Whitestone."

I acknowledged it.

"So you know as much as I do. And you know, if you've got half a brain, which I doubt, there's nothing to it."

"You never reported it."

"There was no news."

"According to Whitestone, the Twitterverse said he might have been the real target."

"Now you're Woody Fucking Hayes, social media expert?"

"Just a question."

"Actually, it was a statement. Like this one: stop calling me."

And with that she hung up.

But two minutes later my phone rang.

"I just thought you should know," Suzanne said.

"What?"

"After your little prank at Lindey's the other night? I got an e-mail the next day. Somebody'd snapped a picture of us sitting there. Sent it anonymously."

"OK."

"Wanna guess what it said?"

"Not really."

"It said, 'Such a cute couple, but I was hoping for ROOF: the sequel.'"

"I'm sorry that happened."

"Know what else? Glen got the same e-mail. From like ten different people. It is a fucking miracle he hasn't walked

out on me yet. Which would be completely thanks to you if
he did."

The line went quiet, but stayed connected, and because I
couldn't think of anything else she'd want to hear from me, I
said, "Bad time to ask if I could look at your copy of the Orton
Avenue file?"

This time the line went good and truly dead.

EVEN I COULDN'T FINISH an entire Danny's corned
beef sandwich, though I gave it my best shot. But eventually,
packaged leftovers in hand, I walked out of the restaurant and
headed back to my van. And I would have made it there without incident, had I not looked across the street at that moment
and happened to see a couple of women I judged to be good-
looking strolling south on Front. Their dark suits said attorneys,
which meant they were probably headed to the Supreme Court
a block down. I followed their progress for the few seconds I
allot myself for such boorishness. Which was why I happened to
be looking to the left when a black SUV—Explorer, or maybe a
Jeep—pulled up in front of the hotel a block down on my side of
the street. The Neil House Inn. As I watched, the driver got out
and walked around to the passenger side. I stepped back, fum-
bled in my pocket for my sunglasses, put them on. Speak of the
devil. Even from that distance, I recognized him immediately:
Glen Murphy, Suzanne's newest boyfriend. The receiver of ten
e-mails of her and me at the bar at Lindey's. *The first guy who's
stayed with me longer than a month. It is a fucking miracle he hasn't
walked out on me yet.* As I watched, he opened the passenger door,
reached out a hand, then helped a woman get out of the SUV.
Another blonde. Not Suzanne caliber, but even at this distance
I could tell she was a close second. Murphy put his arm around
her. They headed for the door, stopping just long enough for
Murphy to say something to the bell cap, then hand him his
keys, before they disappeared into the lobby.

14

BACK HOME, I PROCESSED WHAT I'D SEEN.
It was lousy for Suzanne. But I also knew I'd take the blame
regardless of how long it had actually been going on. My trip
to Lindey's guaranteed it.

Rousing myself for the task at hand, I considered trying the
families of Matt, Jacob, and Tina again but thought better of it.
They either weren't talking or were deciding how to respond.
I could afford to give them time. I still didn't have a number
for Helen Chen, and it was clear I wouldn't be getting it from
Suzanne. I called the state about the report on Eddie Miller's
suicide. Then, because it was the only other thing I could think
to do, I looked up the number for the Environmental Geology
Department at Ohio State. When I reached a secretary I asked
for Tanner Gridley, the professor who cowrote the earthquake
article with Matt Cummings.

"He's got office hours right now," she said. "You can try to
reach him, but he usually doesn't pick up."

"How long do office hours last?"

"One to four," she said. "Are you a student?"

"A student of life," I said, and thanked her before I hung up.

GRIDLEY'S OFFICE WAS ON the third floor of Northstar Hall, a science building on south campus, a postwar limestone-and-brick pile with what looked like a 1990s-era wing bolted onto the side. There was a poster for a movie called *Gasland* on the partially open door at his office, and three different political cartoons about fracking, including one with the "See no evil, hear no evil" chimps wearing State of Ohio badges as they were jostled by an apparent earthquake.

"Come in," a voice said in reply to my knock.

He sat at a desk, staring at a computer screen, right hand on a mouse. To his left, a window, in front of that, a table covered haphazardly with papers and magazines and books. Beyond that a floor-to-ceiling bookshelf crammed with more books and science journals. Plastic file crates lined the floor behind his desk, each bursting with documents. At the rear of the room a second computer with a wide screen sat at another work station, and beside that sat a third computer whose screen was jumping as some kind of statistical program ran table after table of graphs and numbers. A poster for a U.S. Geological Survey conference on hydraulic fracturing hung above the computers.

"Tanner Gridley?"

"Yes," he said, not looking up. He made an adjustment with his mouse, saved the action, then glanced at me.

"Help you?"

"My name's Andy Hayes," I said. I handed him my card.

"What's this about?"

"I'm trying to find people who knew Matt Cummings."

He frowned. "Matt? Why?"

I explained.

When I was done he folded his arms and stared at me.

"That's got to be the most screwed-up thing I've ever heard of," he said.

I LET MY GAZE drift to his desk. A family photo sat to the left of the computer—him, a woman I took to be his wife, and a girl and a boy that looked about Joe and Mike's ages. A smart phone lay in front of the photo. To the right of the keyboard, another pile of papers, topped with a Youngstown State coffee mug adorned with a picture of a scowling, scarf-wearing penguin, the school's mascot. It was enough to make you smirk, until you remembered that Ohio State's equivalent was an anthropomorphic buckeye.

"Let me get this straight," Gridley said. "Aaron Custer's grandmother is paying you to prove he's innocent." He was clean-shaven, with closely cropped hair and black-framed glasses.

"To see if he's innocent," I said.

"Big difference. That what lets you sleep at night?"

"I sleep OK," I said. "Mind if I sit down?"

"Be my guest," he said, lifting a textbook from the chair beside his desk. "Until my next student arrives, when you need to get the hell out."

"Let's forget about Aaron," I said. "Tell me about Matt."

"I'd like nothing better than to forget about Aaron Custer," he said. "Along with half the university."

"Matt must have been a good student. He cowrote a paper with a professor."

"Assistant professor," Gridley said. "And you're wrong—he was a brilliant student. Brilliant and passionate."

"Brilliant how?"

"Straight A's. Math, science, even writing. You name it."

"Impression I got."

"Would have made an outstanding geologist. Could have walked out of here the day he graduated and gone to work for any of the big oil companies in a second."

76

"Was that his plan?"

"Hardly."

"Why not?"

"He's from eastern Ohio. Was," he corrected himself. "Ground zero of the state's fracking boom. His family's farm sits smack over the western edge of the Utica Shale."

"That's a formation of some kind."

"Giant deposits of shale, deep underground. Not as big as the Marcellus Shale in Pennsylvania, but still huge. And lucrative. Natural gas is trapped in the shale. Fracking is how you get it out."

"Big market for natural gas right now."

"True."

"Cleaner than coal."

"Cleaner-burning. Not any cleaner to extract."

"Because of fracking?"

"That's right."

"But isn't it just another kind of drilling?"

Gridley snorted. "Calling fracking a kind of drilling is like calling rape a way you make love," he said. "Pardon the analogy."

"Pardoned, I guess," I said. "Not a fan?"

"Depends what you think of blasting millions of gallons of water laced with huge amounts of toxic chemicals into the earth, then taking that leftover liquid and injecting it into wells, where it sits around contaminating the water supply or causing earthquakes."

"These wells cause the earthquakes? I thought it was the drilling."

"Common mistake," he said. "There's the gas wells and the injection wells."

"OK."

"Liquid from the injection wells seeps into the bedrock and encounters existing faults, which can then cause quakes."

"And this is proven?"

"Injection wells have been linked to minor earthquakes all over the country—Arkansas, Colorado, Oklahoma, Texas. Not to mention right here in Ohio. Up in Youngstown, 2011. Don't tell me you hadn't heard about that."

"I remember those," I said.

"You ought to. Because the state still hasn't learned its lesson."

"Meaning?"

"Meaning there's an injection well sitting right over there in Knox County that triggered a quake three years ago, and the state's in total denial about it. Says the jury's out. More study needed. It's bullshit."

"That's what the paper was about. The one you cowrote."

"You read it?"

"Saw the summary online."

"Then you know we made our case."

"But the well's still open."

"Like I said, state's in denial."

"Are they going to study it more?"

"Not if they can help it."

"What's that mean?"

"It means they're going to make a final decision soon based on existing data. Which is a fancy way of saying they'll ignore our paper and findings and go with what Appletree Energy wants."

"Company that owns the well?"

"Energy company doing the fracking. They also operate the well. But they can't frack until the well's in the clear. Which is pissing them off, which is why they're lobbying hard for the state to get off its ass and sign off on the No. 5."

"No. 5?"

"Knox Excavating Class II Injection Well No. 5."

"The well you wrote the paper about."

"That's right."

"Which proved it caused a quake."

"Which proved the evidence leaned strongly in that direction," Gridley said. "I guess that's not good enough."

"Appletree's fighting to keep it operational."

"With their wallet wide open. And it's a big wallet."

"Are you going to publish another paper?"

He slumped a little in his chair. "I might have," he said. "That was the plan. It all sort of went to hell after Matt died. Which is why this is such bullshit."

"What do you mean?"

"What Matt and I found should be good enough. Enough to scuttle Appletree's case. But it's like they know they have the upper hand, because Matt's death screwed everything up for us. For me. They're exploiting that tragedy for their own business purposes."

"Sounds like you're mad at Matt," I said. "For dying."

"Jesus Christ. Are you kidding?"

"You said it yourself. His death screwed things up for you."

He looked on the verge of getting angry. Then he glanced around his cluttered office and took a breath.

"Came out the wrong way," he said.

"Figured as much."

"His death was horrible. I have a hard time talking about it."

"I can imagine."

"And now you're here, bringing this shit up."

"Was Matt opposed to fracking? Or you?"

"We both were," he said.

"Based on the earthquakes?"

"That, and all the other environmental damage."

"Like what?"

"Like drinking wells tainted with methane. Like water coming from kitchen faucets you can light with a match. Like the disruption of wildlife habitats." He gestured at the poster on his door. "Ever see *Gasland?*"

I told him I hadn't.

"Check it out. You want to know about Matt? That was his favorite movie."

"His, or yours?"

"What's that supposed to mean?"

"Nothing," I said. "I'll look it up."

"It's a great film," he said. "Should be required viewing in any state where they're fracking."

I thought about Glen Murphy, Suzanne's boyfriend. Boyfriend for now. "But isn't there already a lot of drilling here? Traditional oil drilling?"

"Sure," Gridley said. "But it's got a much smaller impact. You don't need the six-acre pads you see with fracking."

"That must have been a pretty big deal for Matt," I said. "Getting a paper published."

"I told you, he was brilliant."

"Sounds like a good kid."

"He was. Until a scumbag named Aaron Custer killed him."

I didn't respond, since there was nothing to say. At this point it was hard to disagree with the prevailing view of Aaron Custer. Instead, I said, "You have a copy of the paper? Only thing online was the abstract."

Gridley thought about this for a second. Then he swiveled in his chair, went to the cluttered table, sifted through papers for a couple of minutes, found the document, and handed it to me. "Hydraulic Fracturing Injection Wells and the Prevalence of Seismic Activity in the Eastern Ohio Geological Corridor," the title read. By T. Gridley and M. Cummings.

"Just for the heck of it," I said. "Anybody not like Matt?"

"What do you mean?"

"Get in any arguments with anyone? Anybody in favor of fracking? Somebody who didn't like your findings?"

"Sure," Gridley said. "The entire fracking industry, starting with Appletree Energy. But the entire fracking industry

SLOW BURN

wasn't a convicted firebug who got drunk and decided to torch a house full of hardworking students."

Before I could reply a shadow darkened the door. I looked up and saw a young man, backpack around his shoulder. He looked questioningly at Gridley, who waved the student in, which I knew was my signal to go.

"Thank you for your time," I said.

Gridley didn't reply. He didn't look at me. He just gestured for me to leave.

15

I RECOVERED MY VAN FROM THE GARAGE next to the university's Wexner Center for the Arts and drove down High a few blocks toward downtown. A few minutes later I parked and walked into the Short North Tavern, ordered a draft PBR, and sat at the bar while I read Matt Cummings's paper. The article was dense and crammed with scientific terminology and took me a while to understand. I girded myself with a second beer. For all of Gridley's passion about fracking, the article, as a piece of science writing aimed at an academic audience, was devoid of emotion. Its gist was the argument, with several caveats and provisos, that the well dubbed Knox No. 5 could have contributed to a series of minor temblors a year before the article was published. Not exactly a smoking-gun document but somewhat convincing nonetheless.

I was almost done with my beer and trying to keep my mind off the fact that each person I talked to about Aaron Custer left me increasingly convinced of his guilt when my phone rang.

"Andy Hayes?" the female voice asked.

"That's right."

"This is Janet Crenshaw."

"OK."

"I'm with Smyth, Sanner, Stacy and Franko."

"Lot of names," I said. "Is that a folk group?"

"It's a law firm, as I'm sure you know. Did you call the parents of students killed in the Orton Avenue fire?"

"This is the part where I say, 'Why do you want to know?'"

"I want to know because I'm their lawyer."

I acknowledged the calls.

"They're not talking," she said.

"How about Helen Chen," I said. "Happen to have her number?"

"She's not talking either. Nobody is."

"Why not?"

"I represent them in a lawsuit against the landlord of the Orton Avenue house. As long as that's pending, they're not giving interviews."

The civil lawsuit. Another of Suzanne's exclusives, reporting first for Channel 7 that the realty company that owned the house was being sued.

"I don't want to talk to them about the lawsuit."

"What then?"

I told her.

"Oh my God. Even less of a reason. You must be kidding."

"It may be a stretch," I admitted. "But I'll be the judge of that."

"Be my guest. But not with my clients. It's a bad idea, legally speaking, and it's a really bad idea on moral grounds."

"What's that supposed to mean?"

"You can imagine what they've been through. Now you come along saying police got the wrong guy? I don't think so. It would shatter them."

"Speaking of Aaron," I said. "Any reason you're not going after him? Wrongful death?"

"Right," she said. "Move to seize the assets of an unemployed, alcoholic arsonist serving a life sentence."

"So you go after the landlord instead? Even though everything I read says there were working smoke detectors in the house."

"*Some* smoke detectors," she said. "There weren't enough."

"Would that have made a difference?"

"We think it would have."

"Looks to me like you just spun the wheel until you found the deepest pocket."

"I'm not going to dignify that with a response. And I'm not sure why we're even having—"

"Why not go after Aaron's mom, then? Or his grandmother? She's wealthy enough."

"Not that wealthy," she said dismissively. "And in any case, they're not the ones who doused gasoline on the porch of that house and killed the innocent children of my clients. And yes, you're right, we could go after Aaron Custer and garnish his prison wages for life and my clients would be a few pennies a month richer. But what good would that do? What point would that serve?"

"As good a point as going after a realty company that wasn't responsible for their deaths."

"Says you."

"Says everyone who looked at this case."

"That'll be for a jury to decide," she said. "I can't spend any more time on this. I just want to make sure we're clear you're not to contact my clients."

"What if I talk to them off the record? Mediated questions. With you there?"

"Forget it."

"I'm not interested in your lawsuit. And believe it or not, I'm sympathetic to the effect of bringing everything up again. I just have a few questions. Bet you we'd be done in less than an hour."

"No," she said.

"Pretty please."

"You know, I was warned about you."

"Warned how?"

"Warned you're an indefatigable asshole who doesn't give up. Few questions lead to a few more. And a few more. Last thing the families need right now."

"Indefatigable."

"You heard me."

And that was about it. She was too professional to hang up on me. She informed me that she had to go, and it was not a good idea to reach out to the families under any circumstances.

And then she hung up.

I MADE IT AS far as the door of the bar when Anne called.

"Hi there," I said, trying unsuccessfully to disguise the pleasure in my voice.

"Hi there, back," she said. "How are you doing?"

"Channeling my inner Don Quixote," I said.

"Aaron Custer?"

"That's right."

"You have an interesting job. Anybody ever told you that?"

"Frequently. Usually with R-rated language."

"Makes what I do seem kind of pedestrian."

"You're a college professor," I said.

"So?"

"So I clean up messes. You're training the next generation to run the world. So hopefully there won't be messes."

"I teach science fiction."

"You say it like it's something to be ashamed of."

"Maybe it is," she said. "Sometimes I'm not so sure."

"Science fiction is a good thing. That book, *World War Z?* I've been enjoying it."

"You know what Kurt Vonnegut said about science fiction?"

"Sure," I said. "But why don't you tell me just so I can see if you do."

"He said, '*I have been a soreheaded occupant of a file drawer labeled "science fiction"* . . . *and I would like out, particularly since so many serious critics regularly mistake the drawer for a urinal.*'"

"I like how you know that by heart."

"It's a college professor thing."

"Given that I have a hard time remembering what kind of dog food Hopalong eats, I'm impressed."

"Don't be."

"Your point being?"

"A rational person could question whether the world needs college professors teaching the next generation about ray guns."

"Good thing I'm not rational."

"You know what I mean."

"Ray guns," I continued. "Good at cleaning up messes."

"Very funny," she said, but there was an edge to her voice.

"I try."

"Listen," she said. "I called because I can't make it tomorrow. There's this in-service thing at work."

"OK," I said, two beats too late. "Sorry about that."

She said, "You forgot, didn't you?"

I thought furiously. Birthday? Lunch? Four-month anniversary? No, I'd already forgotten that. Then, too late, I remembered. A few days earlier, she'd moved up the Thursday run by a day.

"I did," I confessed. "I'm sorry."

"No matter," she said brightly. "It works out anyway. How about Thursday after all?"

"Yes," I said. "Thursday would be great."

"Lost causes. Terrible for the memory."

"Apparently," I said, out of snappy responses.

"Gotta go," she said. "Now don't forget."

"Of course not," I said.

I put the phone away, walked to my van, and got in. I stared out the windshield for a long minute, then started the engine. As I headed for German Village I tried to concentrate on Aaron Custer. But the whole way home, all I could think of was what if Anne hadn't had an in-service thing? What if she'd shown up on the running path the next day to wait, and wait in vain?

Lunkhead run, indeed.

16

MANSFIELD CORRECTIONAL INSTITUTION
sits on a hill off a country road on the outskirts of the small city
it's named for, more or less halfway between Columbus and
Cleveland. People sometimes confuse it with the old prison in
Mansfield, where the movie *Shawshank Redemption* was filmed:
a long-shuttered Victorian-era building whose gloomy, castle-
like appearance makes you think a closer look might reveal
Miss Havisham peering out an upstairs window. Just before
11:00 Wednesday morning I turned off the road and drove up
toward the new prison, whose alternating brick colors gave
it the appearance, appropriately enough, of stripes. I parked,
went inside, surrendered my driver's license, and signed in.

Fifteen minutes later I was led through a barred door that
rolled open at the command of an officer in a glassed-in booth,
then rolled back shut behind me with a menacing finality. I tamped
down memories of my own time behind bars and focused on the
job I had to do. Two minutes after that I was sitting in a room on
one side of a bare wooden table, the only window a small square
in the door. After another minute I heard footsteps and the door

opened and then Aaron Custer was sitting across from me in dark pants and a beige shirt. He was shackled at the ankles and the wrists, with his wrists linked to a chain around his waist.

"Are those necessary?" I said to the guard who escorted him in and was now standing at attention by the door.

"Yes," he said. "You've got thirty minutes. Any profanity or raised voices and the interview's over. Any questions about prison security or discipline, interview's over. Anything else I don't like—"

"I got it," I said.

Aaron was smaller than I'd expected, thin, with a shaved head, brown eyes, and a smooth face that made me wonder if, at age twenty-two, he'd started shaving yet. His shirt, with INMATE stenciled across the front, seemed big on him. He sat with his hands together, fingers intertwined, as though he were in church. Or pretending to be a judge. As I studied him I realized he looked familiar, as if I'd seen him before. Seen him in some other context than the mug shot run over and over again after his arrest. Tried to pinpoint what I was thinking. Realized after a moment I had to be imagining things. The Sandy Hook killer looked familiar too, after the two hundredth viewing of his picture.

"Thanks for meeting with me," I said.

"Sure."

"I've been talking to your grandmother."

"I know."

I decided to jump right in. "Eddie Miller. You believe him?"

"I guess."

"Meaning?"

"Meaning I guess."

"You think he was telling the truth?"

He blinked a couple times. Looked around the room as if he couldn't recall why he was there.

"I don't know," he said.

"You don't know?"

"I don't remember that night."

"Do you remember setting the fire?"

He shook his head.

"Do you remember being at a party at the house? Earlier that night."

"No."

"Do you remember talking to anyone at the party?"

"No."

"Tina Montgomery?"

He shook his head.

"But you know Tina, right?"

"Yeah. Went to school with her."

"Girlfriend?"

"Just a friend."

"People said you were arguing with her. Do you remember that?"

"No."

"Do you remember getting thrown out of the house?"

He shook his head again.

"Do you remember threatening to kill everyone?"

"I know they said I did."

"But you don't remember?"

"No."

"Do you remember getting beat up, afterward?"

"No."

I said nothing.

"I was drunk," Aaron said, picking up on my frustration. "I don't remember stuff when I drink."

"Did you get drunk at the party?"

"No."

"You didn't drink at the party?"

"I didn't get drunk there," he said. "I got drunker. I guess. I don't remember."

"You came to the party drunk."

"That's right."

"Why?"

"Why what?"

"Why did you come to the party drunk?"

He thought about that for a moment. "Because that's what I did, before," he said. "I drank."

"Did it ever occur to you that the fact you can't remember anything might mean you *didn't* do it?"

"Not really."

"Why not?"

"Why would it? Everything points to me. I'd set fires before, when I was drunk."

"I talked to a girl named Chelsea Fowler. Do you know her?"

"No."

"She said she heard you talking to Tina."

"I said, I don't know her."

"She said that you said, '*The boss is gonna take him out.*' Several times."

For the first time, his eyes seemed to focus.

"She said that?"

"That's right. *Boss.* That's your nickname, right?"

"Was."

"Was?"

"I'm like the opposite of a boss in here. Sounds stupid."

"OK," I said. "It used to be. You got it from your grandfather."

"Yeah."

"Take *him* out. That was Jacob?"

"I don't know."

"But you know Jacob."

"I'd seen him around."

"You know he sold pot?"

"I guess. Lots of people sell pot. Even here."

The guard cleared his throat.

I said, "Why would you say you were going to take him out?"

"I don't know. I don't remember."

"People think he might have been flirting with Tina, and that made you mad."

"I told you, she wasn't my girlfriend."

"Did you want her to be your girlfriend? Ever?"

"I don't know."

"You don't know?"

"OK, yeah, I did. But that was a long time ago. In high school."

"You stayed in touch."

"A little. She was a friend."

"Enough to come by a party she was at."

"Maybe."

"Enough to be jealous of another guy she'd been with? You wouldn't be the first jealous drunk, in case you were wondering."

"I guess."

I looked at my watch, decided to move on. "Back to Miller. He say anything more about this witness?"

"Not really."

"Anything," I said.

He shifted a little in his chair. I heard the ankle shackles clink. "He said somebody saw what happened."

"When did he tell you this?"

"Week before he died."

"Where?"

"Recreation," he said. "We were outside, in the yard. He just came up to me."

"Did you know him?"

He shook his head. "He'd just gotten here."

"OK," I said. "Tell me exactly what he said. What his exact words were."

"I told you," he said. "He said somebody saw something."

"That's what he said? Or are you just kind of, you know, summarizing?"

He looked puzzled at this and seemed to be thinking hard. I was starting to get the impression that Aaron wasn't all there. And it was giving me an even worse feeling about this case, if that were possible at this point. Repeated blackout drinking at a young age left the brain permanently rewired, and not in a good way. Even worse when a night of drinking was followed with a chaser of head slamming.

"He said, 'I know a guy who knows you didn't do it.'"

"That's what he said? Those were his exact words?"

"Pretty close," he said.

"What did you say?"

"I didn't say anything," he said.

"Your grandmother said he mentioned something about a Columbus Red Birds cap."

"He said I was wearing it that night. Or, at least, the other guy said I was."

"Were you?"

"I don't remember."

"Could you have been?"

"Maybe."

"Your grandmother said it was special to you. It was your grandfather's. He used to take you to Clippers games."

"Yeah."

"So you could have been wearing it."

He nodded.

"Do you still have it?"

"No."

"You lost it?"

"It was in my apartment. After I was arrested. I don't know what happened to it."

I sat back. He looked at me, waiting for me to speak. The feeling came again, that I'd seen him someplace before. Someplace other than the news.

The guard cleared his throat. "Two minutes," he said.

I looked at my watch. By my count he was ripping me off by at least a minute. But I really couldn't see that it mattered.

I thought about the ground I hadn't covered with Aaron. His parents' divorce. Grandfather's accident. Father's suicide. The juvenile delinquency conviction for the trash bin fire. I considered that if police or firefighters investigating an un-solved fatal arson hired a psychiatrist and tasked him or her with developing a profile of the suspect, they could do worse, a lot worse, than describing the person sitting across the table from me.

I said, "What do you want to come out of this?"

"Out of what?"

"This situation. What you told your grandmother."

"I don't know."

"You don't know?"

He shrugged. I tried a few more questions, with the re-sponses always the same. He didn't know. He couldn't remem-ber. He wasn't sure.

He didn't care.

"Time," the guard said.

I said, "How about getting out? Being proven innocent? Does that mean anything to you?"

"I don't know," he said. "Yes, I guess."

"That's it," the guard said. "Stand up, Custer."

"Are you innocent?" I said to Aaron. "Did you set that fire? Kill those people?"

"I said, that's it," the guard said.

"I don't know," Aaron said. "I really don't know."

AS INSTRUCTED, I STAYED in my seat while the guard escorted Aaron out of the room. He didn't look back at me as he shuffle-clinked down the hall. A minute later the guard returned and led me back toward the main lobby, silently standing beside me as the gate opened again at the signal from his colleague in the booth. I traded my visitor's badge for my driver's license and signed out.

Back at my van I picked up my phone, which I'd left on the seat, checked my messages, and saw the usual mess of electronic alerts. A breaking news update from Channel 7, Suzanne's station, about an overturned vehicle on Interstate 270. A Facebook comment from my sister. A text from Anne with a reminder about tomorrow's run, complete with a smiley face and a little cartoon image of a woman jogging.

In the middle of this jumble, a text message from a number I didn't recognize.

Eric Jenkins. Guy at the party. A phone number followed.

I tried to think who this was. Then a follow-up buzzed its arrival.

Chelsea's ex-boyfriend. Don't tell her i gave you his number. LOL.

Chad, Chelsea's current beau. I thought back to Sloopy's Diner. Him taking my card. The look she'd given him when he'd brought up Eric's name. But why would Chad care?

The answer came with the third text. **I'm a criminal justice major. Cool what you do. Like Breaking Bad.**

Not exactly, I texted back. **But thanks.**

17

COLUMBUS HAS A THING FOR VILLAGES.
More accurately, for neighborhoods called villages. German
Village, where I live. Merion Village, around the corner from
me. Hungarian Village, around the corner from Merion. Victorian Village, home to Pendergrass Research and the coroner's
office and majestic restored homes from an era you'll just have
to guess at. And Italian Village, northeast of downtown, with
Fourth Street running right alongside it. Good luck trying to
find a short line for meatballs in a cup at the annual Italian
festival, though the wait is always worth it. Look on a map and
you'll see that the fastest way to drive to the Ohio State campus from my house is right up Fourth, one-way going north,
cutting out all those stoplights and crosswalks on High Street.
Almost a speedway if you catch it at the right time of day.

Look at the same map and you'll see that working your
way over from German Village to Front Street and driving up
that side of downtown to campus makes no sense at all. Unless
you're out for a Sunday drive, and even then. But there I was,
a few hours after finishing the lunkhead run with Anne and

on my way to campus to meet with Eric Jenkins. And driving right past the Neil House Inn on Front, where I'd seen Glen Murphy and his girlfriend, his other girlfriend, on their way inside a couple of days earlier. It was irrational, I know. So was coming up to Broad Street, turning left and making an illegal left turn on Civic Center Drive. As I headed south to make another loop, I glanced across the Scioto River at COSI, the children's science museum. For some people, the wings extending out from either side of the old, renovated Central High School conjured images of flight. A crown jewel of downtown development, a sign that Columbus hadn't just grown, but grown up as well.

Maybe it was just my mood, but today the wings made me think of something else. Of the ridges of a zeppelin that had crash-landed smack on the school.

This mood was not improved when, after my fourth loop around, somewhat to my surprise, I spied Murphy and the woman repeating the previous scenario at the hotel's drop-off. You'd think I'd be angry at this point. But now, as I slowly drove past, I felt shame at what I'd done to abet this. I had blindsided Suzanne at Lindey's, launching a flood of digital scorn aimed at her and Murphy, a development I should have foreseen. Out of some misguided attempt to redress an old wrong, I'd made our situation even worse.

And she didn't even know it.

UNLIKE CHELSEA FOWLER, ERIC Jenkins was more than happy to meet me at Starbucks. He ordered a fruit drink, which he drained while we talked. He was a good-looking kid, handsomer, I'd have to say, than Chad. Angular face, wisp of a mustache and beard which hinted at a bohemian side, comfortable in a long-sleeve button-down blue shirt and jeans. No Abercrombie & Fitch.

"So you dated Chelsea," I said.

"Yes, I did," he said.

"Were you dating the night of the party?"

"That was near the end."

"Just didn't work out?"

"She's a great girl. I just wasn't ready to commit."

"And Chad is?"

"Chad's a good guy. Different strokes, you know?"

"Sure. So you were at the party that night."

"That's right."

"You know Matt?"

"Friend of a friend."

"And you heard Aaron that night. Talking to Tina."

"Lots of people did. Kinda hard to miss."

"What'd you hear?"

"Same as everyone, I guess."

"Go ahead and tell me."

"They were arguing. It was hard to understand Aaron. He was really drunk. Almost couldn't stand up. And he was angry."

"Angry?"

"Yeah. Or no. Kind of pissed, upset. He was a mess, either way."

"What was he angry about?"

"Don't know."

"Do you remember what he was saying to her?"

"Something about the boss. '*Boss is gonna get him.*'"

"'*The boss is gonna take him out.*' Could that have been it?"

"Something like that."

"Him being Jacob?"

"I guess."

"Did Aaron and Jacob talk?"

"Briefly."

"Where?"

"Outside. On the porch. After he'd been arguing with Tina, but before Matt threw him out."

"Did you hear what they said?"

"Same thing. Something about a boss and the street."

"A boss and the street?"

"Something like that."

"Any idea what it meant?"

He shook his head. "I didn't know either one. I mean, I'd seen Jacob around campus. But not Aaron. He wasn't in school, was he?"

"No. Did you know Jacob sold pot?"

"Yeah," he said.

"Had you bought from him?"

"Maybe."

"Had you bought from him that night?"

"He said he didn't have any. Wasn't there for that."

"He said he wasn't there to sell?"

"Something like that."

"Why was he at the party? Matt invite him?"

"Doubtful."

"Why not?"

"I don't think they got along."

"I thought they were friends."

"They were roommates. Freshman year. I think they hung out a little after that. I didn't get the impression they were that friendly."

"Why?"

"I heard Matt and Helen talking about it that night. In the kitchen."

"Helen Chen?"

"Yeah. He asked her who invited Jacob."

"What'd she say?"

"She didn't know."

"Jacob stayed the night. Matt couldn't have been too happy about that."

"Probably not."

"He hooked up with Tina Montgomery, didn't he?"

"That would be accurate."

So there was a piece of the puzzle in place, why Jacob had been there when the fire broke out. Point to Detective Fielding. Yet, like every other piece so far, it solved absolutely nothing.

"You really think Aaron's innocent?" Eric said.

"I don't know," I said. "Less and less, I think."

"He stood on the lawn and said he was going to kill everyone. I didn't hear that, but lots of people did."

"Yes," I said.

"So what's Helen say?"

"Helen?"

"Yeah. What's she say about Aaron?"

"I don't know. I haven't talked to her."

"She won't talk?"

"I just haven't tried yet. I don't have her number." I left out my conversation with trial attorney Janet Crenshaw of Smyth, Sanner, Stacy and Franko.

"Oh," Jenkins said. "Do you want it?"

WHEN I CHECKED MY e-mail at home I saw the state had produced the report on Eddie Miller's suicide. No mention of the bad news he'd supposedly received just prior, but otherwise looked pretty basic. Wrapped a bedsheet around his neck between guards' rounds, tied the other end to a window latch, and dropped to his knees, strangling himself. Besides that it told me nothing I didn't already know. The one-page report mentioned a concurrent state patrol investigation. I thought about requesting that, then thought about the paperwork involved. Instead, I called the number for the Portsmouth patrol post in southern Ohio.

"Andy," said trooper Billy Maxwell when he called me back ten minutes later, "what's going on? You got another case?"

"Manner of speaking," I said. "Got a favor to ask."

"Ask away. I owe you, man. Got a nice commendation for helping out on that little dealio last year."

That little dealio had involved two murders separated by a couple of decades, false identity, and a whole lot of heartache, not to mention an ongoing federal investigation into a $50 million Ponzi scheme. It took Maxwell's help to bring it all to light. I told him what I needed.

"Way out of my jurisdiction," he said. But before I could voice disappointment, he said, "But I got a favor or two coming my way from central office. Might be a day or two."

"Day or two's fine."

"Still gotta have that beer," he said. "Talk some football."

"I'd like that," I said.

AFTER THAT I LEFT another message for Molly "Mary" Custer. Ignoring me, or referring the calls to Dorothy? Guessing the former. Next, mindful of Crenshaw's prohibition about calling her clients, I texted the number for Helen Chen that Eric Jenkins had passed on. Spirit of the law and all that. No answer either way.

Late in the afternoon I dropped by Dorothy's house to update her on my progress.

"It doesn't sound promising," she said.

"Lot of loose ends," I said. "They're just not leading anywhere yet."

"I appreciate you keeping me apprised."

"I left messages for Molly," I said. "Has she contacted you?"

"No."

"I'll keep trying, if that's OK."

"Be my guest. I doubt she'll call back."

"Because she knows I'm working for you?"

She nodded. "That, and everything else. But it's your case." She smiled. "As long as you remember who's in charge."

"One other thing."

"Yes."

"It's been a week. I'll probably need some additional funds soon."

"I understand," she said. "Can I write you a check?"

"Whatever's convenient."

A check was convenient, and I left with it a few minutes later tucked in my wallet. I thought about finding a bank branch nearby and taking care of it immediately, but decided against it. I had more pressing matters to tend to.

It was a semiarduous journey to India Oak Grill two blocks north, where I went inside, settled on a bar stool, and tackled a couple of draft Yuenglings and an Italian sub sandwich that my spreading gut told me I didn't need. Fuel for the adventure ahead, I told myself.

It was starting to get dark when I drove up the road, got on Interstate 270, and drove west for about fifteen minutes, marveling at the ever-expanding number of all-glass corporate office buildings cropping up on either side, before getting off at the exit for Dublin. A few minutes later, I found myself driving slowly through a well-heeled subdivision, listening to the voice on my phone direct me to the address I was looking for. Within another minute I was slowing as I drove past the home of Glen Murphy, president of Murphy Drilling and Excavating. I had imagined him living in some kind of McMansion monstrosity, but I wasn't even close. He had a bigger two-story house than you might see in less desirable zip codes, on a bigger lot with a bigger garage. But for the most part, nothing you wouldn't find in any other decent suburb in America. It came replete with a couple of yard signs signaling the presence of one high school runner and one high school softball player dwelling within. I tried to imagine Suzanne as a stepmother to Murphy's kids, living a suburban life so far from her hectic job on the grittier streets of the city. "*Snublin*," she'd said derisively of this very suburb more than once, when we'd been together. Yet surprisingly, I found I could see it. She'd always had a homey side to her, bravado aside. And I had changed since those days, or so I told myself. Why couldn't she? I circled once more around the block, seeing if I could catch a glimpse through the living room window of Murphy, the kids, the girlfriend, Suzanne, or anyone, but all was quiet.

I headed home, needing another beer. Or two.

18

I LEFT ANOTHER MESSAGE FOR MOLLY Custer the next morning. I then spent a couple of strenuous hours drinking coffee, reading the paper, trying to solve that day's Easter Egg hunt clue in the *Dispatch,* going over my notes on the fire, and pushing Hobble-along into and out of my backyard. Eventually, with no response and nothing better to do, I decided to just drive to Molly's house. The address was a two-story white home on Indianola in Clintonville with a "Welcome Friends" mat in front of the door. I knocked but got no answer. I slipped my card between the screen and the door jamb and left.

I had better luck late that afternoon, returning after additionally strenuous hours getting the van's oil changed and reading up on all the requirements to renew my investigator's license. Lunch and a nap factored in there someplace.

A teenage girl answered the door. Hair pulled back in a tight ponytail, wearing a Whetstone Braves sweatshirt, jeans, and a frown. She called for her mom, then disappeared.

Molly Custer came to the door with the same frown. I handed her another card and made my pitch. With obvious reluctance, she agreed to let me come in.

"This is a fool's errand," she said as we entered the living room and she offered me a chair. Hardwood floors, stone fireplace set off by a ceramic tile front, big windows. Framed photos lined the mantel. I examined the one in the middle. The girl who'd answered the door, though a little bit younger-looking, standing beside Aaron, with more hair.

"He's a good-looking kid," I offered. "I met him."

"That's Mike," she said.

"I'm sorry?"

"That's my late husband. Mike."

I took a closer look. "Quite a resemblance," I said.

"What people say."

I found an actual photo of Aaron two pictures down. The feeling came over me again, from the prison. A resemblance to someone that went beyond familiarity with his ubiquitous picture. Beyond his resemblance to his father.

"I don't mean to bother you," I said, sitting down. "I just like to touch as many bases as I can on a case like this."

"OK," she said.

"Do you think he's innocent?"

"I don't know. I suppose not. He doesn't seem like the same boy anymore."

"Anymore?"

"As the one who grew up here."

I heard a sound. Looked over and saw her daughter standing at the edge of the room, listening.

I said, "Things went downhill after your husband died. And his grandfather."

Molly stared at me.

"I mean, from what Dorothy said."

"That's right, I guess. She would know."

"They were close. Frank and Aaron."

"Yes."

"How about Aaron and his dad?"

"Close enough," she said.

"Some tension?"

"Like I said, close enough."

I thought about that. Thought about the old joke. Grandparents get along so well with grandchildren because they share a common enemy.

"Sounds like Mike had a difficult time," I said.

"What do you mean?"

"The business. Olen-Tangy-Tots."

"What about it?"

"Going under."

"It wasn't great, no."

"That what Mike did? Restaurant business?"

"He did a lot of things. Some better than others."

"What about Mike and his father?"

"What about them?"

"Did they get along?"

"What does that have to do with anything?"

"I'm not sure," I said.

"Then why ask?"

"Part of the job, I guess."

"Seems like your job is being nosy."

"One way of putting it. So how about it?"

"How about what?"

"Mike. And his dad."

"They had their ups and downs, OK? Like any father and son."

I wondered about that. But I said, "Mike's suicide. That must have been hard on Aaron."

"Yes."

"On top of his grandfather's death."

"You seem to know everything about us."

"I'm sorry," I said. "Just trying to understand Aaron a little more."

"I don't know how much there is to understand. He's a troubled kid. I hate to admit it, because I still love him. But it's true."

"You and Mike divorced."

"That's right."

"May I ask why?"

"No."

"Hard on Aaron too, I'm guessing."

"You guessed right."

"How long had you been married?"

She hesitated. "Twenty years."

"How did you meet?"

"I'm sorry?"

"You and Mike."

"Ohio State."

"Same year?"

"Yes."

We might have been the same class, I thought. Had I graduated on time.

"You're from Columbus?"

She nodded. "Grew up just down the street."

"And you go by Mary now."

"Yes."

"Any reason?"

"My given name. I always liked it better."

"Dorothy called you Molly."

"Yes," she said.

"Why?"

She shrugged. "Old habits."

I said, "What do you do?"

"Me?"

"Yes."

"Sales," she said. "Business marketing for Time Warner."

"Sounds interesting," I said. "How do you like it?"

"Pays the bills," she said. "I like it some days more than others."

I glanced over my shoulder. The girl was gone.

"Your daughter?" I said.

"Yes. Sophia."

"Still in high school?"

"Junior. At Whetstone."

"How's she doing? With everything?"

"OK, I guess. Better now than before."

"She and Aaron close?"

"Not anymore."

"Are they in touch?"

"Not really. She doesn't want to go to the prison. I don't blame her, and I don't force her."

"How often do you go?"

"Most weeks."

"How do you think he's doing?"

"Not really sure. He's sober, so that's something."

"Yes," I said.

And that was about it. We talked a few minutes more, then I thanked her for her time. I stood up, took one last look at the photos on the mantel, and showed myself out. I could see why Dorothy was calling the shots, I thought as I drove away. Molly-Mary just didn't seem to have the energy. Could you blame her?

19

"IT'S NO BIG DEAL," I SAID THE NEXT MORNING as I climbed into Roy's van just after dawn. "I'm usually up this early on a Saturday anyway." Barely an hour had passed since he'd awakened me from a deep sleep with a request for help.

"Right," he said. "I'll remember that the next time the neighbor's cat tries to get into Lucy's chicken coop at 4 a.m. Anyway, you should be grateful."

"Grateful?"

"Think how much time you would have wasted watching cartoons and eating Cap'n Crunch if I hadn't called."

"Now I feel even worse," I said.

We drove the next few minutes in silence, sipping the coffee Roy had brought along in a large steel Thermos. We drove through downtown, which like us was just starting to wake up, and a few minutes later parked on the grass along the running trail by Confluence Park. A few minutes after that we were back in the homeless camp we'd visited a few nights earlier.

Three people sat around the fire, warming themselves against the April chill. The rest of the camp was still quiet.

Most of its residents were asleep in their tents and makeshift cabins. Like normal people on a Saturday. The men around the fire were drinking coffee from cups they'd filled from a pot perched on a grill above the flames. Roy topped them off from a second Thermos he'd toted along.

He said, quietly, "Trouble last night?"

After a moment, one of the men nodded.

"Guys in the camp?"

Another nod. "Drunks. Seen them here before."

Roy introduced him as Benny. I said hello. He ignored me.

"Hurt anybody?" Roy said.

Benny shook his head.

"Do any damage?"

"Knocked a couple clotheslines down. But Sam chased them off."

"She around?"

"Still asleep."

"She OK?"

"Guess so."

"Know who they were?"

Another shake of his head.

"You looking for me?"

We turned at the sound of a woman's voice. She was thin, wearing jeans and two or three sweaters. Age indeterminate, with heavy black-framed glasses that didn't fit with the size of her face and hair hidden under a Columbus Crew pull-down winter cap.

"Hello, Sam," Roy said. "Coffee?"

She approached without speaking, sat down, held out a chipped white mug.

"You know Andy?" Roy said.

She looked at me, holding both hands around the cup. "Nope," she said after a moment. "Don't want to, either."

"He's not a bad guy," Roy said. "Once you borrow money from him."

Sam frowned and sipped her coffee.

"Ran off some troublemakers last night," Roy said to her. It wasn't a question.

"College kids," she hissed.

"Sure about that?" Roy said.

"How the hell should I know?" she said. "Been college kids before. Chased them up High Street one time. Probably college kids now."

I tried to picture this wisp of a woman pursuing a bunch of drunken college kids. It didn't seem probable, but I liked the imagery.

"Shameful," she said.

"Want the police to pay a visit?" Roy said.

"Already tried that," Benny said.

"And?"

"Dispatcher said she needed a better address than 'a bunch of woods by the railroad tracks.'" Everyone laughed.

"You need help, you let me know," Roy said. "Doesn't have to be like that."

"Always been like that," Sam said. "Always gonna be like that."

"Doesn't have to be," Roy said.

We stayed another thirty minutes, drinking coffee and chatting. A couple other men joined us. Roy distributed the rest of the coffee, then handed out some water bottles he'd carried in. Then we stood, said our farewells, and left. Sam had disappeared by that time. The sun was up and joggers and bikers were passing in both directions when we emerged from the woods and walked back to Roy's church van.

"How'd that guy call 911?" I said.

"Two cans with a string stretched between them," Roy said.

"Seriously."

"How do you think? With a phone."

"They have phones?"

"Some of them. Radios, too, sometimes DVD players even. Very twenty-first century."

"How do they charge them?"

"Same as everybody else. They steal electricity from coffee shops, library, wherever. Being homeless doesn't make them cavemen."

"OK, OK," I said. "Next question."

"Yes?"

"I have a hard time believing college students would do something like that."

"You'd be right. That's all in Sam's head. Could have been anyone. High school kids, drunks from the Arena District, headbangers who stay near campus. You name it."

"She said she chased them all the way to campus."

"Maybe she chased them up High *through* campus. Who knows?"

"On foot?"

"She's got a bike. Rides everywhere. Rode to Toledo and back once, so she claims."

"You believe her?"

He shrugged.

"She all there?"

"On her meds, she's pretty cogent. Comes to church every so often. Prettiest soprano voice. By and large, she's in and out. That's why we came so early. You never know where she'll be."

"How long has she been in the woods?"

"She was there when I came back from Iraq in 2006. Then she left and lived with a sister or someone for a while. Then she came back, and then right away got some kind of transitional housing. She showed up again about a year ago, couple years maybe. St. Clare's working with her. Trying to find something permanent."

"If she left the camp, who would chase off the troublemakers?"

"Good question," Roy said.

20

I SPENT MOST OF THE NEXT DAY AT THE zoo on an extended outing with Anne, her daughter, Amelia, her parents, and Mike and Joe. I forgot Mike's *Redwall* book and Joe's Darth Vader shirt again, but all things considered, it was a good day. We piled into an Italian restaurant on Sawmill Road afterward, and I had the boys home to their respective houses with an hour to spare before bedtime.

Trying to turn over a new exercise leaf, I walked to the bank the next morning, finally getting around to depositing Dorothy's check. I had just come back to the house when my phone rang with Mellencamp's "Small Town."

"This is Helen Chen."

"Yes," I said, pulling up.

"You wanted to talk to me. About the fire."

"That's right," I said. "And about Aaron."

"All right."

"When's a good time?"

"This afternoon? My last class ends at four."

She gave me her address.

"Before I come?" I said.

"Yes."

I told her why I wanted to talk to her. Told her flat-out that Dorothy didn't think Aaron had done it.

"Oh," she said when I finished.

"I wanted to make sure that's OK."

"I see."

"I know that's probably not something you want to hear."

"It's fine."

"You're sure?"

"Yes," she said. "I'm not sure Aaron set the fire either."

HELEN LIVED ON WOODRUFF Avenue, just a few blocks over from the Orton Avenue house. Same style of century-old brick building. Two stories with an attic, five steps leading to the lawn, five more steps leading down to the sidewalk. Wheelchair accessible this neighborhood was not.

"I'm surprised you're so close," I said when I was seated on a couch in the living room. "To Orton Avenue, I mean."

"My parents weren't happy," she said. "They wanted me in the dorms. But I couldn't have dealt with that. All those eyes on me. Rent was cheap here, and my roommate and I get along."

"Makes sense," I said, not sure I thought it did. She was slight, with black hair and light-brown skin and a serious expression. She didn't bear obvious scars from the fire, with the exception of a penny-sized scar on her throat, which I knew from Suzanne's extended interview with her parents was the incision from the tracheotomy she'd needed after inhaling so much heated smoke. Which also explained her raspy voice, like that of a two-pack-a-day smoker twice her age. She'd spent weeks in the hospital and months in outpatient therapy and treatment afterward, but overall she'd been lucky. Some fire victims had permanent tracheotomies from the severe scorching as they breathed in superheated air and smoke. Others, of course, didn't leave the scene of the fire at all.

"You're from Columbus?" I said.

"Worthington."

"Nice city. Got that cute downtown."

"I guess. We live in a subdivision."

"What do your parents do?"

"Mom's a doctor. Dad's an engineer at Honda."

"Why'd you go to Ohio State?"

"Lots of reasons, I guess." When I didn't say anything, she went on. "Didn't want to be that far away. Both my parents went here. Got a scholarship. And Mom was in the marching band, so that was always a big deal, hearing about that."

"You said you didn't think Aaron set the fire. Why?"

"I'm not exactly sure," she said. "I know it sounds strange."

"Ever tell the police that?"

"I was never interviewed."

"Your injuries."

She nodded. "I wasn't really with it until at least a month later. And by then Aaron was in jail and had already confessed and been charged."

"Did you have doubts then?"

"I didn't really think anything. I was just trying to survive. To live, you know? But afterward, I just thought about it. I remember seeing him trying to talk to Tina Montgomery. The look in his eyes. Even though he was drunk. He cared about her."

"You know about the security video, from the gas station? The print on the lighter?"

"Sure."

"The threat? To kill everyone?"

"Yes."

"Doesn't change your mind?"

"I'm just telling you what I think. It didn't seem like he was threatening Tina. More like he was warning her."

"He was angry about her and Jacob Dunning. Isn't that the whole thing?"

"More like he was worried about Jacob."

"Worried?"

"About something happening to him. So that made him worry about Tina."

"What about threatening to hurt Jacob? '*The boss is gonna take him out.*' All that."

"That's not what he said."

"What?"

"*The boss.* That's not what he said."

"It's what Chelsea Fowler heard. And Eric Jenkins."

"It wasn't *boss,*" she said. "It was *posse.* He kept saying *posse.* You know, like cowboys? Like some posse was going to do something to Jacob."

"You're sure?"

"Yes."

"Why?"

"I don't drink," Helen said. "I was probably the only sober person there that night. Aaron was slurring his words and all that, but it was clear. '*The posse's gonna take him out.*'"

"Any idea what kind of posse we're talking about?" I said. "We're a little short of cowboys in Columbus at the moment."

She shook her head. "Maybe something to do with drugs? I mean, everybody knew Jacob sold pot."

I told her what Eric Jenkins had said, about Jacob not selling that night.

"That could be true," she said.

"Eric said Jacob sort of showed up uninvited."

"Not sort of. Just did."

"Why didn't Matt tell him to leave?"

"He did, at first. But then Jacob kind of disappeared and Matt was talking to other people. It was a really big party."

"Eric said Jacob and Tina hooked up."

"That's true," she said.

I mulled the possibilities. *Posse,* not *boss.* I thought about Karen Feinberg. *This isn't TV, Andy.*

"So Aaron might have been worried about Jacob," I said.

"Maybe not worried, like, cared one way or the other. But worried that if something happened to him, it could affect Tina. Like that."

"No idea what he was talking about?'

"No."

"Did anyone threaten Jacob at the party?"

"I don't know about threaten," she said. "Tina said something."

"Like what?"

"Something about somebody named Ryan."

"Ryan?"

"That's what she said."

"This is after Aaron and she were arguing?"

"That's right."

"And after Aaron left?"

She nodded.

"How did this come up?"

"I asked Tina what Aaron had been talking about. She said she didn't know. But later, I guess she'd been talking to Jacob, and supposedly some guy named Ryan had come by and threatened Jacob."

"Came to the party?"

"Yes."

"No idea who the guy was?"

She shook her head.

"Anybody else see him?"

"I don't know. It was a huge party. Lots of people in and out all night."

"And nobody told the police this?"

"I don't think so," she said. "I don't think Tina told anybody else but me."

"And she and Jacob were the only two that would have known about it," I said.

She nodded.

I was about to ask her another question when we were interrupted by the door opening. A young woman walked in, dropped her backpack on the floor, said, "Hey, girl!" then stopped, seeing me.

"This is Lori," Helen said. "Lori Hume."

Matt Cummings's girlfriend.

"I'M SORRY," HELEN SAID. "I should have told you he was coming over."

Lori was sitting on a chair opposite the couch, her knees up and her arms wrapped around them. She was quiet, not moving.

"I didn't realize you were roommates," I said. "I'm sorry."

"I guess I thought you knew," Helen said.

"I can't believe it," Lori said.

We were quiet.

"I can't believe you would do something to try to help that guy. After what he did."

"I'm sorry," I repeated.

"I'm sorry, too."

She stared at me a few moments longer, then walked out of the room. Disappeared around the corner past the stairs, into the kitchen. A moment later I heard stomping as she went up a back stairway. I sighed.

"She know about your doubts?" I said to Helen a moment later. "About Aaron?"

"No."

"You never told her?"

"Didn't see any reason to."

"Why not?"

"We both know how we feel about what happened," she said. "What I think of Aaron wouldn't change any of that, I guess."

"OK," I said.

"It definitely wouldn't change Lori's mind," she said. "And she's my friend."

"Friends are important," I said.

"They are when you've lost them the way I did," Helen said.

I'D PLANNED TO STAY in that night, organize my notes, see if I was close to making a report for Dorothy. But my conversation with Helen turned everything topsy-turvy. Instead, late in the afternoon, I walked down to Whittier and over a few blocks, and a few minutes later I was sitting at the bar in the Hey Hey Bar & Grill, "The bar so nice they named it twice," sipping a draft PBR and snacking on fried sauerkraut balls. I stared at the Hawaiian lei-wearing puppet behind the bar, daring her—him?—to stare back. The Cavaliers were on TV, and this sparked a conversation about basketball with a couple beside me originally from Parma Heights. My first beer led to a second, and then a third, and I was finally starting to relax when my phone rang.

"Andy? Billy Maxwell."

I looked at my watch. Nearly 7:30 p.m.

"You're working late."

"Pileup on 23. Nobody killed, but a mess. Just got off. Anyway, I got the skinny on your suicide."

"All ears."

"Only going to need one of 'em. You were right about the bad news. This Eddie Miller? His sister was found dead of a heroin overdose the morning before. That stuff they're lacing with fentanyl. Bad, really bad. We're starting to see it everywhere down here."

"OK."

"Thing I'm told, Miller and her both used, but he saw himself as her protector. Long as he was around, she'd stay off the bad stuff. They did a needle-exchange program together."

"I don't follow."

"When he was out of the picture, there was no one around to look out for her. That's what my guys who investigated it said."

"He blamed himself for her overdose."

"That's about it."

"So the suicide was legitimate."

"Looks that way."

I thought about the power that heroin had had over Miller. Enough to send him to prison for bank robbery. To leave his sister exposed to the perils of the street. To push him to suicide despite sitting on an explosive tip that might have helped get him out earlier, or make him a rich man, or richer than he'd been, anyway. Rich enough to take care of himself and his sister.

Or buy them more drugs.

"Thanks," I said. "Now I owe you."

"No problem."

"We'll talk football soon."

"Love to. Have a good one."

I finished my beer, signaled the barkeeper, paid my tab, and left. I'd had enough of the day. It was time to look into a new one.

21

WHEN I GOT UP THE NEXT MORNING I KNEW
in my heart the right thing to do was go for a jog to work off
the beer and sauerkraut balls from the night before. But I was
still thinking about what Helen had told me, piled on top of
seeing Lori react to my presence, and I made more coffee and
fired up my laptop instead.

The first person I should have called was Suzanne. But
after pondering my unpleasant discovery about Glen Murphy,
I decided to stay clear for now. I couldn't undo the damage I'd
done, but I could keep it from getting worse.

Instead, I considered who in law enforcement to tell about
what Helen had said. Or even if I should. Did the fact somebody
had threatened Jacob matter? It could have been true, and still
not be relevant to the case. The world was full of those kinds of
coincidences. But the information was still new, something investigators never heard. It was worth a chance. I dug a nickel out of
my pocket. Heads, I called Omar Sharif. Tails, Lord Voldemort.

I flipped and got tails. I called Omar after all. And left a
voice mail.

I turned to filling in the gaps about Lori Hume. I already knew about her early departure from the party. I supposed it raised suspicions, but you'd have to say the same about Chelsea Fowler and Eric Jenkins and however many others, probably several dozens, who also left the party before the fire. And her grief was so obviously real. And she didn't remotely resemble any criminal I'd ever encountered. I rewatched Suzanne's Channel 7 interview with Lori, marveling at how good Suzanne looked in the power suit and pearls she'd worn for the occasion. I found a picture of Lori in the Ohio State *Lantern*, holding a candle at a vigil outside the Orton Avenue house two days later. I read a *Dispatch* account of the funeral where she made a few heartfelt remarks. And that was about it.

Some of the most touching comments that day came from Tanner Gridley, Matt's environmental geology professor. The story included a link to his university home page, and I clicked on it for no other reason than to give myself a reason not to stare any longer at the victims' photos. Idly, I scanned Gridley's résumé, charting his life from native of Youngstown, Ohio, bachelor of science received twenty years earlier at Youngstown State, then Ph.D. from Penn State. After a few minutes of searching, a picture of parallel lives took shape. Professionally, he was a widely published geologist with a specialty in seismology. Personally, he was an activist fighting the spread of fracking. His pointed reminder to me that he was an assistant professor meant he didn't have tenure yet. There were also a few outliers in his online life, including frequent references to events involving multiple sclerosis. That gave me pause. I checked out his Facebook page and then his wife's and soon pieced it together. She had MS. He was fundraising for the cause. Turns out he had some pretty decent 5K times. I thought guiltily of the run I'd skipped that morning.

I visited a few more Web pages and learned a couple more things about fracking and MS and the Youngstown State

Penguins, but the well of information was starting to dry up. I was close to calling it a day and setting out to do some real work when I came across an agenda for a hydraulic fracturing conference Gridley had attended in Dallas two years earlier. He'd given a paper on seismological indicators related to a series of small quakes in Oklahoma that had been linked to injection wells, though I was hoping the discussion was more interesting than the title: "Anthropogenic Seismicity Rates and Operational Parameters in the Eola Field." I struggled through the abstract of the paper, but then paused when I came to the list of participants on a panel discussion that had followed. Three names down from his was someone I'd heard of before. But in a different context. I lifted her name and title and plugged them into the search engine, then hit enter.

How odd, I thought, as the results of the search populated my screen. Gridley had sat on a panel at an academic conference with Kim McDowell, the Pendergrass Research scientist whose head Buddy "Killer" Keeler had bashed in.

22

I WAS STILL WEIGHING THIS INFORMATION, and trying to decide if it was a coincidence or just the obvious result of a finite number of Columbus geologists attending an important national convention, when Omar Sharif returned my call.

"What do you need?"

"I came across something I thought I should tell someone."

"It's the police department's case," Whitestone said.

"I'll tell Fielding," I promised. "Just hear me out."

I explained about Helen and *posse* vs. *boss* and somebody named Ryan threatening Jacob and Matt's anger at Jacob's presence at the party.

"Jacob wasn't dealing that night?" he said when I'd finished.

"Supposedly not."

"Have you talked to Custer yet?"

"Yes."

"Wouldn't he have known what he said? That he said *posse*, not *boss*?"

"He's a blackout drunk who suffered a pretty serious head injury that night from the beating. He doesn't remember anything," I said. "Plus, his nickname was *boss*. He knew that much."

"Flimsy. He's either lying or stupider than I think. And still guilty as hell."

"What about the threat to Jacob?"

"Somebody named Ryan. That's all Helen said?"

"Yes."

"First I've heard of it. We talked to a lot of kids."

"But not Helen."

"Because she was in the hospital for weeks. And we already had the guy who did it."

"Still new information."

"So Jacob made enemies selling pot. News alert."

"I didn't have to call you," I said.

"Got that right."

"I just thought somebody should know."

"A real do-gooder, you are."

"So you're not interested?"

"Half the stuff you just told me we know. The other half isn't worth crapola. And to get right back to square one, it doesn't matter because we have the guy who did it behind bars. And now I've got to go. And Andy?"

"Yes?"

"Do yourself a favor. Don't call Fielding with this shit."

I WAS RETURNING MY attention to the coincidence that Gridley had known Kim McDowell when I checked my e-mail and saw a notice from the bank. Dorothy's check for $500 had bounced. Not a welcome development considering how low my bank balance was.

She was apologetic when I called and promised to move things around right away. She said something about problems with automated payments and online banking. I assured her I

wasn't angry and told her I understood. Truth be told, I was
the last person to criticize anyone else's financial affairs. Not
so long ago, my updated version of the old free spender's joke
went like this: if I still had my ATM card, how could there not
be money in my account?

My conversation with Dorothy reminded me of something
she had said about e-mailing Aaron. I went online and signed
up for the prison communication system, bought a package of
virtual stamps, and sent Aaron a message about my conversation with Helen Chen.

I went back over my notes and looked at the number of
potential witnesses I could still talk to. I realized I hadn't heard
back from either the pizza delivery guy or the guy who called
the fire in. Since those numbers were staring me in the face, I
called them first. I got the same recorded message for my pizza
person. Someone kept answering the McDonald's phone, then
hanging up. In the end I decided it was close enough to lunchtime and just drove over there.

D. B. CHAMBERS SEEMED taken aback by my visit,
but once I'd explained my unpleasant mission again he agreed
to sit down with me during a break over a Big Mac and fries. I
offered to buy him lunch, but he shook his head. "I don't eat
this shit, man, I just sell it. I'm mostly a vegetarian."

"Smart choice," I said.

The McDonald's sat on Hudson just around the corner
from Fourth. The lunchtime crowd was a mix of retirees, tired-
looking moms, and a couple of college kids, or kids who looked
like they should be in college, anyway. Had they rousted any
homeless camps recently, I wondered? Chambers was black,
light-complected, his face freckled, both arms covered with a
series of tattoos. I was guessing he'd done time, but I had long
ago stopped holding that against anyone. Just as with my financial affairs, I was the last person to talk.

"Ohio State quarterback, huh?"

"That's right," I said. "Long time ago."

"I remember you. Good till all that shit went down."

"Something like that."

"Ever see that movie *The Replacements?*"

I nodded. I get this question a lot. Keanu Reeves's second outing as an ex-OSU quarterback. First time, in *Point Break,* he was undercover FBI agent Johnny Utah. "Quarterback punk." Second time, Shane Falco. "Fabulous Falco." A big deal until a forty-point meltdown in the Sugar Bowl. Movie didn't come out until long after my fall from grace. But a lot of days I still identified with Falco.

"Paper says you were on your way to work that morning," I said. "You live near there?"

"Not too far."

"What happened?"

"Not much to say. Saw the flames, pulled over, and called."

"You see anybody?"

"See?"

"Out and about. On the street. Like Aaron Custer, for example. Guy in prison for doing it."

He shook his head. "Nobody was around. It was really early."

"Did you stay? After you called?"

"I drove up the block and parked. I was barely out of the car when the fire trucks started getting there. I waited a couple minutes, talked to a cop, but I had to get to work."

I ate a fry. Then another.

"I know that sounds bad," Chambers said. "But there wasn't a lot I could do at that point. And I really needed this job." He paused. "I was on probation. Got a little girl. I couldn't afford to get canned."

"Probation for what? If you don't mind me asking."

"Drugs," he said. "Possession. Little dealing. Stupid shit."

"You happen to know Jacob Dunning? One of the kids who died?"

"No."

"People said he sold a little pot on the side."

"White kid dealing pot," he said. "Imagine that."

"Didn't know him?"

"Didn't know any of them. They were all college kids. How's that one girl doing?"

"Which one?"

"Chinese girl? She got hurt bad."

"Helen Chen?"

"That's the one."

"She's back in school."

"That's cool."

"How about a guy named Eddie Miller? Ever hear of him?"

"Nope. He go to OSU?"

I explained about Miller. It still didn't ring any bells.

"OK, forget about that," I said. "So how'd they get your name? Afterward. You got interviewed, right? On TV?"

"Police traced my phone, I guess. How the reporters got it, probably. That was about it. Cops said they might call me in, but they never did. Guess 'cause they got that kid so fast."

I nodded. Aaron's almost immediate arrest had made things a lot easier for everyone.

"So what's this about?" he said. "You're a private detective? I thought those were just in the movies."

"Used to be. Now we're on Netflix too." I explained about Aaron and Eddie Miller and the Columbus Red Birds cap.

"That's why I was wondering if you saw anyone," I said. "Or saw Aaron, maybe wearing the hat while he ran."

"Somebody else did it? Bad luck for Custer."

"Somebody else might have done it," I corrected. "Or not. It's all a bunch of questions with no answers right now." I pulled out my notebook. "You know a guy named Rory Ellison?"

"He one of the victims?"

"Not unless he died of food poisoning. He was delivering pizzas that night. Dropped a bunch off at the party."

"Never heard of him. Lot of pizza delivery guys. Thinking of trying it myself. These 5 a.m. shifts are getting old."

"I bet."

He looked like he was about to say something when a loud female voice called from the kitchen. "Hey, Chambers."

"Yeah?"

"These Happy Meals ain't gonna sell themselves. Let's go."

He turned back. "Sorry. Kids love them plastic toys. Anything else?"

I handed him a card. "Call me if you think of anything."

"Sure thing, Falco," he said, grinning as he got up.

I was back in my van feeling like I hadn't made any progress at all, and maybe even taken a step back, when a not-friendly-sounding lady finally returned the calls I'd placed to the number for Rory Ellison, the pizza delivery guy. He didn't live there anymore. Hadn't been there for a year. Had gone back to West Virginia. Taken her iPad with him, and did I happen to know how I could reach him since she didn't have his number in Charleston.

No, I apologized, I didn't know his number. As my messages trying to reach him might have implied.

Make that two steps back.

23

IT WAS BECAUSE OF ALL THESE DEAD-ENDS
that I was surprised, to say the least, to get a call the next morning from Helen Chen. I was half a block from my house, standing by a tree in front of the Brown Bag deli while Hopalong, gingerly limping back and forth, did his business. It was his longest outing since sometime in February.

"Lori's still upset," she said.

"I can imagine."

"After you left, she went through some things of Matt's. Stuff she hadn't touched since the fire."

"OK."

"That really set her off."

"I'm sorry."

"She gave it all to me. Said she couldn't deal with it anymore."

"Understandable."

"I don't know what to do with it. So I figured I'd just give it you."

"To me?"

"For the investigation."

"What about Matt's family?"

There was a pause. "I didn't think about that."

"How about if I just look at it instead?"

"Yeah. You're right."

"If there's anything I want, I'll make a copy."

"OK."

"Does Lori know you called me?"

"No."

"Probably better that way."

"Yes," Helen said.

GOING BACK TO HELEN'S house was out of the question. She suggested the Union, but I had no interest in a repeat visit. We settled on the coffee shop inside the Barnes and Noble campus bookstore, which a few years back had replaced Long's down the street, a store that served generations of Ohio State students, even myself on the few occasions I deigned to crack open a textbook.

I got myself a black coffee and bought Helen something hot and frothy containing milk and chocolate and sugar and not a whole lot of actual coffee, and then she pulled out a folder and showed me what she had. I opened it and spread the papers across our table. A couple letters Matt had written Lori one summer. I scanned them, looking for incriminating phrases that would exonerate Aaron Custer, but instead learned a lot about summer chores in the Cummings's household and the rigors of late-night Xbox sessions. Interesting that Lori would give those up. But maybe she was really trying to move on. Several photographs, most of them of Matt and Lori but a few of him and friends. A couple school papers. A selection of stick-on notes in different colors on which he'd drawn little pictures of himself with mock warnings in dialogue bubbles: Study. Eat. Jog. I imagined her finding those hidden in a book or on

ANDREW WELSH-HUGGINS

her seat in the library or beside her laptop when she came back from a bathroom break. I fought off a rush of sadness, thinking about what Aaron had done. Allegedly done.

I pushed the notes aside and looked through the rest. Gazed at some kind of incomprehensible geological document that I took to be related to Matt's research with Gridley. A flier from a showing of *Gasland* on which someone, presumably Matt, had scribbled "7 pm. Meet you there?" A menu for the Varsity Club on Lane Avenue. And that was it. Partial remains of a young life, tucked inside a red school folder, evocative, promising, but thin. So thin.

"Anything interesting?" Helen said, holding her cup in both hands as she took a drink. Her voice scratchy, hoarse.

"All of it," I said. "But I'm not sure it tells us anything. Anything bigger. If you know what I mean."

She nodded. "I sort of figured as much. I just didn't know what to do. She was so upset."

"Appreciate you thinking of me. These should go back to Matt's family at some point. Or at the very least, stay with you in case Lori changes her mind."

"That's no problem."

I looked through the papers again, pausing at the stick figures Matt had drawn. He would have been a fun kid to know. I skimmed the first couple pages of the papers, one on geological formations, the other an anthropology paper about mid-twentieth-century urban migration patterns, then glanced at the header on the geological document. I paused, looking at it again. And a third time.

"On second thought," I said. "Maybe I'll just make a copy of a couple things. Just in case."

"That's fine," Helen said. "I've got class at 11, though. Do you want to bring them back to me later?"

"Hang on," I said. I wandered through the bookstore, quizzing two different employees unsuccessfully about the possibility of a working copy machine. I returned to the table where Helen was sitting and used my phone to take pictures of the letters Matt had written Lori, the stick figures, the first page of his papers, and last but not least, the geological document. When I was done I handed the folder back to Helen.

"Maybe keep this in a safe place for now? Give Lori some time."

"Sure," she said.

We took our drinks with us as we walked out of the bookstore. At the street we shook hands formally, like a professor and student wrapping up a tutorial.

"Thanks again," I said. "I'll be in touch."

"All right," she said. And then she headed across the street to class.

24

"ANDY HAYES," I SAID, A FEW MINUTES LATER. "For Professor Gridley."

"He's not in at the moment," the department secretary informed me. I was back inside the bookstore with another cup of coffee. "I can take a message or put you through to his voice mail."

"Do you know if he's coming back?"

"I don't believe so."

I asked if she knew his schedule the next day.

"Tenure committee first thing, classes and office hours the rest of the day. Busy time of the semester."

I murmured my concurrence, then left my number.

BACK HOME, I TURNED on my laptop, plugged my phone into the computer, and a few minutes later printed out two of the pictures I'd taken of the documents in the bookstore. I e-mailed Gridley, a guy I suddenly wanted to talk to very much.

Next, I placed a call to Appletree Energy headquarters in Oklahoma City. I wasn't exactly sure how to word my message, so I left it somewhat vague after the receptionist transferred me to a marketing and communications number.

I was looking up an address on the Web when my cell phone buzzed.

How's it going?

Chad, I realized, the criminal justice major. Chelsea's boyfriend.

Fine, I texted back. **Thanks for your help.**

To my surprise, he called a minute later.

"Chad?" I said.

"Don't mean to bother you," he said. "Just wondered if I could talk to you sometime. About private detective stuff, I mean. How you got into it. It's cool."

"It has its moments," I said. "It's not really a good time right now. But maybe in a couple weeks."

"That's fine. I'm thinking of being a cop? That's what Chelsea wants me to do. But I've always liked private eyes, too. Pinkerton Agency, you know? Were you a cop? I mean, before this?"

"No," I said. "Not a cop. I know a few."

"I'm doing this street patrol thing next semester? You walk the neighborhoods, talk to people. Kind of eyes and ears of the police. Not armed or anything. Good experience."

"Sounds like it."

"So did Eric Jenkins help you out at all?"

"A little. Although I wonder if you gave me his name for information or because he was Chelsea's ex-boyfriend."

"Maybe I was teasing her a little," he said. "But Eric was there. At the party, I mean."

I agreed with this assessment.

"So he was helpful?"

"Yes," I said, multitasking while I looked up Tanner Gridley's home address.

"Like with what?"

Impatiently, I told him about the *posse* and *boss* confusion, adding that I didn't think it amounted to much.

"Like the Fourth Street Posse," he said.

"What?"

"The Fourth Street Posse. The gang."

I stopped fiddling with the computer. "What are you talking about?"

"It's a gang, you know. We've studied it in class. Been around for years. The Fourth Street Posse. You've heard of it, right?"

I confessed that I hadn't.

"It used to be a big deal. In the nineties. Then the feds cracked down hard. I wrote a paper about it."

The boss is gonna take him out.

The posse's gonna take him out.

"I'd like to read that," I said.

"Really?"

"Could you e-mail it?"

"Sure."

"Thanks."

"That's really cool, you want to read it," Chad said.

"Yes," I said. "Very cool."

25

"I HAVE TO ADMIT," ANNE SAID. "I USED TO BE a little nervous running along here."

"Even in the daylight?"

"Sometimes, yeah."

The Thursday morning lunkhead run. A week and a half out from Anne's half marathon. Her prospects were excellent, to judge by the pace we were keeping. Good thing I was on the bike.

"What changed? Your brute private eye boyfriend tagging along?"

"That helped," she said as we headed up an incline that took us away from the river and into the shadows of Ohio Stadium looming off to the right.

"Good to hear."

"Although your tendency to squeal whenever a Canada goose hisses at you has given me pause."

"Those things descended from velociraptors," I said. "Never forget that."

"What helped was visiting the homeless camp," she said. "With Roy and Lucy."

"How?"

"The homeless guys I'd see on the trail scared me. But after that night, I realized they're just, you know, like me. Except a whole lot less lucky. That lady I met? The one with the baby?"

"I remember."

She reached up and touched the long scar running down her face, the one left by her murderous husband. A gesture I could never be sure was conscious. "Slightly different circumstances, that could have been me at one point."

"I'd still be careful," I said. I thought of Roy's and my visit to the camp the previous Saturday, the troublemakers who'd raised Cain.

"Understood," she said. "It just got me thinking."

"Roy will do that to you."

We paused to let a trio of female joggers pass us, then resumed our journey.

"Visiting the camp reminds me," Anne said.

"Oh?"

"I was watching the news last night."

"All bad, I hear."

"Channel 7 was doing a story on a big heroin bust, on the South End."

"OK," I said.

"The reporter was Suzanne Gregory. First on the scene, she said."

"She usually is," I said, carefully.

"She's beautiful," Anne said.

"I'm sorry?"

"Suzanne Gregory. She's beautiful."

I said nothing.

"It wasn't a question," she said. "I know beautiful when I see it."

We crossed underneath Woody Hayes Drive and headed toward Lane Avenue.

"I hope you don't mind," Anne said. "I watched the ROOF video."

I let this sink in for a minute.

"Why, if I may ask," I said.

"Why what?"

"Why did you watch it?"

"To figure out the e-mails."

"E-mails?"

"The ones people have been sending me. Since I told some friends we were dating."

"Sending you?" I said. But I was thinking that *dating* sounded nice.

"Did you know," she said, "that you were arrested for point shaving the week before the Michigan game twenty years ago?"

"I might have heard something about that."

"It's amazing how many people thought I didn't know. That it might be news to me. It reminded me of an article I read once, about P. D. James, the mystery writer."

"OK."

"She described a motorcycle backing up an alley in one of her first novels. As you probably know, motorcycles don't back up. Thirty years later, people would still write her and chastise her for the mistake."

"That's kind of funny."

"Anyway, I just hit delete on the e-mails. Had a sore finger, at first."

"Har."

"A bunch had been links to the video. Which I finally decided to check out after Lucy brought it up that night at Surly Girl."

"Great."

"It's bad," she said.

"Thank you."

"It's like it's not even you. Not even the same person."

"I'd like to say that's true."

"Mind if I ask you something?"

"Shoot."

"Have you talked to her lately? Suzanne Gregory, I mean."

I looked at her. She returned the glance without malice or censure. But I think she slowed down a little.

"As a matter of fact," I said.

She waited. I hesitated. Then I told her about Lindey's.

"But somehow," I said, "I have the feeling you already know about that."

"Someone sent me a picture. The two of you at the bar. Another e-mail."

"Who?"

"A friend. But it had been forwarded five times by then."

I said nothing.

She said, "I just wonder if I have anything to worry about."

Same line Glen Murphy had used.

I thought about the dream I'd had of Suzanne the other morning. I said, "I asked her for help with the Aaron Custer case. She knows more about it than any reporter in town. Probably more than most people in the fire or police departments."

"Makes sense," she said.

"I also might have seen it as a chance to make amends."

"Just amends?"

"Meaning?"

"You said you're not the same person as the guy in that video."

"I'm not."

"But you wouldn't be the first person to think that cleaning up your act meant you might have a second chance with somebody."

"I suppose not."

"So do you?"

"Do I what?"

"Think you have a second chance with her?"

140

I kept quiet. Thought about the question. Recalled something from Suzanne's and my time together that made me
blush.

I said, "I'd be lying if I said the thought didn't cross my
mind."

It was Anne's turn to say nothing.

"And I should have told you I'd reached out to her. I'm
sorry about that."

She kept running.

"If it's any consolation, the kindest descriptors she used for
me at Lindey's were *turd* and *asshole.*"

More silence.

Then she said, "You know."

"Yes?"

"I've been thinking of moving out of my parents' house."

"OK."

"They've been great, since everything happened."

I rode my bike and listened.

"But every day I'm there is a reminder of the fact I'm
forty years old and living with my parents and have basically
nothing."

I could have disagreed with this sentiment, starting with
her daughter and moving to her job, but instead kept quiet.

She said, "Moving out is daunting."

"I can imagine."

"And it's mixed up with thoughts about you. About us."

"Us?"

"As in, what's next? If I move, should it be near you? Should I
rent or try to buy? Is it a short-term move or a long-term move?"

"OK," I said. I didn't trust myself to say more. The option
she'd left unspoken hung in the air between us, like the fading
reverberations of a distant gong. *Should I move in with you?*

As though reading my mind, she said, "I mean, I don't even
have a key to your house. But I'm there all the time."

"Well," I said. "Maybe we could—"

"I wanted to talk to you about it," she interrupted. "About the move. I was going to bring it up. Then I got the e-mail."

"The video."

"No," she said, sharply. "Not the video. That doesn't matter. Water under the bridge. The picture. Of the two of you at Lindey's."

"I'm sorry. I should have told you."

"Yes," she said. "Yes, you should have."

Maybe it was one of those optical illusions you hear about, a stream appearing to run uphill. That kind of thing. But whatever it was, after we turned around a few hundred silent yards later, the trip back to Confluence Park and our cars seemed a whole lot longer than the first half of the run.

26

THE FEDERAL COURTHOUSE SITS BESIDE A
small downtown park where an eternal flame burns in
memory of Columbus firefighters who died in the line of duty.
Seemed a fitting enough place to talk to Assistant U.S. Attorney
Pete Henderson a couple of hours later. He was midthirties,
maybe six foot, short black hair, with the build of someone
who worked out four times a week but not five. We sat on a
bench and didn't look at each other.

"Fourth Street Posse," he said. "Why do you care?"

I gave him the *Reader's Digest* version of the case, leaving out names here and there, but walking him through
the work I'd done leading up to Chad's connection of dots
the day before and my discovery of Henderson's name in
Chad's paper, which had arrived promptly in my e-mail box
the previous evening.

"First I've heard of this," he said.

"Makes two of us."

"You're thinking there might be a connection between the
posse and the fire."

"I'm not thinking anything," I said. "I'm passing information along to you. And hoping I can ask a couple of questions."

"I'm not in the habit of talking to private detectives about federal investigations."

"You'd be surprised how many times I hear that from assistant U.S. attorneys," I said.

"No duh."

"Followed by the same AUSAs dialing me back to ask, pretty please, could I check up on the hubby or the Mrs., because something just doesn't feel right."

"Get serious," he said.

"Scout's honor."

"Aaron Custer," he said, ignoring me. "They got the guy dead to rights. I know the prosecutor who worked the case. There's nothing there."

"I would have said so too. But I keep hitting bumps in the road."

I told him what Helen had heard from Tina. Somebody named Ryan, talking to Jacob.

"Any Fourth Street Posse dudes named Ryan?" I said.

"Indictments are online. Be my guest."

"Simple enough question."

He didn't respond right away. I glanced out at the river, the confluence of the Scioto and Olentangy, a breeze casting small waves and riffles across the water. Eyed a couple jogging on the newly reconstructed exercise trail. Thought about Anne's and my own run a couple hours earlier.

"No Ryans," Henderson said. "There was a Ryder, back in the nineties. An Ian, more recently. That's about it."

Ryan, Ian. Ian, Ryan. Seemed like a stretch.

I thought about Jacob Dunning. "Posse deal marijuana?"

"More of a loss leader. Hell, it'll probably be legal here in another five years. Their real deal is cocaine, meth, and, more and more, heroin. And guns. And armed robberies. And human trafficking."

"That a fancy word for prostitution?"

"Not when we're talking about fourteen-year-old girls working truck stops."

"Point taken. I've been hearing a lot about heroin."

"You should be. There's a fire hose of the stuff coming in, and they're selling it just about any way you can imagine. Busted a guy two weeks ago sewing bags into Beanie Babies and hawking them to moms picking up kids from Head Start."

"Enterprising," I said. "But they still wouldn't appreciate a guy like Jacob Dunning, either way, right? Orton Avenue's pretty close to Fourth Street."

"Don't get hung up on the name. Original members lived on and around Fourth. But that was twenty years ago. These guys are all over the near east side. Plus a lot of what they do is across state lines. Columbus isn't a destination anymore. We're a hub now."

I thought about the irony of this. The city had struggled for decades to throw off its reputation as a bland, sleepy midwestern backwater. Cowtown. How perfect that, having finally grown big enough to make it onto the national map, to offer more than Ohio State football and a starring role in presidential politics every four years, the reward was to become a center of the drug trade.

"Back to my question," I said. "Possible the gang could have put pressure on Dunning?"

"Maybe," Henderson said.

"Maybe came back that night to send him a message?"

"Using Aaron Custer? No way. That kid's a scumbag. But he's not drug-dealer caliber."

"Someone else, then. This guy Helen heard about, threatening Jacob."

"Aaron Custer brings the gasoline, but somebody named Ryan ignites it? Jesus Christ, Hayes, this isn't *Murder on the Orient Express.*"

Him and Karen Feinberg both. His body language told me we were near the end of our interview. I ran through my now familiar list of names.

"Ever hear of Eddie Miller?"

"No."

"Rory Ellison?"

"No."

"D. B. Chambers."

"No."

I told him about Chambers's background.

"Get real," Henderson said. "We look at every guy on the east side with a possession and dimebag-dealing record and that's all we do every day for the next hundred years. Hell, at least he's got a job. Most of these mopes sponge off their girl-friends and watch HBO all day."

"Mopes," I said.

"Term of art," he said.

"You have a fedora hanging up in your office?"

"Next to the tommy gun."

He stood up. I stood up.

"Don't get me wrong," Henderson said. "I appreciate you calling me. It could have been something."

"But you don't think so."

"I think Aaron Custer set that fire and he's where he should be."

"Thanks for the meeting."

"I'd say anytime, but I'd probably be lying. By the way."

"Yes."

"That crap about people calling you. Other AUSAs. About affairs. You're kidding, right?"

I leaned forward. Whispered in his ear.

He backed away, shock on his face.

"You're shitting me," he said. "He's the most straitlaced guy I know."

"Wish I were," I said. I pulled a card out of my wallet and handed it to him.

"Keep it handy," I said. "You never know when you might need it."

27

DESPITE HENDERSON'S OBJECTIONS, I couldn't help but feel I had come across something. The mysterious Ryan had begun casting a shadow over the Orton Avenue house that I couldn't shake. I could see how a campus pot dealer like Dunning wouldn't have mattered much to a big-time street gang. But what if Dunning had graduated to something harder, like heroin? That might explain the threat at the party, though not what Dunning was doing there to begin with. Matt had been upset to see him. So why had he shown up? Then there were the other, niggling details. The geological document I'd come across in Matt's papers. The fact that D. B. Chambers, the one person who had been near the scene of the fire that morning, *hadn't* seen Aaron, potentially giving my client his first toehold on some kind of innocence claim. And, and, and. Taken individually, the things I'd uncovered were as confusing as random paint blotches on trees in thick woods. Taken together, they were starting to point to, if not an actual trail, something that might lead to one.

I used these thoughts as an excuse to repeat my reconnaissance of Neil House Inn, settling into a steady rhythm of circling the block, thinking about the case, glancing over at the hotel entrance in hopes of spying Murphy and the girlfriend, then turning left on Broad. And repeat. And again.

I lost track of how many times I performed this maneuver. But not of how many times I saw Murphy. Which was exactly zero.

I WAS BACK HOME, opening up jars of peanut butter and jelly for another private investigator power lunch while thinking about what Anne had said, about her feelings of having nothing, a feeling my escapade at Lindey's had unintentionally reinforced, when my phone rang. It was Janet Crenshaw of Smyth, Sanner, Stacy and Franko. She did not strike a conciliatory tone.

"You called Helen Chen," she said. "After I expressly forbade it."

"Texted her," I corrected. "She called me back."

"Are you kidding me? That's how you're going to play this?"

"I have nothing to do with your lawsuit," I said. "Helen and I had a conversation, she gave me some information unrelated to your bottom-feeding activities, and I left."

"You're a conniving SOB. You know that?"

"I've been called much worse by blood relatives. We done?"

"What did she tell you?"

"None of your business."

"The hell it is."

"Then ask Helen."

"She said to ask you. Which was a mistake on her part, but I'm not holding that against a twenty-two-year-old girl who's been through what she has."

"A real Mother Teresa, you are."

"Just tell me what the hell she said."

I'm not in the habit of pissing off lawyers. I work for a good one, who keeps me in Black Label and Hopalong in kibble. I'm especially not in the habit of annoying trial attorneys. I knew Crenshaw was good at what she did. I'm also not sympathetic to manufacturers of defective products, which was her bread and butter. I just didn't like her attitude.

Nevertheless, I told her the nature of Helen's and my conversation. Her doubts about Aaron.

"Christ," she said. "She never told me that."

"Maybe she was afraid to."

"What's that supposed to mean?"

"If it's any consolation," I said, ignoring the question, "I don't plan to contact the other kids' parents. Text or call. Unless they call me, of course."

"No chance of that happening. I can assure you."

"I bet you can."

"So now two people in the world think Aaron's innocent," she said. "Helen and his grandmother."

"Look on the bright side. Maybe the real culprit's a closet millionaire. Then you could quit picking on the realty company."

"Screw you."

"Or are you more the vengeful type? Maybe you'll decide to go after Aaron's grandmother after all."

"I already told you," she said. "You can't get blood from a turnip."

I started to say something, but didn't get the chance. This time, she hadn't bothered warning me she was going to hang up.

Crenshaw's crack about Dorothy Custer reminded me to check my e-mail for an update on the bounced check. But I'd barely made it past an overdue library notice when my phone rang again.

"Andy Hayes?"

"That's right."

"Steve Dickinson, returning your call."

"Thank you," I said. "From where?"

"Appletree Energy."

28

WE MET LATE THAT AFTERNOON AT THE bar at the new Hilton just north of downtown, across the street from the convention center. Dickinson stood up as I walked into the room. He was wearing a tailored dark suit and a red tie and silk handkerchief to match.

"Andy," he said, shaking my hand. "Thanks for meeting me. What can I get you?"

The bartender poured me a draft Heineken and refreshed Dickinson's stemless glass of white wine.

"You're based here," I said when we were served.

"That's right."

"Full-time?"

"I live here. Used to lobby at the Statehouse. Different clients. Now I work for Appletree."

"They've got a lot going on in Ohio, I hear."

"You hear correctly," he said. "So you called Appletree. Something about a document. Related to the Knox No. 5."

I acknowledged it.

"I'm all ears."

"No. 5 is the well linked to an earthquake three years ago."

"I wouldn't say that."

"OK. How would you put it?"

"Unfairly implicated."

"Why?"

"It's not been proven."

"You know Tanner Gridley?"

"Of course."

"He and Matt Cummings wrote a paper that suggested a link between the No. 5 and the Knox County earthquakes."

"I'm aware of it."

"You don't agree with their findings."

"They didn't make their case. As I've pointed out to Gridley."

"You've talked?"

"We were on a panel at the Metropolitan Club last year. 'The Future of Fracking.'"

"How'd that go?"

"Let's just say neither of us behaved as well as we should have and both of us agreed it had been a mistake."

"Magnanimous of you."

"I try," he said, tipping his glass toward me.

"Bottom line, you disagree with their findings."

"That's correct."

"The No. 5 is what they call an injection well."

"That's right."

"Class II, if I have my terminology right."

"Correct again."

"You inject the leftover fracking waste down these wells."

"A little more complicated than that, but yes, that's essentially right."

"Some of these wells have been linked to earthquakes."

"Some," Dickinson said. "Key word being *linked*. There's a lot of debate about this right now."

"The ones in Youngstown in 2011 seemed pretty definite."

"I'll concede those."

"But not the Knox No. 5."

"Definitely not."

"Which Appletree owns."

"We have an exclusive contract with the outfit that operates it," he said. "More or less the same."

"And Appletree is a fracking company."

"We're an energy company that drills wells of all kinds looking for oil and gas. Traditional vertical wells along with the horizontal wells associated with hydraulic fracturing."

I wondered if he knew Glen Murphy. Was not in the mood to find out.

"Appletree's a pretty big company," I said.

"Yes, it is."

"Big, and growing."

"Something we haven't made a secret of. There are tremendous opportunities in Ohio. Our geologists say the Utica Shale could hold trillions of cubic feet of natural gas."

"That's a lot of fracking."

"Which we'll do in a safe and highly regulated environment."

"And the leftovers from the fracking, the brine?"—he nodded—"is going to need to be stored someplace. Like the No. 5."

"The wastewater is a byproduct of the process. It has to go somewhere."

"What's in it? The brine, I mean."

"Numerous chemicals, along with water."

"What kind of chemicals?"

"Proprietary information. No offense."

"None taken," I said. "But you've got a lot at stake with the No. 5. Anybody ever proves that caused the quake, the state would shut it down. Just like in Youngstown. And maybe the company's other wells as well. And where would that leave Appletree?"

"We're a big company," Dickinson said. "Just like you said. We have plenty of options."

"Really?" I said. "Pennsylvania banned additional brine waste storage, and New York State sure as hell doesn't want it. Sending it west, to Oklahoma or Texas? That's going to lop a lot off your profit margin."

"Andy Hayes, hydraulic fracturing expert?"

"I'm just saying Ohio injection wells make the most sense for Appletree operations in the state."

Dickinson paused and took a drink of his wine.

"We anticipate a favorable report from the state's review of the Knox No. 5."

"Gridley says you're lobbying the hell out of regulators. Throwing money around to get the result you want."

"My job is to make our case. Something Gridley seems to have an issue with."

"When's the report due?"

"June 1. Thereabouts. Which brings me to your call."

"Yes."

"This document. Appletree's name is on it."

"That's right."

"Mind if I look at it?"

I pulled a sheet of paper out of the jacket of my sport coat and handed it to him.

He unfolded it, took in the contents. His eyes gave nothing away. After a minute he refolded it and handed it back.

"Mean anything to you?" I said.

"Mind if I ask where you got that?"

"Proprietary information," I said. "No offense."

He smiled. "I'll rephrase. Are you working on something involving Knox No. 5?"

"I don't believe so."

"Meaning?"

I explained what led me to the document, without giving away its source.

"Aaron Custer innocent? That's nuts."

"You wouldn't be the first person to allege that."

"And without telling me where you got this, you obviously stumbled across it looking into the fire."

"I prefer 'obtained' to 'stumbled,' but that's about it. Now my turn: do you know Kim McDowell?"

"I know who she was, of course."

"Worked for Pendergrass."

"That's right."

I tapped my coat pocket. "Pendergrass's name is on this piece of paper. As is Appletree's."

"I don't dispute it."

"So what's the connection."

"Back to Door No. 1," he said. "Proprietary information."

"Handy, that response."

"With the added fact of being accurate."

"So you can't say more?"

"Let's just say I could be persuaded to say more if you could be moved to tell me where you got that."

"Ye Olde Standoff," I said.

"Apparently."

We each paid a visit to our drink.

"Interesting business you're in," Dickinson said.

"Beg your pardon?"

"Private investigator."

"It has its moments."

"I'm sure it does. But maybe not the highest-paying gig in the land?"

"I do OK."

"And to judge by the way you walk, physically demanding?"

"I limp because I played football, not because of my job."

"Ever thought of corporate work?"

"Such as?"

"Corporate security. Protecting the assets and personnel of a business."

"Not really. Why?"

"We could use someone like you. You can imagine what we deal with. The threats. Potential sabotage. Our industry's a bull's-eye for fanatics."

"Like Tanner Gridley?"

"Like fanatics."

"You're offering me a job."

"You interested?"

"I'm interested in why you're offering me a position on our first date. I thought we were talking about Knox No. 5."

"So we were. But I'd rather discuss it with a colleague, a fellow employee. Someone who has the same logo on his paycheck."

I thought about this for a second. "I go to work for Appletree, I find out some things about the well that right now you can't tell me. Proprietary information and all that."

"You go to work for Appletree at a significant bump up from whatever you're making now. *Significant*, if you catch my drift. And yes, we could talk about the well more freely. You and me both."

"What's that supposed to mean?"

"Just that I think there are some things you could tell me, if you had the professional freedom."

"Like what?"

"I'm not sure. Care to offer a teaser?"

I ignored the question. What interested me was the slightest shift in his gaze as he'd asked the question. I turned and for the first time noticed a man sitting across the room, checking his phone and pretending not to look at us. He was big and wearing a dark suit that didn't fit him nearly as well as Dickinson's did him. His short-cropped hair, square chin, and rearranged nose screamed ex-cop or ex-military. Or both.

"Friend of yours?" I said.

"In a manner of speaking. That's Rick Peirce. Head of Appletree security. Thought I'd invite him along."

"But not to sit at the grown-ups' table?"

"He'll join us depending on how this conversation goes."

"How delightful."

"It's Peirce, by the way. E before I."

"OK."

"Very sensitive about it."

"I bet," I said, keeping an eye on said security director.

"So what about it?" Dickinson said.

"All right," I said. "Humor me."

He did so, giving me a ballpark estimate of the money I could earn if I went to work for his thuggish-looking colleague. He was right. It was significant. To my credit, I barely dropped my jaw.

After a moment, I said, "I'd have to drop my investigation. Into the fire."

"Probably."

"That would disappoint a paying client."

"Custer's grandmother?"

"That's right."

Dickinson placed both arms on the bar. "Dropping the investigation really that big a deal? That kid did it. I know it, and I'm guessing you know it, too."

"Jury's still out."

Dickinson looked at his watch. TAG Heuer. I've had more than one car that cost less.

"Another appointment?"

"I made us dinner reservations at Hyde Park."

"Did you now," I said. The steak restaurant in the Short North was a five-minute walk from where we sat.

He said, "Hoping we could celebrate the beginning of a beautiful relationship."

"I'd need time to think about it," I said. "It's a big proposition."

"Yes, it is," he said.

"That's a lot of money."

"I was hoping you'd feel that way."

"Decent bennies, too, I'm guessing."

"The best," he said.

"Figured as much. As long as we're down to brass tacks, OK if I make a counteroffer? In the spirit of negotiation?"

"Be my guest. I'm authorized to hear you out."

"OK," I said. "How about, instead of me going to work for you and Rambo over there, you just drop the bullshit and tell me what I've got in my coat pocket."

"That's your response?"

"That's it. I can't afford a blow job in the form of a fancy steak dinner, but I'd be happy to squeeze your pipe for a couple minutes behind the curtains here. If it's all right with your friend Rick. How about it?"

"Don't be crass. Do you know what you're turning down?"

"I know the difference between a job offer and a bribe, if that's what you're asking."

"We join forces, everyone wins. Otherwise . . ."

"Otherwise what?" I looked in Peirce's direction. He'd stopped pretending to play solitaire on his phone and was staring at me.

"Otherwise we go our separate ways and you have plenty of time to think about the biggest mistake you've ever made."

"Now you're just being stupid," I said. "The biggest mistake I ever made was on national TV for a week. What I did was so bad, I'm in *books*. My threshold for caring about my mistakes is very, very low."

"You need to watch yourself," Dickinson said. "You don't really know what you're saying."

"You're screwing this up," I said. "This is the part where you go, 'You don't know who you're dealing with here.'"

"Are you always such an asshole?"

"Only when I'm with one," I said.

I drained my beer. No sense letting a good drink I wasn't paying for go to waste. Then I stood up.

"Last chance," Dickinson said.

"Get it right," I said. "It's 'Last chance, or else.'"

I turned and walked away from the bar. Peirce stood up and, while not exactly blocking my way, did not exactly not block it either. I thought about giving him a shoulder shove, like in the movies, but I was guessing that, unlike in the movies, I'd be doing an involuntary face plant a moment later. Ex-cop or whatever, he looked like the real deal. Not like a guy who let himself go to seed because of a Labrador's sore paw.

Instead, I nodded as I moved around him. He nodded back, his face unreadable. Calm and collected. Like he had all the time in the world to deal with thickheaded gumshoes like me.

29

I WOKE UP TO THE GOOD NEWS FRIDAY morning that Dorothy's check had cleared and I wasn't facing bankruptcy after all. I tempered this development with the realization that another week had passed and she was in arrears again.

She didn't seem overly concerned when I explained the situation over the phone. An hour later I was in her living room holding another check and accepting more apologies for the snafu.

I updated her on my conversations of the past few days.

"You think there's something to this?" she said. "This gang, going after Jacob Dunning?"

"I'm bothered by it," I said. "It doesn't change anything that we know, including all the evidence against Aaron. But it hasn't been checked out by anybody, and that makes me nervous."

"The U.S. attorney. He didn't think much of it."

"He put on a good show of not thinking much of it. That doesn't mean he's not checking it out himself."

"You haven't heard back from Aaron yet? About what Helen Chen said?"

I shook my head.

"I will admit," she said, "it's not what I'd hoped for when I first called you." Then she added, quickly, "Which is not to say I'm not impressed with what you've uncovered. You've worked hard, and I'm so sorry about the check. I was just hoping for more by now."

"You and me both."

Dorothy's compliments about my work ethic and apologies about the bounced check didn't keep me from driving straight to the nearest bank and pulling up to a pneumatic tube station to deposit that week's payment. I had just sent the check flying toward the teller when my phone rang with an unfamiliar number. The speaker squawked with a question about checking or savings, and I let it go to voice mail. I got another call after that from the American Red Cross, looking for blood donors, and a call after that from someone whose dachshund was missing and was I available. Tired of the interruptions, I gave the phone a time-out in the glove compartment and drove away from the bank and on to my next destination.

PENDERGRASS RESEARCH OCCUPIES ALMOST an entire block along Neil, and although its modern brick architecture hardly matched the restored houses in surrounding Victorian Village, with their gables and turrets and porch spindles, the attention it had paid to landscaping and preserving as many trees as possible gave it the feeling of a friendly nearby campus.

That feeling evaporated when I went inside and handed my card to the grumpy receptionist sitting at an ultramodern desk that looked like something straight off a Dakota Jackson showroom floor. She was young, with short, dyed-black hair, orange-frame glasses, and a stud in her nose bigger than the one Karen Feinberg wore but not nearly as classy. I explained who I was and why I was there. She listened icily. Several minutes passed while she made a series of phone calls she did not appear happy about, and I bided my time on a couch and pawed through copies of *Scientific American* and several specialized journals devoted to chemistry, physics, and geology.

Just as I was preparing to ask Ms. Orange Glasses what the delay might be, a frosted-glass door to the right of her desk opened and a worried-looking man stepped through. He had closely cropped blond hair, a nicely tailored dark suit, and an accent, which I deduced from extensive experience watching back-to-back episodes of *Wallander* sounded Scandinavian.

He introduced himself and we traded business cards, from which exercise I learned he was Erik Petersson, Pendergrass vice president of strategic research.

"Where did you get this?" he said when I showed him the copy of the document from Matt's papers.

"Friend of a friend," I said.

"That's a proprietary report," he said stiffly. "It's not something meant for the general public."

Proprietary. Same word Dickinson had used.

"I guessed that," I said. "I'm just wondering what it is. It seems to be related to the Knox No. 5."

"I couldn't really say. I'd need the entire log."

"So it's a log."

"Something like that."

"If I provided the whole log, would you tell me more about it?"

"As I said, it's proprietary."

"I understand the need to protect your research information," I said.

"Thank you."

"So what if I shred the original when I'm finished with it. To ensure no one else sees it."

"No," he said, a little too quickly. "That would be worse. Destruction of private property."

"But don't you have a copy? Something stored electronically?"

He seemed to wrestle with this question for a moment. Then he said, "Generally, yes, that's true. With this type of material."

"Then why do you need what I've got?"

"It's not a public document," he said. "There shouldn't be any loose copies out there."

"Loose lips sink ships?"

"I'm sorry?"

"Just an expression."

"I appreciate you bringing this to our attention," Petersson said. "I'd be grateful if you could provide us the log. The original."

I glanced at the reception desk and caught Orange Glasses staring at me.

I said, "That was good news about Buddy Keeler."

"I'm sorry?"

"The man they arrested for killing Kim McDowell. It must be a relief."

"Yes, of course," Petersson said.

"Wasn't one of your concerns she might have been the victim of corporate espionage?"

"It's terrible what happened to Kim. She was a promising researcher."

"What was she working on?"

He frowned. "She had various areas," he said.

When he didn't elaborate, I said, "Let me guess. Proprietary?"

"That's right."

I took the paper out of his hand. I don't think he wanted to let it go. I said, "Could it have had anything to do with this log?"

"I couldn't say."

"Can't? Or won't?"

"We're relieved an arrest was made," he said. "We support the full prosecution of this individual."

"Something we both agree on," I said.

"It would be useful to have the document returned," Petersson continued. "The original."

"I bet it would."

"Yes."

"This institute," I said, changing the subject. "You do scientific research."

"That's right."

"For the government?"

"We have government contracts, yes. But we also conduct research for businesses. And we have our own investigations."

"People say you have the bodies of aliens hidden in freezers in your basement. Is that true?"

"Don't be absurd."

"But you've heard that?"

"I know that's the joke."

"Ever think about capitalizing on that?"

"What?"

I gestured at the couch where I'd been seated, waiting for him. "Blow-up alien figures, strategically positioned around the lobby. Or hanging from the railing." I nodded at a second-floor overlook. "Could be kind of fun."

"You're mocking me," Petersson said.

"Just an idea."

"The document," he insisted. "Could I get it, please?"

"It would be useful to know more about it first," I said.

"That's not possible," he said.

"Call me when it is," I said.

We left it at that, and I departed under Petersson's watchful scowl. I tried catching the receptionist's eye again, but she frowned and turned away.

IT WAS LATE AFTERNOON by the time I got around to checking the voice mail from the call I'd gotten while banking. I'd been hoping for someone like Joe Whitestone from the fire department or Karen Feinberg calling with a break in the case. Instead, it was someone named Freddie, her message a mere "Hi. Call me back."

"This is Andy Hayes," I said when she answered. "You called me this morning."

"Oh, hi," she said. "It's Freddie. How's it going?"

"Fine," I said. "Freddie?"

"Freddie short for Frederica. But only my parents call me that. They loved Friedrich Schiller in college. They just didn't expect to have daughters. Not that I mind. It's a cool name, it's just a mouthful."

"OK, Freddie short for Frederica," I said. "Was there something I can do for you?"

"I just wondered if you'd talked to any of the can fairies."

"The what?"

"Can fairies. Least that's what we call them."

"Let's back up," I said. "Who are you again?"

"I'm a friend of Mindy."

"Mindy?"

"She knows Courtney? From Orton Avenue?"

That at least got my attention. I said, "I'm lost."

"Weren't you on Orton Avenue the other day, looking for somebody who might know something about the fire? The one that killed those students?"

"Yes," I said, thinking back. "But that was two weeks ago."

"Really? Because I just heard about it. About you, I mean. Courtney told Mindy and Mindy and I were talking the other day, and she, like, mentioned it."

Courtney must have been one of the students I talked to the day I canvassed the neighborhood. Something came to mind. Something one of the students I'd talked to had said. *This one girl . . . Different kind of name.*

Freddie. Freddie short for Frederica.

I said, "You know something about the Orton Avenue fire?"

"Not the fire, exactly. I mean, I know it happened. Everybody does. But Mindy said you were looking for witnesses. And I thought of the can fairies."

"Can fairies."

"The guys who pick up the cans. You know. After the parties."

"I'm not sure I do."

"You've never heard of the can fairies?"

"Humor me."

"So they're like these guys," she said. "Really early in the morning on the weekends? After parties? They come along the street and pick up all the cans in the yards."

"They just pick them up?"

"To recycle them, I guess. I saw them one time. I hadn't gone to bed yet. They push these shopping carts along and toss the cans in."

"Why are they called can fairies?"

"Because the cans just disappear magically," Freddie said. "That's why you never need garbage bins at parties. People just toss the empties in the yard. Wake up the next morning—poof, they're gone. Can fairies."

I thought about the first boy I'd interviewed that day. His empty yard, despite claims of a big party the night before. I said, "Are they out every weekend?"

"Depends on the time of year. Fall, could be Saturday *and* Sunday mornings, if there's a home football game. Rest of the year, depends what night people are partying. You know? Winter, you don't see them so much."

"Right," I said.

"So I was thinking," she continued. "You want to know if somebody saw something, ask a can fairy."

D. B. CHAMBERS PICKED up almost immediately when I called.

"It's Andy Hayes," I said.

"Fabulous Falco," he said. "How's it going?"

"Got a second?"

"One minute," he said. I heard muffled voices, and in the background the sound of a young girl babbling.

"Sorry about that. I'm over at my baby mama's. With my baby. And her mama." He laughed at his own joke. "So what's happening?"

I told him what Freddie had said.

"Sure," he said. "I've seen them. Never heard them called that, but I've seen them."

"Question is, did you see any out that morning? Morning of the fire."

"Nah," he said. "I already told you. I didn't see anything *but* the fire. I didn't see this Aaron Custer dude or can fairies or anyone. It was quiet."

"Be good to find one," I said.

"I suppose. Knock yourself out."

"When you've seen them, more Saturday or Sunday?"

"Hell, I don't know. I'm not out that early, period, unless I'm opening, and mostly I do weekdays now anyway."

"All right," I said. "Thanks."

"Why you asking? Going can fairy hunting?"

"Maybe."

"Tomorrow?"

"Sunday. Same day of the week as the fire."

"Better man than me. Make sure you go early. They're gone by 7 or 8."

"Can't stand the sunlight?" I said. "Like vampires?"

"Can't stand the students, probably," Chambers said. "Can't really blame them. Those kids are pigs."

30

I SLEPT IN THE NEXT MORNING FOR THE first time in a while. I was feeling good until I rolled over and saw that the clock said 8 and I realized that Anne had been running along the Olentangy Trail with her girlfriends for more than an hour. Suddenly grumpy, I dragged myself out of bed.

Tanner Gridley hadn't returned any of my calls or e-mails since my meeting with Helen. So I decided to go to him. I threw on my coat, grabbed my keys, and headed out my front door. I was walking down the street to where I'd parked my van when someone called my name. I stopped and located the source of the voice sitting inside a silver mini-Hummer parked in front of my house. Rick Peirce. Appletree Energy's director of security.

I stood in front of the open passenger window and looked at him.

"Morning," he said.

"Morning."

"Nice day."

I looked up and down the street. "Yes, it is," I said.

"Little chilly, though," he said. "Good you have a jacket."

"I like to be prepared."

"Like the Boy Scouts."

"Or garbage men," I said. "Guys that take out the trash."

"Too nice a day to get dirty," he said.

"Couldn't agree more. Something I can do for you?"

"Just the opposite."

"OK."

"Steve is concerned we got off to a bad start the other night."

"The night he tried to bribe me?"

"He wanted me to convey to you that our offer still stands with no hard feelings."

"Big of him."

"We're a big company."

"And you're conveying this message by sitting in front of my house until I walk out?"

"I was about to knock on the door."

"Tell him I'm still not interested."

"Sure about that?"

"Sure as shit."

He gave me the same implacable look I remembered from the bar. Neither threatening nor unthreatening.

"Sorry to hear that," he said. The passenger window started to roll up. I said, "Peirce," and it stopped midway.

"Yeah?"

"When I said your name just now?"

"Yeah?"

"I was imagining it spelled 'I, E' in my mind."

The look again. Then the window rolled all the way up, and he started the Hummer and pulled away. I watched him turn left at Whittier and kept watching until I couldn't see him anymore. I turned around, went back to my house, and made sure I'd locked the front door. Satisfied, I walked down the street, got in my van and drove off.

I PULLED UP IN front of the Gridleys' house on Lakewood in Clintonville, a few blocks south of where Dorothy Custer lived, about twenty minutes later. Neighborhood of neat, well-kept clapboard houses, blue and green and beige and white. Plants hanging on porches, front lawns small or in some cases turned over to flower or vegetable gardens. Every other car on the narrow street had a bike rack.

A green Subaru wagon was parked in Gridley's driveway. "No Fracking Way," read the bumper sticker on the rear. His wife answered the door after I'd rung the bell. I recognized her from the picture in his office. She looked frailer in person, and used a cane. I apologized for the intrusion and asked for her husband. She was polite, but I could tell she was bothered as she turned back into the house and disappeared down a hallway.

Gridley came striding up a minute later. He looked more than bothered.

"What are you doing here?" he said, standing in the doorway.

"Needed to ask you something else. Seemed like you didn't get my messages."

"I got them," he said. "Just didn't see a need to return them."

"Only take a minute," I said. "It's about Knox No. 5."

He looked behind him, then back to me. He stepped outside and pulled the door shut.

"My wife's been having a hard week. And I don't have anything else to say to you. Other than I resent what you're trying to do for Aaron Custer."

For the third time in as many days I pulled the document, or the log or whatever it was, out of my coat pocket. I showed it to him.

"Where did you get this?" Gridley said after several moments.

"I keep getting asked that," I said.

"And what do you say?"

"Do you recognize it?"

"No."

"Sure seems like you do."

"I mean, yes I recognize it. It's a seismic log of some kind. I just don't recognize that particular one. I'm curious why you have it."

"I'll get to that," I said. "Let me ask you something else."

"What?"

"You saw that it's something from Pendergrass Research."

"Yes," he said.

"How well did you know Kim McDowell?"

He froze for just a second. Just enough for a formula of a suspicion to work itself out, algebra-like, in my mind.

"Kim McDowell," he said.

"That's right."

"What does this have to do with her?"

"What I was hoping you could tell me."

"I knew Kim," he said. "It's terrible what happened to her. Just terrible."

The lines stiff, like something memorized by a community theater first-timer.

I said, "You were on a panel together. In Dallas."

"How do you know that?"

"It's on the Internet."

"Hard to find unless you went looking for it."

"Wasn't that hard."

"Why do you care?"

"It caught my attention. Were you in the same field?"

"No."

"What did she study?"

He hesitated for a moment. I could see him working out his own algebra.

"Carbon sequestration," he said after a moment. "That was her area."

"Carbon what?"

"Sequestration. Injecting carbon from coal-burning power plants into the ground. The whole clean-coal technology thing."

"Coal can be clean?"

"Personally, I think it's a crock. We're better off investing in renewables."

"But?"

"Theoretically, it could work."

"Does injecting carbon cause earthquakes too?"

He shook his head.

"But the carbon's injected into the ground?"

"That's right," he said. "But this doesn't—"

"Like an injection well?"

"Sort of."

"Explains why you were on the same Dallas panel, then."

"Some of our interests overlapped."

"I bet they did."

"What's that supposed to mean?"

"Just a statement."

Gridley took a breath and gathered himself.

"Is there anything else you need?" he said. "I want to get back to my wife."

"A lawyer I know said Pendergrass was convinced Kim's death was related to corporate espionage. Right up until Buddy Keeler was arrested."

"He's the guy who did it?"

I nodded.

"I don't know anything about that," he said.

"Do you think Buddy Keeler's guilty?"

"I have no idea. I assume he is if the police arrested him."

"Usually that's true," I said. "Not always."

"It's terrible what happened to her," he repeated, just as formally as the first time.

I decided to move on. Felt like the look on his face when I'd first brought up Kim's name had answered at least one of my questions.

"Jacob Dunning," I said. "One of the fire victims."

"One of Aaron's victims."

"He was a friend of Matt's."

"I think so, yes."

"But maybe not a good friend," I said. "I heard they had a parting of the ways. And Matt didn't want him at the house that night."

"I wouldn't know."

"Any idea what might have come between them?"

"No."

"Did you know him?"

"Dunning? I'd met him."

"Ever have him in class?"

"No."

"Matt ever talk about him?"

"Not really."

"You must have worked pretty closely with Matt. On the paper, about Knox No. 5. He never talked about Jacob? Why they weren't friends anymore?"

"It's not the kind of thing we discussed."

"Did you know he sold pot?"

"No," Gridley said, after a pause.

Behind us, the front door opened. His wife appeared. Looked at me curiously.

She said, "I'm sorry to interrupt. We need to get the kids to soccer. And we're supposed to bring snacks."

Gridley glared at me. I smiled at his wife.

"If you think of any more answers to my questions, I'd appreciate a call," I said. I turned and headed up the walk.

"Andy," Gridley said.

I turned around.

"The log."

"What about it?"

"Could I keep it? That copy?"

I looked at him. Looked past him to his wife.

"No," I said.

31

I'D SET MY ALARM FOR 3:30 A.M. SUNDAY, BUT there was no need. My eyes opened thirty minutes before that, and I lay in bed, thinking. I knew I'd been dreaming of a woman again. But I couldn't have told you if it was Suzanne or Anne. Somehow this was not an encouraging development.

As I drove up High Street, all but deserted except for a couple of stragglers either just getting up or just going to bed, I thought about Tanner Gridley and Kim McDowell. Had they had an affair in Dallas? Nice hotel, hothouse atmosphere, away from the hassles of home. Jazz at the bar while they had drinks. Maybe Mrs. Gridley had had a bad week, or month, or year. Things happen. Didn't I know that? His reaction to McDowell's name betrayed a guilty conscience of some kind. On the other hand, does a guy who runs 5Ks to help raise money for MS turn around and step out on the wife he's doing those races for? I wouldn't have put it past me, once upon a time. I wasn't so sure about Gridley.

I wondered about the other, related possibility on my mind. Connected to the document, the log, whatever, that Lori

Hume had come across. That so many people seemed interested in.

Was it possible police had the wrong guy for Kim McDowell's murder?

I FOUND A SPOT at the top of Orton Avenue, parked, and started walking up the street. A couple of houses had lights on, and I saw images on a television in somebody's living room, but it was otherwise quiet. Why wouldn't it be? It was 4 in the morning. I heard a sound and tensed, then relaxed as I saw a cat run between houses. Old-fashioned lamps cast pools of orange light up and down the street, their glowing curved globes atop cast iron black poles like giant matchsticks. The result was a lot of shadows but not a whole lot of dark. Whoever this witness was, if he existed, would have to have hidden carefully to avoid being seen.

I was starting to think that both Freddie short for Frederica and D. B. Chambers were putting me on when I heard another sound. Not a cat. And then I saw him. Up the street, near Orton Avenue's intersection with Woodruff. A man pushing a shopping cart jangling with aluminum cans. I'll be damned, I thought.

I walked in his direction, keeping an eye on him as he turned the corner. Unless he was a real fairy, he probably wouldn't be hard to find. Sure enough, he was standing on a lawn two doors down, patiently filling a bag, when I came up to him.

I cleared my throat from a few feet away.

"Excuse me," I said.

He looked up carefully but not in surprise. As if he were used to people commenting on his nocturnal activities. He was older, white, with a beard far more salt than pepper. When he saw my face, he gave me a hard stare.

"Woody Hayes," he said. "I'll be damned."

"Do I know you?" I said.

He was about to respond when a sound up the street interrupted us, a sound that wasn't the dawn's first bird chorus. I turned and immediately heard a second sound, an alarm going off, and even from half a block away I knew this wasn't good. I looked at my newly discovered can fairy, hesitated, then ran toward the commotion. Judging from the smoke pouring from under the hood of my van as I rounded the corner, I would have been too late no matter what. Up ahead, moving fast, a car made the corner at Eighteenth and was gone.

"COULD HAVE BEEN AN accident," I said to Whitestone as we stood beside his city-issued sedan. "Engines overheat."

"Sure they do," Whitestone said. "Just not on Orton Avenue at 4 a.m."

Flashing emergency lights painted the street in reds and blues. A few bystanders gawked from lawns. My Honda Odyssey, or what was left of it, was a cooling mess of retardant foam, water, and the acrid stink of burnt plastic. Forty-five minutes had passed since I ran into my can fairy.

"This guy you saw."

"Yeah."

"Don't know him?"

I shook my head.

"Couldn't have been him?"

"Don't see how."

Whitestone scribbled in a notebook. He looked up at my van, then back down. He wrote some more.

"This is a mess," he said.

I said nothing.

Whitestone said, "Got any suspects?"

"Me?"

"No, Jim Rockford, hiding behind the bushes." He shook his head. "Yes, you."

I told him about Peirce. Couldn't see any reason not to. Then I reminded him about a member of the Fourth Street Posse who might be called Ryan.

"Pretty thin."

"All I've got."

"Why would either one want to do this?"

"I don't know. Send me a message?"

"More like send up a flare."

He wrote some more in his notebook. He said, "You talk to any of the families yet, about this case?"

"Why?"

"Just curious. I think a lot about them. Good people."

I explained about Janet Crenshaw of Smyth, Sanner, Stacy and Franko.

"Bunch of bullshit. House had detectors."

"Were they working?"

"Far as I know."

"Batteries?"

"Fully loaded."

"What kind?"

"What kind of what?"

"What kind of batteries?"

"Hell if I know. What difference does that make?"

"I'm just asking," I said. "Covering all my bases."

"Good, because you keep striking out."

"Thanks for the reminder."

"We'll tow the van. See if we find anything might explain what happened. Anything valuable in it?"

I thought about it. "A Louisville Slugger I keep in there for protection. Not that it's ever done me any good. Bunch of CDs."

"Who?"

"Bon Jovi. Bruce—'Born in the USA.' Lot of John Mellencamp."

"Heavy on the eighties."

"Sort of my era."

"That's right. I always forget."

"Forget what?"

"How much older you look than you really are."

"Thanks."

"No problem."

Peeved at his crack, I declined Whitestone's offer of a ride and was scrolling through my phone looking for the number of a cab company when I glanced up and saw a Channel 7 news truck round the corner. I turned and looked at the arson investigator.

"What can I say?" he said. "Scanners. Even my grandma has one."

A minute later a red sports car zoomed up and parked behind the truck. Suzanne jumped out and started striding down the sidewalk. She was wearing designer jeans, a tight-fitting red turtleneck, and a Channel 7 jacket, unzipped. She looked dynamite, especially considering she must have been sound asleep not that long ago. She stopped in her tracks when she saw me.

"What the hell are you doing here?" she said.

"Guess I could ask you the same thing."

"Fire on Orton Avenue. Kind of got my attention."

"But nobody else's?"

"There's a reason why I owned this story," she said. "Now answer my question."

I turned to Whitestone. But he had already disappeared inside his sedan.

I looked back at Suzanne and explained my presence.

"Can fairies," she said.

"That's right."

"Find any?"

"Might have. The fire hampered my investigation."

"Hampered."

"What I said."

"I'm waiting."

"I saw somebody, but I didn't have a chance to talk to him."

"Where is he?"

"He's gone, like any self-respecting can fairy when some-body's van catches fire on his watch."

"You think he did it?"

"No."

"Who then?"

I repeated my suspicions about Peirce.

"Anything else you know about this situation you're not telling me?"

I decided not to point out that I hadn't told her things be-cause she'd repeatedly told me to go to hell. I gave her the bare bones on the Fourth Street Posse and the threat against Dunning.

"Somebody named Ryan," she said. "Tina Montgomery told Helen that?"

"That's right."

"What do you think?"

"You're asking me?"

"Yes."

"Provides a possible motive for someone else to have set the fire. With Dunning as the target."

"Maybe."

"Problem is, nobody's heard of a Fourth Street Posse mem-ber named Ryan. And it presupposes Dunning was more of a threat to them than he appeared based on a possession arrest."

"The kid you talked to," Suzanne said. "Eric? He confirmed Dunning was selling pot?"

"That's right."

"That's more than misdemeanor possession."

"Fourth Street Posse moves kilos of cocaine and heroin. Why would they care?"

She considered this. She looked briefly at me, then up the street toward the van.

She said, "You tell anybody else this?"

"You're the first," I said.

"Because I'm the only one here."

I shrugged.

"Whitestone talking?"

"You can ask."

"I will," she said. "Not that there's any point."

"Why not?"

"Like I'm going to do a piece on Andy Hayes's van catching fire. All I've got out of this is lost sleep."

I wondered if she'd been at Murphy's house or her condo when she got the call.

I thought about my conversation with Anne the other morning. Whether I'd seen my visit to Lindey's as something more than business-related.

I said, "Any chance I could grab a ride home?"

"To German Village?"

"That's the general idea."

She looked at my van again, then back at me.

"No," she said. "I'm sorry."

She walked past me and rapped on the window of Whitestone's car.

THREE MINUTES LATER I walked into Buckeye Donuts, ordered a coffee and five for the price of four, called a cab, and tucked myself into a booth while I waited.

The cabbie turned out to be a fellow named Abdi with a doctorate in economics from Sapienza University of Rome, a house in Mogadishu that was mostly rubble, and several brothers and sisters he was trying to retrieve from a Kenyan refugee camp. That managed to put my morning in context. So I was feeling marginally better, if that's the way to put it, until we hit Third Street and were passing Katzinger's Deli, just a few minutes from my house. That's when I felt my phone buzz. I looked down and saw a text.

My offer's still good.

Dickinson. From Appletree Energy.

32

I LEFT A MESSAGE WITH MY INSURANCE
company, texted the basics of the fiasco to Anne, tried unsuccessfully to call Dickinson, then fell asleep on the couch. I was
awakened two hours later by my insurance agent calling back
with information on rentals. I jotted the information down,
hung up, then immediately got a call from Anne. She was at
my house half an hour later and had me at the airport rental
counter fifteen minutes after that. The best they could come
up with on short notice was a Chevy Cruze. A little small but I
took it. Made in Ohio. Better than nothing. I asked Anne if she
wanted to meet me at my house for breakfast, but she needed
to get back to Amelia and her parents. I said I understood.

I somewhat thought I did.

Dickinson was circumspect when he called at noon.

"What's the deal?" I said. "Drop your phone in the toilet?"

"I was at church."

"Why'd you text me that time of day?"

"I'm an early riser."

"Know anything about my van getting torched?"

"I'm sorry?"

"My van went up in flames a couple hours before you texted. Just wondering if there's any connection."

"Don't be absurd. Are you all right?"

"Not really," I said. "Any idea where Peirce was this morning?"

"None. Why?"

"He paid me a visit yesterday."

"As I asked him to."

"Why?"

"I was concerned I'd done a bad job pitching the job to you. I wanted to make sure you understood the sincerity of the offer."

"Felt more like a threat."

"I'm sorry you took it that way."

"I bet you are."

"I'm also sorry you still don't appear interested. Some people don't know a gift horse when it looks them in the mouth."

"Look a gift horse."

"What?"

"You look a gift horse in the mouth. It doesn't look at you."

"You know what I mean."

"I know when I'm talking to a horse's ass," I said.

I HEATED SOME SOUP for lunch and thought about my next move. My first priority was to find the can fairy I'd encountered before my van accidentally on purpose overheated. I thought about enlisting D. B. Chambers to help look for him, figuring he could use some extra income for his baby and his baby mama and his planned exit strategy for leaving behind the early morning sale of Happy Meals. I texted him the query, but all I got in return was a simple **No way Falco. LMFAO**. *Laughing my fucking ass off.* Didn't seem all that funny to me.

My second priority was to pose some questions to Matt's girlfriend, Lori Hume. Questions raised by the papers of Matt's she'd saved, questions my conversation with Gridley the day before hadn't answered. Calling her was out of the question, even if I had her number. Telling Fielding or White-stone my suspicions was premature. Calling Helen Chen was a possibility, but I had to weigh that against the fresh memory of Janet Crenshaw's tongue-lashing. With that in mind, I did the next best thing.

I called Crenshaw herself. At home, on a Sunday.

Because that's what indefatigable assholes do.

33

MONDAY MORNING'S WALK STARTED OFF
promisingly enough. Hopalong made it all the way to Schiller Park at the bottom of the street, where we lingered by the
Umbrella Girl, the bronze statue in the center of a fountain
with water bubbling from the top of her umbrella and dripping
down in perpetuity. We ventured into the grass and I waited
while he did his business, scooping up the mess into a blue
Kroger bag afterward. When he started to limp, I succumbed
to the inevitable, hoisted him over my shoulder, and carried
him back up Mohawk. We cut quite a figure, especially with
the bag dangling from my hand.

I saw Peirce sitting in the Hummer in front of my house
from half a block away. I set the dog down as I walked up.

"Hi," he said when the passenger window rolled down.

"Long time no despise," I said.

"Kill you to be nice once in a while?"

"What do you want?"

"World peace. And for you to reconsider our offer."

"Fair enough," I said. "OK, I've reconsidered. Shove it."

"Not what I was hoping to hear."

"Let me rephrase then. Shove it, and where were you yesterday morning about 4 a.m. while somebody was torching my van?"

"That van was a piece of shit," he said.

"That's your answer?"

"Wheels say so much about a man," he said, tapping the Hummer's dashboard.

"So do their peckers. But you don't see me waving mine around."

He didn't respond, merely looked at me with that same implacable expression. Like someone content to admire a butterfly poised on a flower. Or to pull its wings off, one by one.

"I was asleep in bed Sunday morning," he said. "Like you should have been."

"Like hell you were."

"Yes or no, Hayes? You in or out?"

"Out," I said.

"That's what I'm supposed to tell Dickinson?"

"No," I said. "You can give him a message for me."

I lifted the blue plastic bag holding Hopalong's deposit, reached through the open window, and dropped it on the passenger seat floor.

"That's what I think of his offer," I said. Then I reached down, picked the dog up, and strolled to my house with as much dignity as I could muster holding a seventy-pound Labrador over my shoulder.

THANKS TO MY PHONE call to Janet Crenshaw the day before and a bit of judicious groveling, I found myself at noon in her Brewery District office with Helen Chen, Lori Hume, and Lori's mother.

"This is an off-the-record conversation," Crenshaw said, seated at the top of the table. Her dark hair was pulled away from her face, and she had donned a blue-and-yellow power scarf to set off her navy suit. She looked all business.

She said, "We're not recording and we're not taking notes. I've agreed to let Mr. Hayes pose a couple of questions which I've determined might have relevance to our suit. Nobody has to answer anything, but it might not be a bad idea to hear him out." And that was it. She nodded at me.

I looked at Lori. "I'm going to ask you about Matt, if it's OK," I said. She nodded, then looked at her mom. Her mom frowned at me.

"Matt and Jacob were freshman-year roommates."

"Yes."

"But not after that?"

"No."

"Any reason?"

"Matt wanted to stay in the dorms his sophomore year. Jacob wanted to live off campus."

"They still got along?"

"More or less."

"Did they hang out together?"

"A little. Couple parties. I think they worked out once or twice."

"That changed, though."

She nodded.

I said, "They didn't get along so much anymore."

"Not really."

"Which is why Matt was angry when Jacob showed up at the party."

She nodded.

"So what happened between them?"

Lori looked at her mom again, then at Crenshaw, who nodded.

"Jacob was selling pot. Matt thought it was stupid."

"Was Matt opposed to drugs?"

"No," she said. "He'd smoked pot before. A little."

"Lot of kids do," I offered. "One time or another."

"I guess."

"Did you?"

She looked at her mom again. "Once. I didn't like it."

"Jacob wasn't selling at the party," I said.

"I don't know. I don't think so."

"But in general, Matt was angry at Jacob because he was dealing."

"Sort of."

"Sort of?"

"Matt didn't really care. He thought it was stupid, mostly, and that Jacob was wasting his time and should have been studying more."

"But?"

"But he was really mad because he found out Jacob wasn't selling just to students."

"Not just students."

"That's right."

"Who else? People around town?"

She shook her head. "Professors, too."

"Professors?"

"I guess. Just a couple."

I had not expected that response. But I knew right away what my next question had to be.

"Was Jacob selling marijuana to Tanner Gridley? Matt's environmental geology professor?"

Lori stared at the table. And nodded. Helen reached out, rubbed her back.

"And that's what made Matt angry?"

"Yes," she said. "But that's where I think he was wrong."

"What do you mean?"

"Professor Gridley met Jacob through Matt. On the green or something. Matt was mad about that, because he thought he could get in trouble for introducing them, and he didn't want to jeopardize anything with his degree. Or the paper he and Professor Gridley wrote together."

"Understandable."

"But the thing is, the marijuana wasn't for Professor Gridley. That's what I tried to tell Matt."

"It wasn't for Gridley?"

"No."

"Who then?"

"His wife," she said.

"His wife?"

"She was sick. And it helped her. I know it's not right, or legal. But it seemed OK to me. If it's helping somebody. But Matt didn't see it that way."

Of course. Jacob Dunning had been selling Gridley marijuana to help his wife with the MS. Medical marijuana.

I said, "That's why Matt was so angry when Jacob showed up at the party."

Lori nodded.

"So why did he?" I asked, the obvious suddenly occurring to me. "Why did Jacob show up that night?"

"I don't know," Lori said.

"Really?"

"I have no idea. None of us did."

"Jacob came to Matt's party, knowing full well he probably wasn't welcome there," I said.

"Yeah," Lori said.

Jacob had to have been there for some reason, especially if he wasn't dealing that night. The only thing connecting him to the party was Matt, and the only thing connecting them was Gridley. Had Gridley sent Jacob? If so, why?

Only one thing was certain. Jacob's presence at the party had apparently attracted the attention of the Fourth Street Posse. Of "Ryan." Maybe not happy he was on their turf. Been keeping their eye out for him. Word gets around. But had the warning they'd given him, that Ryan had given him, ended with whatever confrontation Helen had heard about? Or had the threat to Jacob gone farther? Had it somehow included the arson fire?

"One other question," I said.

"OK," Lori said.

"You had some papers of Matt's."

She nodded.

"Helen told you she shared them with me? After you gave them to her?"

"Yes."

"There was a document in there, related to Matt's research with Professor Gridley."

"I'm not sure about that."

I took the log out and slid it across the table. Crenshaw snatched it up, examined it, then placed it front of Lori. Helen leaned over, took a look.

"Any idea where Matt got that from?" I said.

"No."

"You're sure?"

"Yes." Although her eyes said differently.

"You're sure about that."

"Yes."

I looked at Crenshaw. She looked at me. I looked at Lori, then back to Crenshaw. And nodded.

"Thank you," Crenshaw said. "We're done here."

34

"SHE KNOWS SOMETHING ABOUT THAT document," I said, when Crenshaw and I were alone.

"I don't disagree," she said. "But what's its relevance?"

"What I was hoping Lori could tell me."

"Her right not to," she said. "She gave you plenty about Dunning and this professor."

"Yes, she did."

"So was there anything else?"

"Any chance I could talk to her alone? Without her mom there?"

"No."

"Why not?"

"Because I bent the rules for you far enough and because I said so."

I thought of some retorts. Reminded myself I'd given up pissing off trial attorneys for Lent.

"Different question, then."

"Make it quick."

"Dorothy Custer."

"What about her?"

"You've made two different references to her not being worth it financially to go after."

"So?"

"So her late husband published a best-selling history book that's been optioned as a movie. I'm not saying she's Gloria Vanderbilt. But she ought to be semi-flush. Right?"

Crenshaw didn't respond. I thought about the bounced check. The apologies. The vague references to automatic payments and the bother of online banking.

I said, "I'm just wondering if you know something you could share with me."

"I don't have anything to tell you," she said.

"We're on the same side. You know that, right?"

"What?"

"We both want justice from this case."

"Spare me."

"You've got your way, I've got mine. Same church, different pews."

"Not how I see it."

"Simple question. About Dorothy."

"Same answer."

"What if I told you there was another angle?"

"Angle?"

"About the smoke detectors."

"Like what?"

I pulled out my phone and scrolled through my e-mail until I found the message Whitestone had sent me that morning. After my question about the smoke detector batteries had gotten the better of him. I tapped "Forward," entered Crenshaw's e-mail address, pressed "Send."

I said, "Like with the smoke detectors."

"I'd say you were bullshitting me."

"What if I weren't?"

"Fat chance of that."

"Humor me. Check your e-mail."

"Why?"

"I give you something decent, you trade me for it?"

"Like what?"

"Like whatever it is you seem to know about Dorothy Custer's bank account."

She stared at me. "Are you saying you really have something?"

"You didn't answer the question."

"All right," she said. "I'd consider it. Satisfied?"

"There now. Wasn't that easy?"

"Nothing's easy with you."

"You still haven't checked your e-mail."

She dug out her phone, scrolled through messages. Looked at the information from Whitestone. About the batteries.

She placed both hands on the table and let out a breath.

"All right," she said. "Let's go back to my office."

PETE HENDERSON WAS ADAMANT WHEN HE
reached me three minutes later as I walked down Third toward
home, thinking about what Crenshaw had just told me.

"What's so important we have to meet in person?" I said,
nearly to St. Mary's Catholic Church.

"The NSA might be listening in."

"That's *you* guys."

"I wish. Same place as before?"

"You aren't worried the trees are bugged?"

"Twenty minutes?"

I agreed and picked up my pace.

UNLIKE MY RECENT DRIVE to campus, it really was a
direct route to maneuver over to Front Street from my house to
Marconi Boulevard and the little park outside the courthouse.
As a result I didn't feel too bad as I passed the Neil House Inn,
slowed to almost a stop, looked into the parking garage and
then the drop-off area, before continuing on. Nothing. The
realist in me had started to wonder if maybe I was imagining

things. That there was another explanation. The skeptic in me knew that if I were Murphy and I had even the slightest inkling I'd been seen, I'd be extra careful.

There was something different about Henderson's expression when he walked up to me a few minutes later.

"I heard you had an interesting Sunday morning."

"Fancy that."

"Any idea who did it?"

"Speaking of the NSA, mind if I ask how you heard about it? Wasn't exactly broadcast widely."

"Little bird," he said. "You know how it is."

"I know little birds used to die in caves from breathing carbon monoxide."

"I'll keep that in mind next time I need anthracite," Henderson said. "In the meantime, any connection to what we were talking about the other day?"

"What do you mean?"

"Fourth Street Posse. Orton Avenue is right on the edge of their territory."

"You're the one who told me not to get hung up on their name."

"Work with me for a minute."

"You asking if I think a gang banger torched my van?"

"Something like that."

I thought of Peirce, watching my house. About Dickinson's text that morning.

"I don't think so."

"Why not?"

"I have an alternate suspect in mind."

"Who?"

"Someone not related to a violent drug gang."

"Why would they torch your van?"

"To make a point."

"About what?"

"Has to do with a job offer."

"Interesting recruiting technique."

"I've seen worse," I said. "Why am I talking to you again?"

"Ever hear of a guy named Richard Ronnell?"

"No."

"Dealer with the posse. And part-time enforcer. Father was in the gang in the nineties. Uncle too."

"All in the family?"

"Ronnell was around for a while. Back at the time of the fire. Then he disappeared. We think he was in Detroit. Now he's back."

"OK."

"He's got a nickname."

"Which is?"

"Run-Run."

"Run-Run?"

"That's right."

"Why?"

"He ran fast as a kid. Back then he was good at running away from his grandmother. Now he runs fast from street corners where someone's got a bullet in his head."

"Not seeing your point."

"We're picking up chatter about things happening in neighborhoods controlled by the Fourth Street Posse. And Run-Run's name keeps coming up."

"OK."

"Run-Run. Similar to Ryan, don't you think? If you heard it at a crowded party. And maybe you'd had too much to drink or smoke?"

"Ryan," I said.

"Ryan. Run-Run."

I thought about my meeting with Lori Hume that morning. About Jacob Dunning and Gridley. Gridley's wife and medical marijuana.

I decided to tell him what I knew.

"Ronnell threatens Jacob Dunning at the party," Henderson said when I finished. "Maybe comes back later to drive home the point?"

"Maybe. But like you said, what would he care about a kid selling pot?"

"Unless Dunning had upped his game."

"Any evidence of that?"

"No. But worth thinking about."

Henderson reached into a briefcase, pulled out a sheet of paper.

"Run-Run," he said, handing it to me.

I stared at the face. Cold, hard eyes, hint of a smirk. Scar on his right cheek like a thin band of badly folded clay. Not someone you'd take lightly. Something in his expression reminded me of Peirce.

"When was this taken?"

"Couple years ago."

"What am I supposed to do with it?"

"Familiarize yourself with his face so you can avoid him at all costs."

36

THE INFORMATION CRENSHAW PASSED ON
to me about Dorothy Custer inspired a call to Karen Feinberg,
who was more than happy to talk to me as long as it wasn't
about Aaron Custer or Buddy "Killer" Keeler or any of the
other sick motherfuckers (her word) she numbered among her
clientele. She gave me Gabby's number, whose office I called in
due course, asking for some help. She agreed to look into the
matter I brought to her.

On a lark, I texted D. B. Chambers to see if he'd been
heading to work Sunday morning and noticed anything un-
usual in the neighborhood. Silence ensued. I was circling back
home when my phone rang. I didn't recognize the number,
nor the woman's voice on the other end, quiet and maybe a
little scared.

"Are you the guy who was at Pendergrass the other day?
Asking about Kim McDowell?"

"That's right. Can you speak up a little?"

"Sorry," she said. A little louder: "I'm the receptionist.
Out front."

"Orange glasses," I said. "I remember."

"I was wondering if we could meet. If I could talk to you."

"I suppose. You didn't seem thrilled to see me the other day."

"It won't take long."

"Did you want me to come over there?"

"No. Not at Pendergrass."

"Drink? After work?"

"Tonight's not great. Maybe before work? Do you eat breakfast?"

"As often as possible."

After we made the arrangements, I said, "Mind if I ask what you want to talk about?"

"I've got to go," she said. "I'll see you tomorrow."

WE MET AT A café on Pennsylvania Street in Harrison West, a rapidly gentrifying neighborhood not far from Pendergrass. Her name was Melissa Kramer. She didn't look icy, as she had the other day. She looked miserable.

"We've been instructed not to talk to anybody about Kim," she said. "I could be in big trouble just meeting you."

"Why?"

"Kim's death is off limits. You stirred up a lot of people the other day."

"Good to hear. So why'd you call, if this is so hush-hush?"

"Kim was my friend," she said. "It seemed like you knew something about her. About what happened."

"Why do you say that?"

"The way Leif reacted to you."

"Leif?"

She blushed. "Sorry. Erik. Erik Petersson. We call him Leif, like Leif Erikson? The explorer? Please don't tell him I said that. That could definitely cost me my job."

"Mum's the word."

"They were always super-secretive about what happened to Kim. Like it was this big deal to do with Pendergrass. Like it was about them, not her."

"There were rumors of corporate espionage," I said.

She nodded. "There's always been a suggestion it wasn't as clear-cut as a burglary."

"You mean like somebody else killed her? Besides Buddy Keeler?"

"There was talk she was working on something that couldn't be found after her death. And people thought it was suspicious."

"Something like what?"

"I don't know."

"She never mentioned it?"

"We didn't talk much about work. We went out a couple of times, had some drinks. She was pretty private. But then, when you were here, I saw you show Petersson something. Something that got a reaction."

"It's a log of some kind," I said. "That's what he called it."

"Where did you get it from?"

"I can't tell you that right now. But it might be part of a case I'm working on."

"What kind of case?"

I told her the basics about Aaron Custer.

"I don't understand," she said. "What would that fire have to do with Kim?"

"I'm not sure it has anything to do with Kim," I said. "But that log, or document, or whatever it is, turned up as part of what I'm looking into. That's why I asked Petersson about it."

"What did he say?"

"Not much."

"He didn't tell you what it was?"

"No. And I didn't give it to him, either. It meant something to him, though. I'm just not sure what."

"They're very guarded."

"Why?"

"Pendergrass is a private company. We may look like a university to outsiders. But we're a business."

"And businesses keep secrets."

"Everybody keeps secrets," she said. "Ours just carry a price tag. We have millions of dollars in contracts."

"Kim's field," I said. "Clean coal technology?"

She nodded. "Carbon sequestration. Big deal right now." She looked at me. "Are you saying it's related to that?"

"I don't know. It's a thought."

She picked at her breakfast burrito. Ate a bite. Continued to look miserable.

"Mind if I ask you a question?" I said.

She shook her head.

"Was Kim seeing someone? Before she died?"

She didn't answer right away. Moved some food around her plate.

"I think so."

"Think?"

"Like I said, she was a private person. She'd listen to me complain about my boyfriend all night. But she didn't share a lot back."

"Any idea who it was?"

"Not really. Seemed like something she wanted kept a secret."

"Was it possible he was married? Is that why she didn't talk about it?"

"Do you know something? Know who it was?"

"I have some ideas," I said.

"Who?"

I told her my suspicions, in confidence. Couldn't see any reason not to.

"You said they were on that panel together? In Dallas?"

"That's right."

"That would make sense."

"Why?"

"She seemed preoccupied after she came back. Now that I think about it, it's around the time she started dropping hints."

"She never used his name?"

She shook her head. "You don't think he had something to do with, you know, killing her?"

"I have no idea. He doesn't seem the murderous sort." I thought about Karen Feinberg's courthouse syllogism. *Just because someone's a screwed-up motherfucker means they probably did do it.* "Sometimes that means something, sometimes it doesn't."

"What about the guy they arrested for it?"

"Strong possibility, little I know of him. Career criminal. Not a violent past, but burglaries have been known to go bad when someone's unexpectedly at home. No question he was in the apartment. They matched his prints once they arrested him and he had some of Kim's things."

"It's so horrible."

"Yes."

"What are you going to do? About Kim? And the document?"

"I'm not sure. I don't know if it's even related to Aaron Custer, which is who I really need to focus on." I had a thought. "Don't suppose there's any chance you could show it to someone at Pendergrass?"

"I can't risk it," she said. "I'm sorry. Kim was the only researcher I really knew. And if word got back to Leif . . ."

"Understood," I said. "Vikings—very volatile."

She smiled at the joke. But it was a sad smile. Definitely sad.

37

THE CAFÉ WAS AROUND THE CORNER FROM Pendergrass, and the research institute was not far from the coroner's office, and that's where I ended up a few minutes later, thinking about my conversation with Melissa Kramer. George Huntington didn't seem all that surprised to see me, until he found out I wasn't there about the fire.

"Kim McDowell's still an open investigation," he said, when we were back in his office.

"I know that," I said. "I'm just trying to find out how she died."

"That's in the coroner's report. Which is a public record."

"'Blunt force trauma.' Yes, I know. Which could mean just about anything."

"I can't show you the file. Not on this one."

"Anything more specific? About the blunt part?"

"Why the sudden interest? I thought you were busy springing triple arson-murderers."

"It's possible they're related."

"You're kidding."

"Maybe, maybe not," I said. "Just looking at some loose strings."

"To hang me with."

"Wouldn't think of it."

"Cops know about this? About Kim and the fire?"

"Not yet."

"You going to tell them?"

"Soon enough. Quicker I know how Kim died, quicker I can make that happen."

He wrestled with my request for a minute, rubbing his goatee several times. Then he got up, walked around his desk, closed the door to his office, sat down, and typed furiously at his keyboard.

"All right," he said.

"Can I see?"

"No."

"Can you tell me?"

"A little."

"What'd she die of?"

Some typing and scrolling.

"Interesting," he said. "Looks like she had a subdural hematoma."

"And in English, that's?"

"Buildup of blood between the brain and skull. The hematoma presses on the brain and starts to affect heart rate and breathing and temperature, things like that. Pretty easily treated if you catch it in time. Obviously not in this case."

"Obviously," I said. "Because she would have been unconscious."

"Not necessarily."

"What?"

"Your blunt force trauma is what initiates the bleeding that causes the hematoma. But it's pretty common for people to seem fine, at least to be conscious, at first. Then the headaches and the nausea start and temperatures spike. Once that happens it's usually lights out."

"You're saying McDowell didn't die right away?"

"I'm telling you what she died of. I'm saying it's possible, based on the hematoma, she could have been awake for a while first."

"Why didn't she call 911? Or go to the hospital? I mean, wouldn't there be a lot of blood?"

"Not always, if it was all internal," he said. "It's a deceptive injury. Possible she thought an ice pack would do it." He consulted the computer. "She was found in bed, so maybe she lay down first."

"In bed, like for the night?"

He tapped a couple of keys. "On top of the covers, in regular clothes. Sounds like a nap to me."

"Lying down to take a nap is not consistent with someone who was just attacked by a burglar."

"No," he said. "No, it's not."

"Wouldn't the police think the same thing?"

"Possibly, except that sometimes people do conk out immediately after they're hit. It's hard to correlate the time of attack with time of death in cases like this. You factor in Keeler's prints in her apartment and her stuff in his possession and it's a logical leap: he hit her over the head in her bedroom while robbing her place and left her lying there."

"But why the bedroom? Why not the living room?"

"Maybe she ran in there, trying to get away."

"Which is it?" I said. "In your opinion? Conked out or awake for a while?"

Huntington scrolled up and down several screens and rubbed his goatee over and over.

"Awake," he said finally. "I'd have to say she was awake."

207

BACK OUTSIDE, I GOT in my rental and called Karen Feinberg.

"Don't tell me you lost Gabby's number," she whispered.

"Gimme two minutes," I said. I explained what Huntington had told me.

"I'm not getting it," she said.

"If Kim McDowell got hit on the head and was knocked unconscious right away, then Keeler's looking pretty good for it. But if she were awake for a while, and then died, it couldn't have been him. What victim of a stranger assault in her own apartment takes a nap first without calling police?"

"But if that's true, how'd she get the injury?"

"She either had a bad household accident," I said, "or she knew whoever hit her."

"What do you mean?"

"I mean, like a domestic incident gone bad. Tempers cool, they kiss and make up, injury doesn't seem so bad at first."

"I never heard anything about a boyfriend."

"You wouldn't have."

"And you did?"

I told her my suspicions. When I was finished, the line was quiet for so long I thought she'd dropped the phone. Then she said, "I've got to go. I'm in contempt of court in thirty seconds. I'll call you back."

MOHAWK WAS FREE OF silver Hummers when I pulled up in front of my house a few minutes later. Mixed blessing, I thought, since it meant I didn't know what Peirce was up to.

I had done more listening than eating during breakfast with Melissa, and to ward off famine I made myself a couple of slices of toast. I was adding jelly to one and peanut butter to the second when Chambers called.

"Falco," he said. "I got your text. What's going on?"

I could hear voices in the background, and what sounded like a series of beeps.

"Are you at work?"

"Every day, man. Moving those Happy Meals. Took a break to call you."

I explained about the van fire and what Henderson had told me about Richard "Run-Run" Ronnell. He didn't respond right away.

"You there?" I said.

"Yeah."

"Everything OK?"

"Except for the fact you're pissing me off a little bit, sure."

"Pissing you off? How?"

"You heard me."

"I'm not following."

"You think because I'm an east side dude with a record that I know all the 'inner workings' of a drug gang?"

"No," I said. "I just thought—"

"I know what you thought. And I don't appreciate it. I like talking to you. I wish I saw more that night. But like I already told you, all I did was call 911."

"Listen," I tried to say.

"This 'Run-Run,' guy," he went on. "That ain't no state secret your U.S. marshal or whoever is floating around you. That guy's been in the news before. All those guys have. Everyone knows. It's no secret what they do."

"All right," I said. "Sorry I asked."

"I don't mean to get upset. But I'm trying to make my way. You know?"

"I know," I said.

"Who's telling you all this about Ryan or Run-Run anyway? That kid's grandmother? The one who set the fire?"

"One of the survivors. Look, I'm sorry. Again. How about I come by, take you out, make things right? We'll go to White Castle; my treat."

That got a laugh. "All right, Falco. Break's almost over. Gotta get back to work."

"All right."

"But Falco?"

"Yeah?"

"I told you Run-Run's been in the news, right?"

"Right."

"If the news is right, he's nobody to be messing around with. Just keep that in mind."

I assured him I would.

"Guys like that?" Chambers said. "Reason why I moved over to Happy Meals."

38

I WOULD HAVE PREFERRED SPENDING THE next couple of hours leaping tall buildings in a single bound or warning the bad guys of Gotham City to clear out once and for all. Or maybe, if I were lucky, giving Dorothy Custer something besides a status quo update. Instead, I found myself sitting in the waiting room at Merion Place Veterinary Clinic on South High staring at charts of heartworms and cursing the person or persons who'd smashed a beer bottle at the park two months earlier that was continuing to cost me a small fortune in bills for Hopalong.

I spent most of my time at the vet's engrossed in *World War Z* and so hadn't checked my phone regularly. It wasn't until I got home, late in the afternoon, that I plowed through my e-mails, deleting them left and right—the electronic message equivalent of zombie killing, come to think of it—until I paused above a return address I didn't recognize. Aaron. From the prison e-mail system.

i might have remember something. maybe i said that about the posse i don know. i cant remember a lot from that night. i'm also the

211

boss that's my nickname. One thing i remember is i heard Jacob might be into selling smack. not smart.

I wrote a quick response, telling him about Richard Ronnell, asking if the name rang any bells. Next I called and left a message for Henderson, telling him what Aaron had recalled. And then, deciding to go out on a limb, way out, I hit "Forward," typed in Suzanne's address, threw a host of capitalized caveats in my message, starting with "OFF THE RECORD FOR NOW," and sent her the e-mail.

When Mellencamp's guitar riffs emitted from my phone five minutes later, I was disappointed to see it wasn't Suzanne on the line. I didn't recognize the number.

"Hi. It's Freddie."

Freddie. Short for Frederica.

"What can I do for you?"

"I found your can fairy."

"What?"

"He says he saw you the other night."

"You found him?"

"Saw him on the street. Got to chatting."

"When?"

"Just now."

"He was out in the daytime?"

"He's a can fairy, not a vampire."

"You know what I mean."

"He's an interesting guy."

"Interesting how?"

"He mentioned the other night. I put two and two together, you know? Figured that was you?"

"Where is he now?"

"With me. On my porch."

I PARKED THE RENTAL in a campus garage on North High near the Wexner arts center. I didn't think anyone would try to torch it in the remaining hour or so of daylight, but I wasn't taking any chances.

I crossed the street with a pack of students, then started jogging toward Orton Avenue. For a moment I wondered if Freddie short for Frederica was putting me on. Then, at a house across the street and two down from the boarded-up site of the blaze, I spied a girl with rainbow streaks in her hair talking to the man I'd seen the previous Sunday.

"Woody," the man said as I arrived, out of breath. "Where'd you go the other night?"

HIS NAME WAS WILLIE Smith. He was a little shorter than me, compact. He was not homeless. I know because he told me that three times. We sat on the porch at Freddie's house, drinking cups of herbal tea she made for us. She sat and listened, wide-eyed.

He said, "You're the only Big Ten player ever shaved a couple of points, I'll eat my hat." He took a drink of tea, made a face. "Just think you was robbed."

"Water under the bridge," I said. "And just because other people did it doesn't make it less of a crime." Then I added, "But thank you. I guess."

"Private detective, huh?" he said.

"Investigator. Same difference."

"That what you majored in? At OSU?"

"I majored in girls, with a minor in trouble," I said. "Got into this a little bit later."

He smiled. Winked at Freddie. He said, "You want to know about the fire."

"That's right. Looking for anyone who saw something."

"Why?"

I told him.

"Kind of crazy," he said.

"What do you mean?"

He ignored the question and posed one of his own. "If somebody did see it, what then?"

"Guess I'd try to talk to them. See what they know."

"But after, I mean. They gonna get arrested?"

"Arrested?"

"For not saying anything. Obstructing justice. Whatever."

"I wouldn't think so," I said. "Would guess the police would be more interested in what they knew. And if they'd never talked to them before, it wouldn't really be obstructing justice."

"Reward?"

I shook my head. "Officially, the crime's solved, so there's no reward out there."

"What about the grandmother. Lady you mentioned. Would she pay?"

"I'm not sure," I said, thinking about my conversation with Crenshaw and my follow-up request to Gabby, Karen Feinberg's probate lawyer fiancée. "Guess I could ask her."

"You ask her. Then we'll talk."

"You know something?"

"I know you need to ask her about a reward. That's all I'm saying for now."

I LEFT SMITH ON Freddie's porch, thanked her for my tea, walked over to High Street, retrieved my car, and called Dorothy. She said it wasn't a problem to come by.

"He's the witness?" she said, seated on the couch a few minutes later.

"Looks like."

"And he wants a reward."

"He wants to know about one."

"Did he say how much?"

"No."

"Why didn't he go to the police?" she said.

SLOW BURN

"I'm not sure," I said. "I don't think he's a bad guy or anything. But maybe he didn't want to get involved. Or maybe he
didn't realize what he saw, maybe thought Aaron was the guy.
Only realized later on. Hard to say."

"Should I meet him?"

"I could arrange something. I think right now he just wants
to know about money."

"I'd rather know an exact amount," she said. "But of course
I can pay. For Aaron."

"You sure?"

"Of course. Why would you ask?"

I didn't say anything.

"The check," she said. "That was a one-time thing."

"The thing is," I said. "*Old Hickory.*"

"What about it?"

I thought about what Crenshaw had told me.

"You haven't been getting any royalties for a few years,
have you? Since your husband died."

"That would be none of your business."

"Sales dried up."

"It's simply not your concern."

"I don't mean to pry. But if things are tight for you, financially, we need to look at this another way."

"Things are fine."

"The reward. We could negotiate."

"Get the amount," she said.

"I'm just trying to help."

"I recognize that. And you've done a lot so far. What I paid
you to do, finding this Smith fellow."

"We're close," I said.

"Not until we have his story. Tell him I'll pay. Let me worry
about the details."

Smith didn't have a phone, so I had to drive back to his
apartment on Ninth Avenue to find him. It took him a minute
to answer the door after I'd knocked.

215

"Didn't think I'd see you again," he said.

"Why not?"

"Thought you might be making the whole thing up."

"Wish I were."

I explained that Dorothy had approved a reward, but she needed to know a number.

"I don't know," Smith said.

"Ballpark it," I said.

"I can't."

"Why not?"

"Because it's not for me, Woody. It's for the person who saw what happened."

I SAT ON THE couch in his living room, which would also have been his kitchen but for a counter separating the two. The air smelled of fried food and coffee. A woman he introduced as his mother dozed in an armchair, an oxygen machine clicking and chuffing beside her.

"I met Eddie Miller on the streets one day," Smith said. "He tried to rob me. Junkie, you know."

"I know. Him and his sister."

"Told him I couldn't give him anything. Needed everything to take care of her." He nodded at his mother. "She's eighty-seven. Emphysema and bladder cancer."

"I'm sorry."

"Offered him something else. Information. Name of somebody who knew about the fire. It was all I could think to do. Couldn't afford to have something happen to me, because of her."

"It wasn't you who saw what happened. You knew somebody."

"That's right."

"This person knew about Aaron. And the baseball cap. Which nobody else knew about."

"That's what they told me."

"Who is it?"

"Lady that's homeless."

"A lady?"

"You heard me."

"What's her name?"

"Aaron's grandmother," he said. "She'll pay?"

"She said she would."

"Not for me. For this lady. She can use the money."

"The name," I said. "I need the name of this witness."

"She goes by Sam."

"Sam?"

"That's right."

Sam. Samantha.

I described Samantha to Smith.

"That's her," he said. "Bit feisty. Not all there, either, if you know what I mean."

Samantha Parks. Lady from the homeless camp. The one who'd once chased a bunch of rabble-rousers all the way to High Street.

All the way up to the neighborhood around Orton Avenue?

I punched Roy's number into my phone as quickly as I could.

39

THE SKY WAS JUST BEGINNING TO LIGHTEN the next morning when Roy and I got out of the van parked beside the Olentangy Trail and hiked into the camp.

Samantha wasn't there and no one had seen her.

"Where could she be?" I said as we sipped coffee in Roy's van a few minutes later. "I thought she lived here."

"She tends to wander. Has some demons that keep her up at night."

"But what if something happened to her?"

"Like what?"

"Like I don't know. What if someone found her? Someone who knew she was a witness."

"Like who?"

I told him about Pete Henderson and Jacob Dunning and the Fourth Street Posse and "Run-Run." I showed Roy the flier with Richard Ronnell's photo.

"Sam knows how to take care of herself," Roy said. "She'll be fine. It's just a question of finding her."

"How do we do that?"

"We look."

We swung back to German Village so I could pick up the rental. Then we split up and each drove around for a while. I went down Broad, past the science museum, past the old train depot converted to a firefighters union hall, past Spaghetti Warehouse, under the rail trestle and up to McDowell, where I spied my first two semiauthentic-looking homeless guys. I rolled down my window and asked if they knew Samantha or had seen her. One of them shook his head and the other one called me Woody and told me I sucked. I drove to Town, worked my way behind the science museum, crossed the river over the new bridge, then drove back up Front. As a bonus, no sign of Glen Murphy and the girlfriend at the Neil House Inn.

We called the search off at just past 8:00 and met at Tommy's Diner in Franklinton, a few blocks up from Roy's church.

"You calling the police?" Roy said.

"Not yet. I need more than the word of a can fairy shaken down by a heroin addict that a homeless woman might have seen something."

"Such high standards now."

"I try."

"We'll find her," Roy said. "I know a lot of people out there."

"Even if we do, what's the point?"

"What's that supposed to mean?"

"You said it yourself. She's in and out. Not the most reliable witness."

"It's true she would muddy the waters, in this situation," Roy said. "Her past and everything. But she's more than you've got now."

"I suppose. It felt promising when Willie told me about it. Now it's seems like a dead end."

"Dead ends can be useful."

"How?"

"Keep you from going off a cliff," Roy said. "We'll find her. Don't worry."

40

THERE WAS NOTHING FOR IT BUT TO GET
on with the day. Roy was already late for a Wednesday medical
clinic he ran at his church. I beeped at him as he turned off a
few blocks east of Tommy's, then did two more halfhearted
loops of downtown with no success.

I was almost home when Karen Feinberg called.

"You certainly got people's attention," she said.

"Meaning?"

"I took another look at the police report on Kim McDowell. That and the autopsy."

"Figured you might."

"Turns out CPD's crime scene techs found trace blood and
hair on a corner of the coffee table in her living room."

"OK. Except she was found on her bed."

"Where she ended up. Maybe not where she started."

"Go on."

"They weren't quite sure what to do with it at first. Idea
being maybe she got hit in the living room, fell on the table,
then he finished her off when she ran into the bedroom."

"Sounds plausible." George Huntington had ventured something along those lines.

"But not if she were awake for a while before she died. Like you said."

"Point being?"

"What if her only injury came from hitting the coffee table?"

"I suppose. If she hit it hard enough."

"What if she hit it hard enough because she was arguing with someone and got pushed or tripped?"

"Arguing with someone?"

"With a married boyfriend, for example."

"Interesting," I said.

"Not the word the prosecutor used when I brought it up."

"What are you doing now?"

"Ball's in their court. They may want to talk to you."

"You tell them you heard it from me?"

"Not yet."

"Thanks."

"But I may have to. Or—"

"Or?"

"Or you could just tell them yourself."

"I was afraid you were going to say that."

"I'm going to make a couple more calls, look at a couple more things. But then we should talk about it."

"All right."

"Believe it or not, that's not why I called."

"Surprise me."

"Thing is, Gabby's parents came into town last night. Mr. and Mrs. Donatelli. A bit unexpectedly."

"The ties that bind."

"Or strangle. They're having a heart-to-heart about our upcoming nuptials. She's a little distracted at the moment."

"I can imagine."

"Probably not. But she told me to tell you something. Something about Dorothy Custer? What you asked her about."

"About the movie option?"

"Something about the royalties."

"There are no royalties."

"I'm just passing her message on. She might have something for you tomorrow. If she survives today. Also?"

"Yes?"

"She wondered if you had his accident report."

"Whose?"

"Frank Custer. From the crash."

"No. Why?"

"She likes to cover all her bases. Like you. Just an idea."

"All right," I said. "I'll check it out. And tell her I said thanks."

"If she or her parents are still alive by dinnertime, I'll pass that on."

I POURED MYSELF A cup of coffee, then took a couple minutes and faxed a request for Frank Custer's accident report to the police records department. When I called to make sure it had arrived, the clerk said it should only be a few hours. I read a chapter of *World War Z* sitting at my kitchen table. Then another. Had more coffee. Fielded two calls from women worried their husbands were straying who were interested in engaging my services. I listened patiently, failing to mention that if they were worried they were probably right and didn't need me to confirm the inevitable. Instead, thinking about my bank account, I explained my fee structure and what I could do for them. One signed up, the other was put off by the expense. If trying to prove the innocence of triple murderers didn't pan out, at least I had another job to fall back on.

I was debating whether to start looking for Samantha again or figure out the best strategy for approaching the cops about my Kim McDowell theory when Suzanne called.

"This is way off the record," she said.

"Can reporters do that?"

"Shut up and listen. That message from Aaron? I did some checking around. Called in more than one favor."

"Thank you."

"Talked to a guy on a county drug task force. Who knew a guy. Who said Dunning's name had come up in connection with a heroin possession arrest near campus."

"When was this?"

"Couple weeks before the fire."

"Anything to it?"

"Nothing to go on air with. But it confirms Dunning was into more than pot."

I thought about this. It was good news, and yet, in a way, not good news.

"What are you going to do with it?" I said.

"At the moment, nothing. But I'm keeping a file."

"You need anything else? From me?"

"The exclusive, remember?"

"And you remember what I told you? Like, what's to keep this McGruff the Crime Dog source of yours from blabbing?"

"Good manners. Give it a try sometime."

"Good manners don't solve cases."

"They just keep relationships going. Don't burn me, all right?"

I let the dig slide. I thought about Glen Murphy and the Neil House Inn. I thanked her for calling. I started to say something and realized she'd hung up.

41

AN HOUR LATER I WAS AT POLICE
headquarters, paying for my copy of Frank Custer's report. I
stood in the second-floor lobby while I read the results. Nothing seemed out of the ordinary until I read it a second time
and looked at the officer's conclusions. Custer had run a red
light going fifty-four in a thirty-five-mph zone. Met up with a
dump truck with injurious results. Very injurious. That seemed
mighty fast, which got me wondering about his driving record.
A question that would have to wait, however. It was time to get
back to Samantha.

I began circling downtown again. Civic Center Drive. Front
Street. Over to Spring, then Souder. Back Long Street. Back and
forth on Broad. Up and down the north-south streets in the Bot-
toms, the city's oldest neighborhood, just west of downtown.
Past the Florentine restaurant, starting to pull in the dinner
crowd and looking pretty inviting at this point. Resisting tempta-
tion and back down Broad. Around COSI. Rinse. Repeat.

It was on my fourth version of this circuit, headed north
on Front, not even paying attention, that I saw them. Murphy

and the girlfriend. Leaving the hotel. Maybe it was my mood, and maybe it was the thaw I was feeling from Suzanne. Either way, before I really knew what I was doing I pulled a U-turn two blocks down, turned around. and started to follow the SUV.

I tracked him across downtown as he took Broad over to Fourth, careful to stay not behind him but in the lane to the left in case he decided to run any long yellows. After a couple of minutes we drove north on Fourth, up the bridge over the railroad tracks, past Abbott Labs on the right and the old Smith's Hardware building on the left, then up and around and onto the interstate.

Afternoon commuter traffic was headed out of downtown and the going was slow, which made it both harder for me to lose him and easier for him to make me if I wasn't careful. We ground to a crawl at the turn by the Ohio Historical Society, then picked up momentum past the soccer stadium. Almost clear sailing by the time Murphy took the Morse Road exit and headed west. I followed him past the Ohio School for the Blind on the right, then onto a street to the left, and then another left.

Our cars were the only ones moving on the street. I drifted back. A minute later I braked, then parked when I saw him pull over. After a minute both doors of his car opened, and they each got out. I watched as Murphy walked her to the door of a small, green house, stood while she unlocked and opened it, gave her a hug, and then, looking inside once as if to catch a last glimpse, walked back to his car. That's when I opened the door of my rental, climbed out, and walked up the street. He glanced at me without recognition, then looked again.

"What are you doing here?" he said.

"Suzanne know about this?"

"Know about what?"

I nodded at the house.

"About her."

"Her?"

"That's right."

"Did you follow me here?"

"Answer the question."

"What are you talking about?"

"I'm talking about you, and Suzanne, and whoever that is."
I nodded again at the house.

"For Chrissake," Murphy said.

"I'm waiting."

He looked ready to say something else, when the door to
the house opened and the woman reappeared.

"Glen?" she said. "Everything OK?"

He waved at her. A moment later, a young man in jeans
and a blue T-shirt appeared at the door behind her, slight, with
disheveled hair as if he'd just gotten up.

"What's going on?" the young man said.

I looked at Murphy. "Who's that?" I said.

Murphy glared at the boy, then at me. He pushed his hands
through his hair.

"That, you genius, is my nephew."

"Nephew?"

"What you call the son of your sister."

"NEIL HOUSE INN," I said, weakly. "You and her."

Murphy brushed his hand through his hair again. He
looked much older than his few years beyond forty.

"How would my kids put it?" he said. "Hashtag, worst private detective ever?"

I said nothing.

"Jen works at the hotel," he said.

"She works there."

He nodded. "Hostess in the restaurant. I was giving her a
ride home just now."

"A hostess."

"What I said, Sherlock."

SLOW BURN

"I saw you there before. Dropping her off. Going inside."

"Let's see," he said. "Maybe that was the time I was begging her manager not to fire her because of how much time she'd missed. Or the time I dropped her off because Wayne had stolen her car. Or pawned the wheels. I lose track."

"Wayne," I said.

"Her son." He looked toward the living room.

"What's wrong with him?"

"He's a recovering heroin addict," Murphy said. "Recovering in quotation marks most days."

"Jesus. I'm sorry," I said.

"You're exactly how Suzanne described," Murphy went on. "A half-assed Maxwell Smart who thinks he's Spenser for Hire." He laughed. "She was right. She had you nailed."

"Suzanne said that?"

"Verbatim."

"Maybe I misinterpreted things."

"Misinterpreted? You got the whole fucking thing wrong. Hate to be the gal who hires you to check up on her husband for real. He and his girlfriend are gonna be lying on the beach in St. Croix before you figure out what kind of car he drives."

"I was worried about Suzanne," I said. "I know I didn't do her any favors at Lindey's. I didn't want her hurt any further."

"You. Worried about Suzanne."

"That's right."

"She know you've been following me?"

"No."

"Sure about that?"

"Yes."

"One ray of hope," he said.

"How about her?" I said. "Does she know . . . ?"

"Does she know about Wayne?" Murphy said. "Told her on our first date. 'Love that series you're doing about the heroin epidemic. Speaking of which, small world!'"

"Just a question."

"A dumbassed question," he said. "No, Suzanne doesn't know. Not yet. If you want to know, I was building up the courage to tell her when you showed up that night, thank you very much."

"Not the best move I ever made."

"You think?" he said. "So tell me this. How long were you driving up and down Front Street today looking for me?"

"I just happened to be driving past."

"Bullshit."

I explained what I'd been up to, without naming Samantha Parks.

"You really think Aaron Custer's innocent?" His voice incredulous.

"Some things aren't adding up," I said.

"Like what?"

I told him. It's not like he was going to spill the beans to anyone. And I was feeling a need to make amends.

"I'll say this," he said when I'd finished. "A lot of the companies that are fracking are getting hosed, PR-wise. Guys like this Gridley are painting with a really broad brush. Half of what he says is crap."

"But?"

"But anything negative you've heard about Appletree is probably true."

"That reminds me." I reached into the left-hand pocket of my sport coat. I pulled out the copy of the log and handed it to him. "Any idea what this is?"

He studied it for less than a minute. "This is from Knox No. 5," he said.

"That's right."

"Very interesting," he said. "I didn't realize they'd run one of these."

"One of what?" I said.

228

"An MReX log."

"MReX?"

"Magnetic resonance," he said impatiently. "It measures permeability in a rock formation."

"Permeability?"

"Listen," Murphy said. "I'm a little busy at the moment. And you'll forgive me if I'm not inclined to pass the time of day with douchebags who follow me and my sister around town for no reason."

"OK," I said. "I deserved that."

"Yes, you did."

"What I did was stupid. Very stupid."

"It was more than that," Murphy said. "It's borderline stalking."

I wasn't sure I agreed on that point but wasn't going to argue. I said, "You're free to call me all the names you want. They're probably all accurate. And deserved, like I said. But."

"But what?"

"But as long as we're agreed that I'm the world's worst detective and a douchebag and an asshole and probably not headed for your company Christmas party this year, I'd appreciate your help."

"My help? With what?"

I nodded at the log. "With this drilling stuff. What you're telling me is useful. It could help me put this case to bed, one way or the other."

"And why should I care?"

"You shouldn't, when it comes to me. But if Aaron Custer is innocent, that's something. And if he is innocent, and I figure it out, the first person I'm going to tell is Suzanne."

"Right."

"I promise. I mean it."

"Sure you do," he said. "And even if you're telling the truth, which I doubt, what do I care if you tell Suzanne anything?"

"You care," I said, "because if I tell Suzanne, she gets the scoop. A big one. And when Suzanne gets scoops, she's happy. Very happy. And I know that because, like it or not, she was my girlfriend too, once upon a time."

Murphy didn't say anything for a minute. He looked at his sister's house, then at his car, then at the log, then at me.

"OK," he said, finally. "You douchebag stalker asshole. What do you need to know?"

"Well," I said, taking a deep breath. "You said something about permeability."

"Yes."

"What is it?"

"Ability of fluids to flow through rock," Murphy said. "Key to fracking."

"And this shows that? The permeability?"

He ran his finger over the middle portion of the page. "See this splotch here? It's a zone of low permeability."

"I'll take your word for it."

"Whatever you want. That's what it shows."

"Header says Pendergrass Research. What would they have to do with anything?"

"Hard to know exactly," Murphy said. "They're doing a lot of work with carbon sequestration right now. Could be related."

Carbon sequestration. Kim McDowell's field.

"But what's the, I don't know, context of the log? Is it from drilling that Pendergrass did?"

He shook his head. "They're a research operation. Not set up for actual drilling. Way too expensive. They probably piggy-backed on someone."

"Piggybacked?"

"Somebody drills a well, there's a lot of interest in what's down there. So drilling companies will let scientists, geologists, whoever, run piggyback logs. Run analyses. For a price, of course. But a lot less than if the research outfit had to pay all the drilling costs itself. By piggybacking, they only pay for the logs and analyses they're performing. Plus the rig time they use for the tests."

I thought about my conversations with Erik "Leif" Petersson at Pendergrass, and with Steve Dickinson at Appletree Energy.

"There's a lot of interest in my copy of this," I said. "But aren't there electronic copies out there? At Pendergrass, or Appletree?"

"Pendergrass, sure. And technically, they're supposed to provide copies to the state."

"Technically?"

Murphy shrugged. "It's very competitive out there, right now."

I was starting to gain a new appreciation for why Dickinson wanted what I had so badly. He might have been stuck, unable to get the log elsewhere. Then, voila, I show up with a copy.

"This permeability zone stuff," I said. "It can measure earthquakes?"

"Not measure them," he said. "That's completely different. This is more a predictor. The log can point out zones of high and low permeability in the rock. Knowing the characteristics of the rock can also indicate the likelihood of whether the well might have intersected with a fault based on the permeability. And it's limited to the borehole location."

"Which means?"

"Borehole data is generally the best for a given location, but it helps to have other data, maybe from other boreholes."

Something was starting to dawn on me. I said, "So a magnetic resonance log can tell whether one of these injection wells is likely to cause an earthquake?"

"One of the things that can," Murphy said. "But yeah, that's right."

"So on this log," I said. "Where does it show that?"

"Show what?"

"Where's the part on there that shows the Knox No. 5 caused those earthquakes?"

"Nowhere," he said.

"What do you mean?"

"I mean it doesn't show that," he said.

"I thought you said it did. The whole permeability zone thing."

"The log *measures* permeability," Murphy said, new impatience in his voice. "The results of that are what indicates whether the injection could have led to tremors."

Still confused, I said, "It doesn't show that on here? Why not?"

"Because the measure of permeability is tiny."

"Tiny?"

"We measure permeability with something called millidarcys. The more of those units, the more permeability in a formation, the more likelihood a well could be linked to an earthquake."

"All right."

"The quakes around Youngstown a few years back? It's pretty technical, but that well had a relatively high mD rate deep down within what are called crystalline basement rocks. Pretty indicative of a fault zone."

"But not the Knox No. 5?"

"Not according to this. The injectate, the saltwater and fracking fluids they pump into the well?"

"Right."

"It's clear as day on here. There's no way that entered the deep portion of the well."

"Meaning?"

"Meaning Knox No. 5 had nothing to do with any earthquakes."

AS I DROVE HOME, headed south on 71, a tractor-trailer flashed his lights at me near the Hudson Street exit. I considered flipping him off until I realized I was driving forty-five miles an hour while I tried to process what Murphy had told me. I sped up, but kept thinking.

Kim McDowell had acquired the magnetic resonance log as part of her research for Pendergrass into carbon sequestration. Whatever it meant to her work, it also disproved Knox No. 5's alleged connection to earthquakes. As a result, it negated Tanner Gridley's entire thesis about the well, and backed up everything Appletree Energy had been saying. That was interesting enough. But it also put Gridley's affair with McDowell, if that's what it was, in a new light.

Up until a few minutes ago, I'd assumed their conjoining had been your standard issue professional conference fling, a bit more odious than usual given Michelle Gridley's medical condition, but no different than what happens in a hundred hotel rooms around the country every day, clothes flung to one side of the bed, name tags to the other. The twist being they were both from Columbus so the fun could continue. But what if there were something else going on? If Matt Cummings had the magnetic resonance log, he had to have gotten it from his mentor, Gridley. And if Gridley had had it, he could only have gotten it from McDowell.

Had he been using the Pendergrass researcher? Using affection as a guide to get the log? Had she refused to show it to him as a fellow professional, so he'd taken a different route? Melissa Kramer had said McDowell was a private person, that she hadn't dated much. A brilliant but shy woman warming to the attentions paid by a type A personality like Gridley? Tale as old as time. But how far had he taken that attention in his desire to get the log? Could Gridley have killed McDowell? Or at the very least had something to do with her hitting her head? Either way, he had acquired the document. And for some reason, instead of destroying it, had sat on it. But why? To study it? See if it could be used to his advantage? Whatever his motives for keeping it, his reasons for taking it were clear: while it was good news for the residents of eastern Ohio, it was bad news for his jeremiads against fracking, not to mention his shot at tenure. Nothing like having your entire thesis on a topic disproved.

But all of this still begged the question: What was Matt doing with the log?

42

IT WASN'T QUITE THE END OF THE WORLD.
But it felt like it the next morning when I flipped to the metro
section of the paper and saw the headline:
Authorities probe gang role in triple fatal campus-area fire.
Stomach sinking, I read the first paragraph:

> Arson investigators are exploring a possible street
> gang connection to a fire at an off-campus rental
> house that killed three Ohio State students, sources
> say. The role the man sentenced to life in prison after
> admitting he set the fire might have played with the
> gang is unclear, but police decided to study new infor-
> mation related to the case, according to the sources.

That's as far as I got when my phone rang.
"You shit," Suzanne said. "You absolute shit."
"I don't know anything about this," I protested. I recalled
with a sickening feeling my conversation with Glen Murphy
the night before.
"Like hell you don't. Did you literally just hang up yesterday and call the paper?"

"You hung up on me," I said. "And no, I didn't do that. I want you to have this first. You know that."

"Bullshit," she said. "You've been playing me this whole time."

"No. I told you I couldn't guarantee—"

"That was just a ruse, wasn't it? Something to cover your ass after you gave it to somebody else."

"I wouldn't do that."

"Please."

"I'm telling you the truth."

"When have you ever done that to me? Ever?"

"I'm doing it right now."

"Just leave me out of this from now on. OK? Don't call anymore. No tips."

"That's it? Biting off your nose?"

"Fuck you."

"I'm telling you, it wasn't me."

"You know what? It doesn't matter either way. Just stay away from me. That's all I ask."

"Suzanne."

"Stay away. Please."

I THOUGHT ABOUT CALLING Kevin Harding at the *Dispatch* to see if he'd give up his source for me. Then I thought about the last time I'd tried that and decided I didn't need the aggravation. I considered calling Whitestone or Henderson and seeing if they knew where the leak had come from. I thought about calling Suzanne back. Oddly, of the three choices, it was the one that appealed the most. I knew if she thought about it she'd see she was being unreasonable. That she had no more reason to expect a scoop on this story in such a competitive media market than I did in expecting she'd keep anything quiet that I told her. The problem with this premise, I knew, is that I had thrust it upon her. Given her druthers, she'd go back in time to the bar at Lindey's and keep drinking her martini while Murphy sipped his Lagavulin.

Instead of calling any of them, though, I dialed the number for Janet Crenshaw.

"YOU ALREADY TALKED TO Lori," she said when I reached her. "You had your chance."

I explained what I needed to ask and why. I told her about Gridley and McDowell.

"We're way past protecting Matt," I said.

"Maybe."

"Not maybe."

"That whole indefatigable thing again," she said.

"In the genes."

"I pity your kids."

"You and everyone else."

But a few minutes later Lori's cell phone number arrived. I called and left a message, explained about my conversation with Crenshaw. Was guessing Crenshaw had probably called too.

When Lori didn't call back right away I used the time to address the other puzzle nagging at me. I flipped through my notes and surfed the Web and as best I could compiled a time line of the worst few months of Aaron Custer's life. Mike and Molly had divorced five years ago, according to online probate records. Frank Custer's accident came a year later, and Mike's suicide just after that. And not long afterward, Aaron started acting up, behavior that ultimately led to an arrest a few months later for lighting a fire in a trash can in Pearl Alley near campus.

I thought back to Olen-Tangy-Tots, Mike's business. Maybe that's what was bothering me. Still seemed like a decent concept for a food truck business at a time in Columbus when such enterprises were booming. On a whim, I looked up the business on the Secretary of State's website. Two principals were listed: Mike Custer and Todd O'Brien. I found a number for O'Brien but ended up leaving a message. I checked the time and shut the computer down. Time to head to the real Olentangy.

FOR HER LAST RUN before Saturday's half marathon, Anne had scheduled a short four-miler, two miles up the trail, two back. She seemed in a better mood, and I listened while she talked about the race and her strategy. Then I told her about trying to find Samantha but left out everything with Murphy. Last thing I wanted to do was explain that I'd been trailing Suzanne's boyfriend, no matter the revelations he'd provided about the Knox No. 5.

We were approaching the bridge at Third Avenue, close to the end of the workout, when the biker passed us going toward downtown.

"*Shameful.*"

I'd sunk so deep into my thoughts that the insult didn't register at first. My eyes on Anne's back, I barely noticed the speaker as she passed. The only thing that brought it to my attention was Anne slowing her pace a tad. She looked back at the figure retreating quickly down the path and shook her head.

"It's OK," I said. "Really."

"I'm sorry," she said. "I'm just never going to get used to it. People need to let it go. You haven't touched a football in, what, two decades?"

"Does a pickup game last Thanksgiving count?"

"You know what I mean."

"I've never gotten used to it either," I said. "It just is what it is."

"It's wrong," she said, but she kept running.

And that's when it registered.

Shameful.

I squeezed hard on my hand brakes.

"What is it?" Anne said, reacting to the squeak of the bike and the scoot of the arrested tires.

"Not what," I said, turning my bike around. *"Who.* That's Samantha Parks."

43

SHE RODE FAST, AND IT TOOK ME ALMOST A minute of hard pedaling to catch her.

"Do I know you?" she said when I'd persuaded her to stop.

"We met in the Spring Street camp."

"So?"

"I'm a friend of Roy," I said.

"Who?"

"Pastor Roy."

"*Shameful,*" she said.

"I was hoping I could talk to you," I said.

"About what?"

"Orton Avenue."

"What about it?"

"Something you might have seen."

"I see a lot of things."

"Like what?"

"Like *things.*"

"That's what I'd like to talk to you about."

"But I don't know you," she said.

I looked up. We were pushing our bikes along a small rise on the path, the protective wall blocking out the 315 expressway on our right. In another couple minutes we'd be at Spring Street, and in a few minutes after that she'd be back at the camp—if that's where she was headed.

I glanced behind me at Anne. She put her hand to her ear with thumb and pinkie spread in the universal representation of a phone. I gave her a look of noncomprehension.

"Roy," Anne mouthed, exasperated.

"Roy?"

"*Call Roy.*"

"Read my mind," I lied, pulling out my phone.

He didn't sound overjoyed when he picked up.

"I've got fifty people coming for lunch in an hour," he said. "I run a soup kitchen, in case you'd forgotten."

"Samantha Parks," I said. "I found her."

"Where?"

I told him.

"Put her on," he said.

IT TOOK ROY SEVERAL minutes of cajoling, during which Samantha hung up on him twice, but eventually we arrived at a plan. Samantha agreed to let me add her bike to mine on the rack I'd strapped to the back of the rental and drive her to the Church of the Holy Apostolic Fire where Roy could talk to her in person. Meantime, Anne would take a house key and drive down to German Village to shower and change at my place. I tried not to dwell on the look in her eyes as I handed her the key, a spare I keep in my wallet. A cross between sadness and resignation.

I had just arrived at the church and was walking Samantha inside when my phone buzzed. I looked down and saw that Lori Hume had texted me back.

Matt made me promise I'd never tell anybody where he got it.

I went inside, handed off Samantha to Roy.

Understood, I replied, stepping into the church dining hall. But things changed. Did Janet Crenshaw talk to you?

A minute passed.

Yes.

What do you think?

IDK, she texted. *I don't know.*

It's important to find out, I said. For Matt, and for other people.

Aaron Custer, she wrote, adding an emoticon devil's face.

For Aaron. And for Matt. And Tina. And Jacob and Helen, I texted. A couple minutes passed. I looked up from the phone and peered around the hall. Roy was in a corner, deep in conversation with Samantha, leaning in toward her like a hermit ministering to a troubled pilgrim. He broke his concentration long enough to glance at me without expression, then went back to what he was saying. Volunteer workers clanked pans and silverware in the kitchen. Two women I knew had been working the streets six months before were setting tables. The smell of bean soup filled the air. I was bursting with impatience to do a formal interview, to find out, finally, what Samantha had seen, but it was clear it wasn't going to happen quickly. Not like on TV, I reminded myself.

My phone buzzed. Six texts in rapid succession.

Matt found it in Professor Gridley's office someplace. One day when he was doing research.

OK. That was no surprise. I remembered all the clutter.

Matt said Professor Gridley was very angry when he found out he had it. Said he needed it back to challenge the findings.

So a possible explanation for why Gridley didn't destroy it. He couldn't let it go.

Couldn't give up the possibility he was still right.

Matt said he didn't know what to do.

He said he was worried.

He said he was scared.

44

LORI HAD CONFIRMED GRIDLEY HAD A LOG that had come from Kim McDowell. A log whose disappearance set off alarms at Pendergrass. A log whose subsequent discovery by Matt Cummings had made Gridley angry.

No doubt about it now. It was time.

First I called Karen Feinberg.

Then I called Columbus homicide detective Henry Fielding.

ON CONSULTING WITH ROY, he made it clear Samantha wasn't ready to talk yet and wasn't going to be for a while, and he had to take a break to start serving lunch.

"Understood," I said. "I'll just grab a plate and we can start up later."

"Might be better if you take off for a little bit. Give her some breathing room."

"Why?"

"She says you make her nervous."

"I make her nervous?"

"That's what she said. Frankly, I agree."

"Thanks a lot."

"It's my pastoral duty to speak plainly."

"A duty you never shirk. What time should I come back?"

"Give me a couple of hours."

Reluctantly, I agreed to return later in the afternoon. I walked back to my rental and was mulling a return visit to Tommy's, this time for lunch, when Chambers called me. I could hear the sound of drive-through orders in the background.

"Falco."

"Hi."

"You see the paper?"

"Yes."

"You the source?"

"No."

"Told you those dudes might be bad."

"Yes, you did."

"So they did it," he said. "Not your guy."

"I don't know," I said. "Maybe. He may still have done it."

"They did it, need to warn that Chinese girl."

"Helen Chen."

"'Run-Run,'" he said. "He's bad news. Told you that."

"She'll be fine."

"Hang on," he said. I heard him take an order, ask how many Happy Meals they wanted. "Four," I heard in response. Lot of kids.

"Falco," he said a minute later.

"Still here."

"Just thinking that girl's got problems."

"She's fine."

"You ain't worried about her?"

I explained that I wasn't. Anyone brave enough to go back to living in the same neighborhood would be OK.

"That ain't brave. That's stupid. She's living on Orton?"

"Woodruff. One down from the corner."

"Hang on," he said again. Took an order for three Big Macs and three large fries. And people wonder why we look the way we do in this country.

"Falco," he said.

"Still here."

"Just think I'd warn her. Or tell that marshal you were talking to."

"U.S. attorney."

"Whatever. Hang on again."

"D. B.," I interrupted.

"Hang on."

A call was coming through on my phone.

"I'll talk to you later," I said.

I took the other call. Gabby Donatelli. Karen's fiancée.

WE MET AT HER office around the corner from the courthouse. She had circles under her eyes, and her usually kempt blond hair was looking not kempt.

"Thanks for doing this," I said. "I know—"

"Don't say it," she said. "It's OK. It'll pass."

"I'm sorry," I said.

But then she blurted out, "What you told Karen? About grandkids? I'm going to have fucking triplets. That'll show them."

"Good on you," I said, uncertainly.

"Anyway, I looked into this business with Frank and Dorothy Custer."

"I appreciate it."

"The royalties from that book."

"Dried up. What Dorothy said."

"No," Gabby said. "Not dried up at all."

"What?"

"Frank Custer changed his will. Right after the accident."

"Changed how?"

"New beneficiary."

I thought back to *Old Hickory and Young America*. The dedication.

"Aaron," I said.

"That's right."

"How much?"

"A lot."

"How much a lot?"

"Tens of thousands of dollars."

"That's how much Aaron's worth?"

"Yes. But no."

"What's that supposed to mean?"

"He's not worth anything in prison. Inmates aren't allowed access to benefits like that."

"But if he weren't in prison?"

"Fat chance of that. I know about his case."

"Humor me. What if?"

"If he weren't in prison, Aaron Custer's a rich young man."

I HAD A VOICE mail when I left her office. Todd O'Brien, Mike's business partner in Olen-Tangy-Tots, had returned my call. He was free that day. Like me, he was hungry. I checked my watch, then headed to the car.

We met at his latest venture, a food truck selling mini-burgers and Korean barbecue parked on High a few blocks north of campus. After his lone employee served us, we sat in a couple of scarlet Ohio State folding chairs he'd brought along.

I said, "You meet Mike through the business? The food truck?"

He shook his head. "In school. Ohio State."

"But first venture together?"

"First food truck. We'd tried a couple of sandwich joints."

"His mother said he had a terrible head for business."

"That's true," O'Brien said. "More a people person."

"The business going under. He blamed himself for that?"

"Not really, no."

"No?"

"Restaurant business is tough. Lots more fail than make it. We knew that going in."

"Must have been a little upset," I said. "I mean, obviously."

"Obviously? Why?"

"Isn't that why, you know, he killed himself?"

"Is that what Dorothy said?"

I nodded.

"That he killed himself because the business went under?"

"That's right. Also."

"Yeah?"

"She said you were skimming from the till."

He stopped in mid-chew and stared at me. "Mike's mother said that? About me?"

I nodded.

"Jesus Christ," he said.

"I take it she has her facts wrong?"

"Not just wrong. She's got them reversed."

"Reversed?"

"*Mike* was the one with sticky fingers. I had to confront him about it."

"What did he say?"

"Made excuses. Said things were a little tight. He owed people money."

"Like who?"

"Like people at liquor stores, for starters. He had a big problem. Why Aaron's issues weren't a surprise."

"That why the business failed? Mike's stealing?"

He shook his head. "Contributing factor."

"What else?"

"Propane prices, meat prices, insurance prices. Really cold winter, really rainy spring. You name it, we got hit with it. Like I said, food business is tough."

"So if Mike didn't kill himself because of the business . . ."

"You're asking me why he did it."

"I guess."

"You talk to Molly?"

"A little. Why?"

"Mike had a lot of issues. Personal finances, the marriage, his father."

"You get this from Molly? Or Mike?"

"Both."

"You're friends with her?"

"A little."

"She goes by Mary now."

He looked surprised at this. "Really?"

I nodded.

"OK," he said. "News to me."

"You knew her at OSU?"

"That's right."

"Where she and Mike met."

"We had class together. With Mike's dad, actually."

"What?"

"Mike's dad, Frank. We had a history class together."

I thought about this. "Molly was in Frank's class?"

"What I said."

"She didn't tell me that."

"Not sure why she should have. She took a few with him. She was a history major. Always seemed funny she went into sales."

"How was he? As a teacher?"

"Frank? Good. Very entertaining."

"Quite the celebrity, in his way," I said.

"Guess you could say that. Come to think of it, Frank was the only one who ever called her Mary. I just remembered that."

"Formal guy?"

"A little."

"Probably hard for Mike. Father like that."

"They had their moments, like I said. Mike didn't talk about him that much."

"Mike was upset by the accident?"

"Who wouldn't be?"

I didn't say anything. Took a bite of my burger. Wrestled with an idea.

"Funny thing was," O'Brien said.

"Yes?"

"Mike was actually doing OK. Even after his dad had the accident. Why his death was so surprising."

"What do you mean?"

"It seemed for a few days like it made them closer or something. But then he got really down one day. I remember it clearly. Like something flipped a switch in his head. It happened right after that."

"Know what it was?"

He shook his head.

"Molly mention anything?" I said.

"Haven't really talked to her much since then. Wish I had. Just always seemed funny."

"Know what you mean," I said.

But maybe not so funny.

45

BACK IN MY CAR, THINKING ABOUT OUR conversation, I called Dorothy Custer and asked her for Molly's cell number. She seemed curious, but I didn't offer any details. I told her there might be a development in the case, but left out Samantha Parks. She said to keep her posted. I said I would.

"It's Andy Hayes," I said when Molly answered a minute later.

"How'd you get this number?"

I explained.

"I'm at work," she said. "It's not a great time."

"I just had lunch with Todd O'Brien," I said. I told her what he'd said about Mike, about a sudden change in mood after his father's accident.

"I don't know what he's talking about," she said.

"Did you know that Frank changed his will at the end, made Aaron the beneficiary of the book royalties? *Old Hickory and Young America.*"

Silence on the other end.

"Could it have had something to do with that?"

"I don't know."

"Did you know about the royalties?"

A pause. "Yes."

"Todd said you took a few classes from Frank Custer. When you were in school."

"That's true."

"How you met Mike."

"What's this have to do with anything?"

"Seems funny you didn't mention you'd had Frank Custer as a professor. When I was at your house the other day."

"Maybe it's none of your business."

"Maybe."

"And what difference does it make to anything anyway?"

"I don't know," I said. I told her what Todd had said about Mike and the business.

"Mike was troubled," she said after a moment.

"I gather."

"I don't think he would have done anything to purposely hurt Todd."

"Seems that way. Possible he was just broke." A pause. "Thanks to his dad?"

"That's not true," she said. "Mike wasn't great with money."

"Maybe that's what pushed him over the edge at the end? Money problems?"

"Maybe."

"Upset the royalties were going to Aaron?"

"I really need to go. I'm sorry."

"Todd said Frank Custer was the only person who ever called you Mary in those days."

"Todd said that?"

"Yes."

"I don't know why he would have told you that."

"Is it true?"

"I have to go," she said.

ROY HAD AN ODD look on his face when I walked back into his church later that afternoon. He was at the desk in his small office just off the kitchen. Samantha was curled up, asleep, on a cot in the hall.

"Let me guess," I said. "Cold feet?"

"Not exactly," he said.

"What's that supposed to mean?"

"You remember that morning in the camp? You were surprised that guy, Benny, had a phone? He used it to call 911 after the camp was rousted."

"I remember."

"Guess who else has a phone?"

I looked at Samantha. Roy nodded.

"That's interesting, I guess," I said.

"That's what I thought. Not that she had one. But that I hadn't seen her with it."

"Maybe she never took it out when you were around."

"Maybe. But I could tell something wasn't right when I was asking her about the fire. After you left."

"Something not right."

"That she wasn't telling me the whole story."

"That would be the situation with this entire case."

"Turns out Samantha has a phone, but she hasn't used it in a while. She's kept it hidden in camp."

"Did she say why?"

"Said she was scared of it."

"Scared of the phone?"

"That's right."

"This one of those 'scared by the radio waves coming from the phone and telling her what to do' kinds of situations?"

Roy shook his head. "This is more, scared by what's on the phone."

"Still not following."

"I told you before, how she muddies up the case, as a witness."

"I remember."

"You didn't ask me why."

"Thought it was kind of obvious."

"You'd think that," he said. "But you'd be wrong."

"So what is it?"

"It's not that she's homeless. It's why."

"OK."

"She was a heroin addict. Ten years ago. On and off the stuff."

"An addict."

"An addict with two little girls. Just her and them."

"Father?"

"Dead. Overdosed. And so her daughters . . ."

"Her daughters," I said.

"One day they were hungry."

I said nothing.

"She started cooking eggs. Then she got high. Then she forgot about the eggs."

"Don't tell me."

"Isn't that always the way? She survived, girls didn't make it. Smoke got them both. Huddled in a bedroom. Three-year-old and a five-year-old. Samantha sprawled on the porch outside. OD'd but alive."

"Jesus."

"She pled down to reckless homicide. Served three years. Been on and off the streets ever since. But never the same again."

I glanced at Samantha, asleep on the cot.

"You said she was scared of what's on the phone."

"That's right."

"Meaning what?"

"Meaning like pictures."

"Pictures?"

"Or more precisely, video."

"Video."

"That's right."

"Samantha's scared of videos on her phone."

"One video in particular."

"Which one?"

"The one she says she took of the Orton Avenue arsonist."

46

AFTER ROY WOKE HER UP, THE THREE OF US
went to the Spring Street camp, where Samantha retrieved the
phone she'd hidden in the tent she called home. It was completely dead, its charger long gone, loaned months earlier to
someone whose name she couldn't recall. Not that she seemed
that interested in bringing it to life, after what she had seen on
Orton Avenue. Back at the Church of the Holy Apostolic Fire
we tried all the chargers Roy kept in a drawer in his office, with
no luck. A few minutes after that I found myself in my car on
I-70 on my way to the commercial district along Hilliard-Rome
Road on the far west side. I rushed into every electronics department I could find, Target, Walmart, Meijer, losing track of
how many chargers I tested. Finally, at a Radio Shack sitting
opposite the new Casino on the old National Road, I found
the one I needed. I knew I was close to finishing the case now.
I thought about the picture of Run-Run that Henderson had
given me. What he would look like in the flesh. In action.

Fielding called me as I drove back down Broad.

"Gridley's lawyered up," he said.

"That didn't take long."

"Usually doesn't."

"Is he under arrest?"

"He's a person of interest."

"How interesting?"

"Very."

"You're welcome?" I ventured.

"I'm going to need that log."

"All I've got is a copy."

"Might work for starters. Need the original if it exists."

"I can get it."

"We can get a search warrant."

"Not necessary. Gimme a few hours."

"Not that urgent. But close."

It was nearing 5:00 when I called Roy and told him about the charger. He told me Samantha wanted to leave, go back to the camp. I told him I thought that was a bad idea. He told me I had shit for brains, that he had already figured that out.

I thought about Samantha finding herself in a position to videotape the fire. What Roy had said, that morning in the camp. *Rode to Toledo and back once, so she claims.* College kids or not, she'd found herself on Orton Avenue at the right time. Or the wrong time, depending on your view of things.

I parked around the corner from my house and had so much on my mind I didn't notice the silver Hummer until I was almost at my door. How the hell did Peirce do that, get the primo curbside space every time? If I didn't hate his guts, I would have hired him as a parking valet.

"What?" I said, striding onto the street, to the driver's side.

"Stunt with the dog crap. Not cute."

"Ask me if I care."

For the first time in our acquaintance, his implacability showed the slightest signs of strain.

"Word is cops are questioning Tanner Gridley. About a certain document."

"News to me," I lied. "Why don't you ask them?"

"We asked you first. Pretty politely, if I recall."

"I declined the offer. If you recall."

"Time's running out, Hayes."

"You're right about that. I'm late as it is."

"For what?"

"For none of your business."

"It would behoove you," he said, "to stop fucking around."

"Behoove."

"You heard me."

I was about to respond when my phone went off.

I looked down, thinking maybe it was Roy calling me back. My stomach fell when I saw the caller ID. Then I felt bad for feeling bad.

"Mike?" I said.

"I really need you to bring my *Redwall* book," my oldest son said. "It's overdue now. And Joe's shirt."

It came back to me in an unwelcome rush. A wall-climbing expedition one of Mike's friends was having for his birthday party. And Mike, being Mike, had insisted he bring Joe. And we were due there in an hour. I thought back to the disastrous Sunday morning call about the Boy Scout trip a couple of weeks ago. Anne's smarting comment, "How could you forget?" I glanced at the plastic bag in my hand holding Samantha's phone and the newly purchased charger. I realized I was dying to see the video, to finally learn the truth. But I also realized the case was months old now. And the sting of my near miss with the outing to Mohican Park two weeks earlier was still raw. There was nothing for it. I'd have to put off the revelation for which I'd been searching a couple more hours.

"Book and shirt," I said, headed into the house. "Got it."

Peirce was gone when I rushed out a minute later. Just as well. I'm terrible at small talk.

257

47

COLUMBUS HAS FIVE MAJOR HOSPITAL systems, and until that night I'd been in all but one of them. Sometimes for myself, sometimes for a friend, sometimes for an enemy. Twice for a birth, one per ex-wife. All of them, that is, except, for some inexplicable reason, St. Clare Sisters Health System on the northeast side. The same outfit that sponsored Lucy and Roy's expeditions into homeless camps. As they say, first time for everything.

Turns out Joe's hand was sprained, not broken, which possibly saved me a trip back in front of a judge on a child custody hearing in the near future. Sprained, not by anything to do with wall climbing, which was run by such a safety-conscious business it appeared to me closer to wall hoisting, but by the mandatory roughhousing in the parking lot at the pizza place afterward involving Joe, Mike, and two other boys.

It was nearly 11:30 by the time I got Joe back to his mother's house, Mike back to *his* mother's house, and myself back to German Village. I found a place to park—miraculously, in front of my house for a change—pushed Hopalong into the backyard, opened a Black Label, sat down at my kitchen table, and plugged Samantha's phone in.

After it came to life and I'd found the photos folder, I saw right away that Samantha had taken a lot of pictures. It took several minutes of swiping the screen back and forth until I found the video I was looking for. I sat back and pressed the "Play" arrow. After so long investigating Dorothy Custer's tip about her grandson, it was surreal to watch the event unfold. Surreal, and yet heartbreaking, since there was no mystery about the outcome.

The first few seconds were just of the house, with nothing happening. Twigs and leaves kept jutting in and out of the screen. Samantha must have hidden behind the bushes on the lawn across the street, as I'd surmised. Then a figure skulked into view. Skinny, dark clothes. Baseball cap. Columbus Red Birds. Just like his grandmother had said. Aaron. Had Samantha hidden from him, mistaking him for one of the louts she said she'd followed up High Street after the camp was rousted?

As I watched, my heart starting to race, Aaron half walked, half stumbled up the steps from the sidewalk to the yard, the plastic jug of gasoline in his left hand. He approached the steps of the house, stopped, then looked up at the porch, almost as if he were waiting for someone to open the door. He swayed once, then walked the rest of the way up. Once on the porch, he twisted the lid off the jug, swayed again, then splashed the gas onto the porch. He turned to the couch as if seeing it for the first time, and soaked it. He swayed more, then opened the unlocked door, half disappeared inside, poured some more. The coup de grâce, I thought. The fuel that helped the fire shoot up the stairs like flames up a chimney. He backed out of the house. Went down the steps. Stood on the lawn. Swayed again. Poured the rest out on the grass. Seemed to hesitate. Collected himself. Then he carefully tightened the lid back onto the empty jug, dropped it on the ground, and pulled something out of the pocket of his sweatshirt. The lighter.

Then something I hadn't expected. As if Aaron's head had suddenly cleared, as if he were emerging from the fog of drink he'd spent the past few hours in. The past few years. He straightened himself. Looked around. Seemed to realize for the first time what he was doing. Backed away from the house. Started to put the lighter back in his pocket. He was having second thoughts. More than that. Giving it up. I was just taking in the significance of this moment, that he might really be innocent, that the baseball cap and Eddie Miller and the witness might all have been legitimate, when his head cocked. He heard something. Looked around. Looked at the house. Then, faster than I would have predicted, he stepped back, looked around again, dropped the lighter into the yard, and started to run.

The camera followed Aaron up the street, then moved back to the house. Nothing happened for almost a minute. I found myself admiring Samantha's concentration. Most others, including myself, would have stopped recording. Then, to my surprise, a figure emerged onto the porch from inside. I squinted, trying to make him out. Nothing, at first. Then—yes. Jacob Dunning. He looked around, then down, shaking his head. Reacting to the gasoline. He made as if to go back inside.

Then he stopped. A sound from the sidewalk. Someone approaching from the right. Man wearing a hoodie. Run-Run. He came up the steps to the lawn. Stopped, seeing Dunning. It was obvious he hadn't expected him. But also obvious he recognized him. Words were exchanged. Shouting, back and forth. Almost a minute's worth, the conversation angry but indistinct. At one point the guy with the hoodie looked as if he might make for Dunning. But then, gazing around, he saw the milk jug. He kicked it. Then he looked at Dunning again. And with the briefest of movements, so quick I almost missed it, pulled something from his mouth. A cigarette, unlit. His hand reached into his pocket, reemerged, a flame flickered, and then the tip of the cigarette glowed. And then, with a swift, practiced movement, he flicked it toward the porch, right toward Dunning. Flames erupted. Dunning stumbled, fell on the couch, stood up, clothes ablaze. The video image suddenly shock, as if an earthquake had hit and Samantha couldn't keep her balance. I thought of what Roy had told me. Her two little girls. What it must have been like for her to watch this. Then the picture stabilized, and for just a moment it seemed that Jacob might fall then and there. Instead he turned and stumbled back into the house. I thought back to what I'd learned at the coroner's office. Dunning would only make it a few feet before collapsing for good, too badly injured to warn anyone, his demise giving the couch time to erupt in full roar, sending its flames into the soffits above and from there into the interior walls. Meanwhile, the fire was already pushing into the house and up the stairway. I realized Dunning went to his death thinking that this gang member, Run-Run Ryan, had poured the gasoline. He never knew it was Aaron.

For his part, the man in the hoodie leaped clear to safety, taking the steps to the sidewalk in two bounds. He turned, looked once at the flames, then turned back. And just for a moment stared into the camera. I reached out and tapped the video to stop it. I took a close look. Wasn't sure I was seeing right. Looked again, and realized I was. It wasn't a guy named Run-Run or Ryder or Ian or anything close.

It was D. B. Chambers. The guy who'd called the fire in.

48

THE FIRST THING I DID WAS SOMETHING I knew I should have done days ago. I got online and tried to look up Chambers's case in Franklin County court. *Little dealing. Stupid shit,* he had said. But nothing turned up, nothing for a D. B. Because the court system didn't do initials. And there were several screens of Chamberses just for Davids and Derricks and Dustins. I looked at my watch. Nearly midnight. I thought about calling Whitestone or Fielding, but the thought of persuading them this was of crisis proportion at that time of night exhausted me. But a sense of urgency was starting to overtake me, though I couldn't have said why, exactly. Something beyond the fact I had unmasked the real Orton Avenue arsonist. I puzzled it out unsuccessfully, then gave up and made another decision. I called Suzanne's cell phone, letting it ring until voice mail picked up. I tried again, and then a third time. Nothing. I scrolled through my phone until I found Murphy's number. No answer the first time, but he answered after four rings the second time around.

"I need to talk to Suzanne. Is she there?"

"Do you know what time it is?"

"It's important. She won't pick up."

"She doesn't want to talk to you."

"Please," I said.

"You're a pain in the ass, you know that, Hayes?"

"You've pointed that out previously."

The line went silent. I thought he had hung up. Then, a moment later, Suzanne's voice.

"What the hell."

"Listen," I said. I explained what I had just seen. Suzanne might have been the most justifiably aggrieved ex-girlfriend in history, but I knew she was also a reporter at heart.

"Christ," she said. "You're sure?"

"I need you to do me a favor," I said. "I need to know what Chambers's initials stand for."

"It's not online?"

I told her about the docket.

"Could you check?" I said.

"Check?"

"The witness statements. You have them all, right? His name's gotta be on there. His full name."

"I guess. I'm supposed to be off tomorrow, but I could swing by the station. Look at the file."

"Now," I said. "Can you check now?"

A few seconds of silence.

"Now?" she said.

"We need to know."

"We?"

"You heard me," I said.

A few more seconds of silence.

"Give me an hour," she said. And hung up.

WHILE I WAITED I downloaded the video onto my laptop. Then I put it on a flash drive and locked that in my safe. I went back and watched it again. And again. Noticed that Chambers had sprinted up the street afterward. Toward Aaron? Thinking maybe he'd seen him?

I thought about Chambers. How he'd played it. Gone along with my questions. Pried me for information as I'd pried him. Remembered the question he'd asked me the first time we talked. *How's that one girl doing. Chinese girl.* I tried to put it together in my mind. Dunning starting to sell heroin. Chambers, connected with the Fourth Street Posse, trails him to the party. Warns him. Maybe returns to warn him again, but this time more seriously. But then that same question. Why was Dunning at the house to begin with? Why would he go to Matt's party, knowing how Matt felt about him? The only thing that connected them was Gridley, the very person whose relationship with Dunning set Matt against him.

Was Chambers the one who'd beat up Aaron? Worried he'd seen him?

But either way, why had Chambers called the fire in?

My phone rang. Suzanne.

"I'm at the station. I've got the files."

"Anything in there? About Chambers?"

"Looking now."

I pictured her there in the mostly abandoned newsroom, lights dimmed or off. Banks of TVs on the walls, muted, flickering images illuminating the room. I'd been there once, years earlier, when she'd shown me around. Shown me off.

"Got it," she said.

"I'm listening."

"Dwayne," she said.

"Dwayne?"

"That's right."

"Middle name?"

"Hang on."

I hung on.

"Brian," she said a minute later. "Dwayne Brian Chambers."

"Brian," I said.

"Brian."

We said it almost simultaneously: "Ryan."

"Brian, Ryan," Suzanne said. "Could that be it?"

"Tina overheard it, loud party, maybe didn't completely make it out. Has to be. It's him on the video. That part's for sure."

"What now?"

Something. Something nagging.

I said, "You're at the station?"

"Yes."

"I'm going to bring you the video."

"Now?"

"Why not? I promised it."

"Can't you e-mail it?"

"I don't think so. It's too big. I've got it on a thumb drive. Easier that way."

"I won't turn it down."

How's that one girl doing. Chinese girl.

"How long do you think it'll take you to get here?"

"What?" I said.

"How long will you be? I should let Glen know what's going on."

"That ain't brave. That's stupid. She's living on Orton?"

"Andy?"

"Woodruff," I had said. "One down from the corner."

"Oh, shit," I said.

"What?"

My conversation with Chambers from earlier today came back to me. I looked at the time on my computer. Yesterday. Our conversation yesterday.

"Brave girl," I'd said. "Living around the corner from the fire."

"That ain't brave. That's stupid. She's living on Orton?"

"Woodruff. One down from the corner."

Chambers knew where Helen Chen lived. The one person Chambers, who didn't know about the video, thought could link him to the fire. Could potentially put him in the house.

"I've got to make a call," I said.

"What?"

"I'm sorry. I just figured something out."

"What?"

"I'll call you right back."

"The video," she said. "You promised."

"One minute," I said.

I hung up and scrolled through my contacts. Found Helen's number. Called, my heart beating fast. No answer. Nothing to worry about, I told myself. Maybe she was asleep. Maybe she was burning the midnight oil in a study carrel. Maybe she was just out late someplace—she was a college student, after all. No biggie.

That must have been what Chambers was up to all along, once I contacted him. Trying to see if Helen remembered seeing him. His role as the guy who called the fire in hadn't mattered at the time, not with Aaron in custody two days later and confessing almost immediately. But now, thanks to the late Eddie Miller, things were different. And Chambers knew that. Knew there was a witness he needed to take care of.

"Shit," he had said. "That's amazing she recovered like that."

I tried Helen again. No answer. And again. Then, thinking about it, I called Lori. Same luck. Left a message. Did it mean anything? It was approaching 1 a.m. Time was I'd be catching a second wind right around then myself. College kids. No big deal.

I wasn't fooling anyone. I put my phone in my pocket, grabbed my coat and keys. I would just drive there, despite the hour. Worst that could happen was I would wake them up. We could decide what to do at that point. But at least I would know Helen was safe. I would call Suzanne on the way, arrange to drop off the thumb drive. Or she could meet me at

Helen and Lori's. Or even the doughnut shop around the corner. Why not?

I walked through my living room and into the hall and threw open the front door. And stopped.

Standing in front of me was Appletree Energy's director of corporate security.

"Where the hell you think you're going?" Peirce said, as he stepped forward and pushed something small and hard into my chest. Too late, I heard a sound like a mosquito hitting a bug zapper.

Except the bug being zapped was me.

49

"STAND UP," A VOICE SAID.

I opened my eyes. Looked around. Looked up. Peirce was standing over me, stun gun in his hand. I tried to move, realized my hands and feet were tied. And a rope was around my neck. I struggled, tried to get up. As I did, Peirce reached forward and pulled on the rope, and I felt myself rising up, choking, as he lifted. I was standing in front of my closet door. He stepped to his left, looped the rope over the door, then tied it off on the knob on the other side.

"You fuck around, I hit you with this"—the stun gun, raised in his hand—"your legs buckle and you're going to strangle yourself. Takes a long time, what I'm told. Where's the Knox No. 5 log?"

"You tased me," I said.

"And I'll do it again, like I said, and I might stay just long enough to see if what they say is true and people strangling get an involuntary hard on. It's called angel lust. Read it in a book. Answer the question."

"I, E," I said.

"What?"

"I'm thinking of your last name right now in my mind. Spelling it 'I, E.'"

The punch was quick, practiced, hard. To the right kidney. I gasped, bright lights bursting before my eyes.

"The log," he said.

Recovering, breathing deeply, I said, "Where'd you learn to hit like that? Interrogation room, up at the station?"

Another punch, just as quick, just as practiced. More stars and jolting, agonizing pain.

"Your knees are shaking a little," he said. "Rubbery. They go, you go. I just want the log."

"I don't have it."

Third punch, this time to the right kidney again. This time I blacked out from the pain. Then came to, a couple seconds later, awakened by the rope digging into my neck. Lucky—I'd been able to regain my footing. Still had use of my legs. For now.

"You had your chance," Peirce said.

"Like hell."

"At the Hilton. The other day. Earlier this evening. Plenty of opportunities."

"Raw deal," I said.

A kick to the groin. Hard, black shoes. Shit-kicking shoes. The pain bad enough that I sagged involuntarily, sweat pouring off my face, knees like water. Barely able to stand up in time.

"Log," Peirce said.

I didn't respond. Because it was slowly dawning on me. They don't know what's on it. They don't realize the log puts them in the clear. Dickinson in all his wisdom thinks it proves No. 5 caused the quake. Why they were still trying to get it.

"Don't have it," I said. "Don't know where it is."

This time, a shot to the ribs. As I struggled to stand, I could tell if he hadn't broken something, he'd gotten close. I didn't have that kind of tolerance for pain. I almost told him then and

269

there, pointed him to the document in my safe in my bedroom. But I knew Helen still had the original. And of course I'd shown it to Glen Murphy. I wasn't going to put those two in danger. Either of them—Helen for what she'd been through, Murphy for what I'd put him through with his sister and nephew and Suzanne. Not if I could help it.

If, I thought.

"Don't be a hero, Woody," Peirce said. "Just tell me."

I shook my head, afraid to try speaking.

He drew closer, and I winced at what was coming. Instead, Peirce took his right hand and pushed the stun gun between my legs. Pushed it hard.

"Shit," I said, gasping.

"Newer models shut off after a five-second pulse," he said. "Safety mechanism. Reduces the number of hopheads who die of accidental heart attacks."

I said nothing. Met his gaze.

"This is not so new. Goes until I let up. Who knows how long." He pushed it harder into my groin.

"You'll lose control of your legs," he said. "Log."

"You kill me, you don't get it."

"*Log*," he said, pushing so hard my eyes welled with tears.

"Why'd you torch my van?" I gasped.

He laughed. "That van was a piece of shit," he said. "But that wasn't me. Should have been, but wasn't."

So: Chambers. I dimly recalled telling him I was going out that morning. Looking for a can fairy. Another thing he'd pried from me, something I hadn't realized. So fixated had I been on Peirce.

If I'd figured out that day it was Chambers who'd set my van on fire—a not so subtle warning to stay clear of Orton Avenue, I was guessing—and not Peirce, I wouldn't be standing here now, rope around my neck. Contemplating a new vocabulary phrase. Angel lust. One I could have done without.

"Last time," Peirce said, jamming the stun gun so hard that by itself, not even turned on, my legs gave way just a bit.

I was about to say, "OK," screw it, I couldn't take what he was threatening, would work it out another way. And then I thought of Helen, and all she'd been through, and changed my mind, and leaned toward him, and whispered, "'I, E.'" And then I thought I was going to throw up from either the second kidney punch or the pain in my ribs or the sickening ache in my groin. And then my cell phone went off. Mellencamp's "Small Town." The actual song, of course, with that concluding line: ". . . prob'ly where they'll bury me."

Peirce took a step back, reached into my coat pocket, pulled out the phone, looked at the number, then showed it to me. Helen. He swiped the phone to answer it, then set it on speaker. He held it in front of my face with his left hand while he forced the weapon back into my groin.

"Mr. Hayes?"

"Yes." Teeth gritted.

"You called? A couple times."

"Yes."

"Is everything OK?"

Peirce pushed the device, hard. I gasped and said, "Everything's fine."

"You sure? You sound funny."

"I'm sure."

"Why were you calling?"

"Are you OK?"

"I'm fine. I was just at a party. I didn't want to carry my phone, so I left it at home."

"Smart," I said.

I relaxed just a bit. A party. Phone at home. She would be OK, assuming I could get out of this mess and get there, warn her about Chambers.

Then she said, "You think tomorrow we could deal with Matt's papers? And that log thing, about the well? I really don't want them here, and I'm afraid Lori may see the folder. She went home for the weekend, but she's coming back tomorrow. Too many memories. You know?"

"Helen—" I tried to say, but it was too late. Peirce cut the connection.

"You would have made a lousy employee," Peirce said. "Keeping secrets like that."

He stood back, and just for a minute I thought it was over, that he was going to leave me and go to Helen's and that was that. Then he hit me with the stun gun in the stomach and I convulsed and saw bright lights and my legs buckled and the rope bit hard, very hard, into my neck as I slipped and started to choke.

50

I OPENED MY EYES. I WAS LYING SIDEWAYS on the floor. In front of me, a few feet away, stood Hopalong. Staring at me like this was an everyday occurrence. Tied-up master. Game!

I shifted, struggled with my bound hands. Looked around. On the floor, off to my right, at the edge of my peripheral vision, a doorknob. I took a breath. The knob had given way. Snapped off. My weight had been too much for the old door.

I was alive because I was fat. Because somebody had smashed a beer bottle in Schiller Park that my dog had cut his paw on and my exercise had ground to a halt for a couple of months.

Funny, the way things work out.

IT TOOK A FEW minutes of inching my way through the living room and then into the kitchen, and another long minute straining to lift myself, ignoring the aches and bruises and possible cracked ribs, but eventually I found a kitchen knife and managed to cut my hands free, nicking myself only five or six times in the process. I untied my feet and then stood, shaking, nauseous and lightheaded, trying to figure out what to do next. Helen, I thought. I had to get to Helen. I looked around for my phone. No luck. Realized Peirce must have taken it. I debated what to do for about ten seconds before I headed out the door the second time that night. Much slower, this time, but no less determined.

Only one or two other cars shared Fourth Street with me as I raced north toward campus. I ran three red lights, once to the sound of an angry horn. I turned left on Sixteenth Avenue, wound my way down and around, then finally stopped someplace on Seventeenth and parked halfway up on the curb in someone's yard. I stumbled in the direction of Helen's house as quickly as Peirce's working over allowed. I swore as I turned the corner onto Woodruff and took in first, Peirce's Hummer, and second, D. B. Chambers, standing on the lawn.

I saw Chambers before he saw me, a stroke of luck which probably saved my life. The shot from the gun in his right hand went wide, and I threw myself behind a car on the other side of the street. He stood in the front yard of Helen's house, near the porch, a can of gasoline by his feet.

"You don't want to do this!" I shouted.

The second shot shattered the windows of the car I crouched behind.

"It's all over, Brian," I yelled.

"No way, Falco. No way."

"Cops'll be here any second."

"Plenty of time."

"Where's Peirce?"

"Don't know any Peirce."

"Guy driving the Hummer."

"Guy driving the Hummer's inside with a bullet in him."

"We can work this out, Brian."

"Not an option, Falco. And quit calling me that."

"There's a video," I said.

"What?"

"There's a video of the Orton Avenue fire. I've seen it. You shouted something at Jacob Dunning, then flipped a cigarette onto the porch."

"Bullshit."

"You do this, they've still got you for Orton Avenue."

"You're lying."

"You were wearing a hoodie. Dunning called you an asshole. It's all there."

"Bullshit." But sounding less certain.

"Dunning was on your turf. You came to send him a message. Maybe kill him. But you smelled the gasoline, decided to take care of him that way instead."

"Fuck you, Falco."

Third shot of the night. Car's right rear tire blown out.

"He was asking for it," Chambers said.

"Asking to die?" I shouted. "I don't think so."

"Bullshitting me. Said he hadn't come to sell."

"That's true."

"That's bullshit."

"Maybe you should have listened to him."

"Listened to the bullshit he was spinning me instead? Like I'm some kind of idiot?"

"What did he say?"

"Told me he was looking for something. Something some guy who lived there had."

Looking for something?

"Like I had time for that kind of crap."

Something some guy had.

"Looking for what?"

"Some paper. Total bullshit."

Some paper.

Dunning had been looking for the log. Gridley must have sent him over. Who better than Dunning to crash a party like that? Not welcome, and yet, for kids like Eric Jensen, very welcome. Gridley couldn't have known the Fourth Street Posse was keeping an eye on Dunning for different reasons. That he'd attract the wrong kind of attention to the party.

Gridley had inadvertently caused the murder of three people in his desperation to recover the log. Add their deaths to Kim McDowell's? A point I'd raise with Fielding. Assuming I lived through the night.

"You the one that beat up Aaron?" I shouted.

"No more questions, Falco!"

"I'll take that as a yes."

"Had to be sure," he said. "Might have seen me."

"That why you called 911? Cover your ass?"

"Wasn't me, Falco."

"What?"

"Custer grabbed my phone. Called when he was on the ground. Right before I started beating his head in. Would have finished the job, too."

"What stopped you?"

"Got interrupted."

"By who?"

"One of your can fairies, Falco."

The ultimate irony. Aaron, the guy serving life for the fire deaths, had called 911 with the real killer's phone. Another thing to tell Fielding. I glanced around the corner of the car. I'd gotten Chambers talking, which was good. The subsequent lack of gunshots was also good. I was thinking of something else to say, some other way to reason with him, when I saw him pull a lighter from his pocket.

That's when I remembered what Whitestone had told me. The danger of waiting too long to light gasoline. Vapors build. *See it all the time.* Chambers had been standing in the yard too long. Talking to me too much.

"No—" I yelled, but in the next instant a ball of flame erupted. I ducked, covering my eyes. When I looked again, Chambers was rolling on the grass, engulfed, screaming, and the front of the house was on fire.

51

I MADE THE STEPS TO THE PORCH IN TWO bounds, ran through flames, and got inside.

"Helen!" I yelled.

Immediately, I encountered someone on the floor. I crouched down, scooted forward and looked at the face. Peirce. I couldn't tell if he was alive or dead.

Then I heard the sound, around the corner. Between a moan and a cry. Helen.

She was collapsed half in and half out of her bedroom. Frozen with fear. I can only imagine what she must have been thinking. *Again?* Thank God she slept downstairs, I thought. Ignoring Peirce for the moment, I inched forward, keeping my head low, then reached out for her, scooping my arms beneath her shoulders and knees. I tried to lift her, then stumbled backward as a wave of pain and nausea overtook me. Peirce had done his job well. I leaned over, lowered my head, took a breath of relatively clear, smoke-free air, and tried again. I felt a wave of relief as Helen raised her arms in reaction and placed them around my neck. I stood up, faltered as the pain hit again, rested a moment, back braced on a wall, then made it all the way up. Something exploded near the front steps and singed my right cheek. I staggered forward, toward the door.

The porch directly in front of me was a wall of flame. But the lawn was just a few feet away. I didn't have any choice at this point. I went ahead, half jumped across the porch, shocked for just a moment at the heat and the bite of the flames, then tumbled down the stairs, somehow stayed standing, and reached the lawn, where I stood, swaying, pulling in great drafts of fresh air.

After a moment, I set Helen down onto the grass, then sat back and put my hands on my knees, sucking in air. I looked at her and saw that her eyes were open and she was breathing. Saying something I couldn't make out. But she was going to be OK. I glanced at Chambers where he lay, moaning, having stumbled into the next yard before collapsing. With an immense effort, I roused myself, stood up, braved the flames to get back inside, grabbed Peirce by the ankles and dragged him out and onto the steps. Best I could do. Behind me, I could hear the fire growing in size and destructiveness. In the distance, the sound of sirens. I became aware of people around us, of voices, of lights starting to turn on. I went back to Helen.

This time I caught the word through her sobs.

"Upstairs."

52

TAKING THE FRONT HALLWAY STAIRS TO the second floor was out of the question; the fire had vented straight up onto the landing between floors. That left—what? I thought back to the day I'd met with Helen in the living room. How Lori had come home, surprised by my presence Stomped out of the room. Stomped . . . upstairs. A back staircase. Other side of the kitchen. I bent over, duckwalked in that direction. Found the stairs and headed up.

She was huddled at the end of the hall, curled into a ball, covering her mouth, trying to shield herself as the cloud of smoke coming from the fire leaping up the front staircase began to descend. I reached out, touched her arm. She started, cried out, her eyes widening as she recognized me. I still had the comforter on, the one I'd wrestled from the inopportunely dressed girl outside, and I took it off now and wrapped it around her. I held her tight as we shifted and scooted toward the back stairs.

But already that way was blocked. The fire downstairs had spread faster than I'd anticipated. The kitchen, full of plastics, the fuel of modern fires, had already ignited, sending smoke up the staircase I'd climbed just a minute or two earlier. Madness to go down now. Help would be there soon enough, if it hadn't already arrived on the street, but now it was a simple calculus of time. The Columbus Fire Department prided itself on quick response. Add to that the report of a blaze anywhere near Orton Avenue and they were going to be here in no time flat. But fires burn fast, much faster than people realize. Would no time flat be fast enough?

We scooted the other direction down the hall. I despaired as I realized the air was already too hot to breathe and I could barely see from the smoke. At the last moment, we reached an open door and I pushed us both inside. Flames illuminated the interior. Tile, a white tub, aluminum legs of a sink. The bathroom. Which meant water, which might buy us a few moments. With what felt like the last bit of strength I had I lifted Lori up, then placed her inside the tub. Grabbed a towel from a rack, soaked it in the sink, then set it over her face. A little protection from the smoke even now starting to fill the room. I got down on my hands and knees. If only I could shut the door. I had almost made it, had my left hand on its corner, when something started to happen with my eyes and the smoke was suddenly overpowering, a gust from a campfire you can't hide from. I tried to breathe but took in only impossibly hot, scorching air. What was the old saying? *Smoke follows beauty?*

I lay flat, pressing my left cheek onto the cool tile floor. Pressed hard, as if by pushing myself down far enough, down into the tile itself, I'd be all right. We'd be all right. Everything would be all right.

In a dream, I heard a sound and raising my head, reluctantly, from the cool respite of the floor, saw big, black boots in the doorway.

53

I CAME TO IN A SMALL, NARROW ROOM. I reached up and felt something cold and hard and plastic over my mouth.

"Easy," someone said.

I looked up. A young man in a blue uniform with some kind of patch on the front of his shirt was staring down at me. Medical equipment on either side of him. *Ambulance,* I thought, the word coming to me. *Paramedic.*

I pulled off the oxygen mask. "Lori," I said.

Then: "Helen."

"Everyone's all right." A second voice. I raised my head. Omar Sharif, standing off to my left. "Lori and Helen. Thanks to you."

Or no thanks to me, I thought.

"Peirce," I said. "Guy on the steps."

"Not doing so well. But he'll make it. Also thanks to you?"

I didn't respond. "Chambers," I said. "On the lawn?"

This time Whitestone didn't answer.

I'D BEEN LUCKY. So had Helen. And Lori. We were all discharged from the hospital within a couple hours. Not so for Peirce, who was in a secure hospital room at the Ohio State medical center with a Columbus police officer parked outside for good measure.

Chambers lived a few hours, but his burns were too severe. He'd moved too quickly, splashed too much gasoline too carelessly, knowing his window to get this right was narrow. Nothing to be done.

It was nearly ten that morning when I finally woke up. The first thing I noticed was that I wasn't alone in bed, and my companion wasn't a yellow lab named Hopalong. Anne lay beside me, still asleep, her red hair cascading across the pillow like hair floating upward underwater. Eyes open, not moving, I thought about the trauma that Samantha Parks must have experienced watching the arson unfold that night, the memories it must have literally sparked from her own life. Little wonder she hid the phone rather than reveal the truth. Then I thought about Columbus waking up to the news that a drug dealer and not Aaron Custer had set the fire that killed three college students. Then I thought about the city learning that a college professor was equally responsible and might have a fourth murder hanging over him as well. Then I coughed, clearing smoke from my lungs, and Anne stirred. She rolled over and put her hand on my chest.

"How are you feeling?" she said.

I thought about the question.

"Happy and sad," I said.

"No need to use such big words," she said. "You saved the day. Again."

"Not yet," I said, after a moment.

"What do you mean?"

I coughed some more, and then slowly sat up. I took her hand. I cleared my throat.

"Aaron Custer," I said.

"Yes?"

"I finally realized who he reminded me of."

54

"WONDERFUL NEWS," DOROTHY CUSTER SAID when she greeted me at her door a couple of hours later.

"Undoubtedly," I said.

Karen Feinberg and Gabby Donatelli were already in the living room, sitting on the couch, as Dorothy escorted me in. She took the chair where I had sat three weeks earlier, the day she told me about Eddie Miller.

"Here you go, Andy," Gabby said, patting a space beside her.

"I'll stand," I said.

"It's been all over Channel 7," Dorothy said.

That it had. Suzanne had pulled out all the stops, and the other stations were breathing her fumes. In addition to the exclusive interviews she'd already scored with Samantha and the family members of the students who'd been killed, she still had Samantha's video by herself, since Columbus police had not received their own copy until an hour or so ago, and were not releasing it yet.

Just as I'd planned.

"So Aaron will be coming home," Dorothy said.

"Not right away," I said. "Things have to happen first. Has to be a motion to set aside the conviction. Prosecutors are going to look hard at the fact he doused the house with gasoline. He could still face serious charges."

"But not life in prison."

"Probably not," I said.

"So it's going to be all right," she said.

"*Old Hickory and Young America*," I said.

"What?"

"Your husband's book."

"What about it?"

"Frank altered the will. Directed the royalties to Aaron. And the movie rights."

A look of surprise crossed Dorothy's face. She didn't say anything.

"I missed the significance of that at first," I said.

"There is no significance," Dorothy said. "It is what it is."

"On the surface, maybe. But he did that against your wishes."

She said nothing.

"Without telling you, in fact. Right after the accident."

"That's none of your business."

"He did it because of what Molly had told him," I continued. "Or Mary, as she calls herself. When she worried he might not make it."

I looked at Gabby again. "Most of it's spelled out in your personal bankruptcy filing. Frank's medical bills and home health aides drained your savings, and his retirement income wasn't enough to restore your funds."

"That's not your concern."

"Actually, it is," I said. "That's because you needed the money left to Aaron. But as long as he remained in prison, it was a target for family members of the victims of the Orton Avenue fire. As soon as they found out about it. Until a couple of months ago, that was a foregone conclusion. It would have taken a court battle, but what judge would have sided against the families? But when you found out about Miller, everything changed. If Aaron's innocent and out of prison, challenging the codicil is much easier."

"That's not true," Dorothy said.

"You needed Aaron to be innocent to survive financially," I said.

"Nonsense."

"And that galled you, didn't it? To have him proved innocent. Because of what he meant to you."

"Meant? He's my grandson. I was the only one willing to take this on."

"Yes, he is," I said. "But he wasn't Frank's grandson, was he?"

"What are you talking about?"

"I couldn't figure out who Aaron reminded me of, the time I met him in prison. I knew I'd seen him before. Then I saw a picture of Mike, when I went to visit Molly. I mistook him for Aaron. They were like brothers."

I tried to meet her gaze. She looked away.

"But that's where I had it wrong, wasn't it? They weren't like brothers. They *were* brothers."

"No."

"What triggered it was looking at the dust jacket for Frank's book. His picture on there. I didn't realize it at the time. He's the spitting image of Aaron."

"Why wouldn't they be?" Dorothy said.

"This was the truth Molly told your husband, after the accident. What made him change the will."

"No." But so softly I could barely hear her.

"The secret she'd lived with all those years."

Dorothy sat silently, hands in her lap.

"Aaron was Frank's son," I said. "Wasn't he? Fathered with his former student, Molly. Or should I say Mary, his name for her. An affair outside of class that lasted until she married Mike? Or was it a lapse, one last fling?"

"Does it matter?" Dorothy said.

"And Molly kept it hidden all those years. Until the end. When she felt Frank had to know. And that's what finally got to Mike, wasn't it? Because she had to tell him too. Tell him the truth about Aaron."

"She didn't have to do that," Dorothy said.

"Learning the truth about his son, and then learning that his father had changed the will. Because Frank thought that with Aaron, he had a beneficiary he could count on. Not like his other son. The one who could never measure up."

Dorothy said nothing.

"It wasn't his business going under," I said. "He couldn't bear his father's betrayal."

Dorothy stayed silent for a few moments longer. Then she said, "Such a Custer."

"What?"

"I told him a thousand times to slow down. He never listened."

I didn't say anything. I didn't have to. I'd looked up Frank Custer's driving record that morning. Multiple speeding tickets over the years.

"He never listened," Dorothy said. "Custers never do."

55

I'D HAD MY FILL OF DOMESTIC TRANQUILITY and left the house a minute later. I was leaving it to Gabby to drop the final bomb: that she had heard through Janet Crenshaw that the victims' families were already making plans to pursue the bequest on the grounds that Aaron was still guilty, at the very least, of attempted murder. And if that didn't work out, Crenshaw had the civil lawsuit against the realty company to keep her busy. Grudgingly, she'd admitted that the information I'd forwarded her that day in her office about the smoke alarm batteries—that they were knockoffs with a tenth of their advertised duration—might be useful to her cause.

In any case, I had one more thing to do. And believe it or not, it was going to be the hardest conversation of the day.

SUZANNE ANSWERED ON THE second ring.

"I'm a little busy right now," she said. "You won't believe how crazy it is. I just got off the phone with *60 Minutes.* But what's up?"

"I need one more favor," I said.

"Of course. Anything."

"It's a big one."

"Forget it. Shoot."

I told her what I wanted.

There was a long pause.

"No," she said at last. "Anything but that."

"You can do it," I said.

"No. I can't. I just can't."

"You have to," I said. "We have to. It's the only way. I've thought it out."

"You've thought it out? You?"

"You heard me."

"I won't do it."

"Yes, you will."

"No."

"Pretty please?" I said.

The phone went quiet, and for a moment I thought that, once again, she'd hung up on me. Then I heard a sound and realized she was crying.

It's a gift, this way I have with women.

56

I GROANED WHEN JOHN MELLENCAMP'S voice awakened me from a dead sleep the next morning. I rolled over, looked at the phone. Five a.m. I couldn't figure out what was happening. My kidneys and ribs and groin ached from Peirce's beating. My throat hurt from the smoke I'd inhaled. My heart was pinched from the look on Dorothy Custer's face as I'd left her house, and my stomach was roiled in anticipation of what I'd told Suzanne. So why in the world was I awake so early? I lay back and collected my thoughts. Then sat up quickly. I remembered what day it was.

And then I remembered something else. I'd been dreaming, just before I woke up. Dreaming about Anne.

I made it to her parents' house by 6:15. She was waiting just inside the front door and came out as soon as the lights of the rental hit the garage. She was wearing a dark training suit and carrying a bag of supplies.

"Good day for a run," I said.

"Chilly," she said nervously.

I dropped her off as close to the start of the half marathon at Broad and Front as I could get before the cops turned me away. Start almost exactly by the Neil House Inn. I kissed her on the cheek and wished her good luck. She returned the gesture with a real kiss, put her hand on my own cheek, and said, "Nice job not getting killed."

"Thanks," I said.

"Because I would have killed you myself if you hadn't been around to cheer me on today."

"Comforting," I said.

I parked in a surface lot south of Main, unloaded my bike, rode back to Front for the start, then began riding north as fast as I could. I was still out of shape and my aforementioned aches and pains weren't helping, but, mindful of Anne's chipper farewell, I knew it was not a day for excuses. Pedaling furiously around town for the next ninety minutes or so, I was able to see her at three different points of the race, including the loop around Schiller Park in German Village, where I cheered hardest of all. A few minutes later, as I watched her charge up High toward the finish at Columbus Commons, a look of determination on her face I recalled from my own past, I allowed myself a quick, hopeful thought about our future together. She finished in well under two hours. Top ten in her age group. We toasted her effort with cups of Gatorade in the park, where we met up with her parents and Amelia.

"Bravo," I said.

"I can hardly wait to run it next year," she said.

"That's great," I said.

"Because next year," she said, wrapping her arm around my waist, "we're doing it together."

57

YOU WOULDN'T THINK POLITICS WOULD come into play with a cause as noble as housing the homeless. Yet divisions in philosophies regarding the best way to approach the problem, coupled with splits in strategies over funding, had plagued local efforts for years. The whole enterprise seemed destined for disaster until a decade earlier, when the warring parties came together over the creation of a separate development wing for fundraising. Even that wasn't problem-free, with heated arguments over the name of the thing. But though the title that was proposed was a mouthful, no one came up with anything better, and so Raising Optional Opportunities Foundation, or ROOF, came into being. Soon its annual May gala was a must-attend event on central Ohio's social calendar.

By noon Saturday Suzanne had called twice to back out. Both times I talked her down. I never directly said she owed me, although I could have gone that route in fairly good conscience. *60 Minutes* was the tip of the iceberg of the attention she was getting, starting with appearances on all the major cable news stations, a trip to New York the following week for

Good Morning America, talk of a made-for-TV movie and a book deal. Not to mention rumblings of another Emmy.

There was also the other little matter pertaining to D. B. Chambers, which had come out in the hours after his death hit the news. People had started talking. The Happy Meals he'd been selling at McDonald's had contained more than toys. If customers knew the code words, they got a baggie of heroin along with their McNuggets. Chambers may have graduated from the Fourth Street Posse, but trying to take care of his daughter, he hadn't gotten very far. Suzanne broke that story too, in time for the 11 p.m. Friday newscast.

At 3:30 Saturday afternoon I picked up my rental tux. At 4:00 I walked into Zettler's Hardware on Main to run an overdue errand. I picked up Anne at her parents' at 5:00 and at 5:30 sharp arrived at the Columbus Athenaeum, an old Masonic lodge pulling duty these days as wedding and banquet reception central downtown. I got out, handed my keys to the red-shirted college kid on valet duty, walked around to the other side, and opened the door for Anne. She exited nimbly, scarcely showing the effects of the race, wearing a purple dress with a black belt and silver earrings. I was moving not so nimbly and promised myself for the umpteenth time that day that injured dog or not, I was turning over a new exercise leaf on Monday.

Murphy pulled up a minute later, and we stood on the sidewalk while he performed the same routine with Suzanne. She was wearing pearls, black pumps, and a sleeveless red dress that fit her like a smile on a wedding day and that I hadn't seen her in for a long, long time. Since the last time we'd been at the Athenaeum together, as a matter of fact.

"In for an inch," she said, reading the look on my face.

WE WALKED UP THE front steps together, Suzanne and I, her arm in mine, as I'd suggested. Anne and Murphy were right behind us. Once inside, through the oak-paneled lobby, down the hall, then upstairs to the big theater space, round tables filling the room, jazz combo on stage. Room got a little quiet as we entered. Phones rose in some of the braver hands to capture the moment. Flashes from a real camera went off. I moved us farther inside, making sure everyone saw us. Then I turned and walked us to the bar, a long, slow, deliberate stroll. It seemed to last my whole life up to that point. I could feel Suzanne trembling beside me. I got us both a glass of white wine. Murphy and Anne did the same. About that time Roy and Lucy approached, and each got a beer. Then we all clinked glasses as a ballroom full of people gawked.

"Appetizer?" I said.

"Love one," Suzanne said.

She moved toward the tables where the food was laid out. I put my hand out gently.

"Why don't you let me bring you something?" I said.

"Why?"

I nodded in the direction of the crowd beginning to surge toward her.

IT HAD BEEN A few years back when everything went to hell between Suzanne and me. At that other ROOF ball.

And for the record, I don't really blame the kid who filmed it all.

We'd been at Lindey's, as a matter of fact, when I proposed. Before heading to that year's gala. The rock was big, three carats, and it sparkled the way big rocks do. Suzanne looked fantastic that night. I was happy, very happy, as I slipped the ring on her finger, but in the old, entitled way. Happiness with a dash of swagger. People in the restaurant greeted my proposal and Suzanne's acceptance with light applause.

After arriving at the ball we'd had more drinks. The people who knew who I was treated me the way they always did at such events, polite with an undercurrent of disdain. The ones who didn't just ignored me. Neither category of people could get enough of Suzanne. The combination of her looks, her charm, her growing celebrity as a reporter—and that night, the ring on her finger—drew small, excited crowds. I was pleased for her. Pleased with a dash of swagger.

After a while, I found myself on the edge of the chattering circles. Understanding, at first. But then a little resentful. Soon, more than a little peeved. And then I was alone by the bar.

That's when I saw her. Blonde, curvy in an athletic way, wearing a smashing little black dress. I bought her a drink. Why not? It's not like I was needed at the moment. She was chatty. Didn't seem to know who I was. One of the Columbus Crewzers, the dance squad that cheered on the city's professional soccer team at halftime. Cheering a bit of a euphemism for their dance moves. Since disbanded, but still around in those days. Yes, they were. She was there with a player, a Brazilian midfielder in the twilight of his career but still rich enough and good-looking enough to keep girls like that on his arm. Like Suzanne, he'd been corralled by well-wishers. Now his date, like me, was alone by the bar. Except we were together.

Somehow we ended up stepping outside the hall. Toward the cloakroom. Then into the cloakroom. And suddenly we were doing more than chatting. I told myself it was wrong, but the entitlement trumped all. *How dare I be relegated to the periphery? After what I spent on that ring?* And of course, the dress. That little black dress.

Like I said, I don't blame the kid. He had his instructions. Film mini-interviews with all the celebrities. Which I guess I still was at that point. Saw me leave, followed me out, didn't put two and two together. Camera running, captured Suzanne stalking out of the ballroom. Beelining for the cloakroom. Had someone tipped her off? Or did she just know me too well? Doesn't really matter. He got it all. Suzanne shouting at me. At the Crewzer. The Crewzer shouting back. The Brazilian's arrival. More shouting, on all sides. Then the ring comes off Suzanne's finger and flies through the air and bounces off my chest and the camera follows Suzanne in tears as she runs from the lobby. Wearing the same red dress she's wearing tonight.

And then the long, slow pan back to me.

It's gotten 4.2 million views to date. Apparently some kind of record.

SUZANNE TOOK A SMALL step back. People were flocking toward her. Toward the woman who broke the story, the real story, about the Orton Avenue fire.

"I'm not sure I can handle this," she said.

I leaned a little closer, smelled the fragrance I still remembered from all those years ago, thought about something from our time together, then kissed her on the cheek.

"You were born to handle this," I said. I turned and guided her by her elbow toward Murphy. They took a few steps forward and soon were enveloped by fans. I took a last look at Suzanne. Then I felt an arm through mine and turned and smiled at Anne.

"Wouldn't mind an appetizer myself," Anne said. "Half marathon and all, you know."

"Top ten in your age group," I said. "You deserve something special."

"Darn straight."

"Reminds me."

"Yes?"

I reached into the left inside pocket of my tux. Anne's eyes widened in what might have been alarm but might have been something else, too. The opposite of alarm. Tucking that thought away for the moment, I pulled out the house key I'd had copied at Zettler's that afternoon, now residing on an Ohio State keychain.

"It's about time," I said, handing it to her.

"Wow," she said. "Sure about this?"

"Sure," I said.

She held it up, examining it. "Any video cameras around?"

"Probably. Every Tom, Dick, and Harry has one on his cell phone now."

"Good," she said, putting her arms around my neck, then pulling me close. "I expect a full in-box by tomorrow morning."

Acknowledgments

Many of the places in *Slow Burn* are real, but not all. You'll look in vain for Neil House Inn on Front Street, although there was a Neil House for decades around the corner on High. William McKinley stayed there when he was governor, and he used to wave across the street to his wife, Ida, each morning from the Statehouse. There is an Orton Hall at Ohio State but no Orton Avenue nearby. There's also no such place as Pendergrass Research, although people have been known to joke about frozen aliens in the basement of Columbus's Battelle Memorial Institute. No Columbus homeless camp is named Spring Street, but such camps sit on the outskirts of downtown, some no more than a fifteen-minute walk from City Hall.

There is also no Knox No. 5 injection well, but the connections between storing fracking waste and earthquakes are real and established, including the 2011 quakes around Youngstown. I'm grateful to Jeffrey Dick, chairman of the Youngstown State University Department of Geological and Environmental Sciences, and Larry Wickstrom of Wickstrom Geoscience in Columbus for educating me about injection wells and piggy-back logs and permeability; any errors in that realm are strictly mine. Rodney Pevytoe, an arson investigator with Kubitz and Associates in Wisconsin, generously explained the science behind arson fires. Thanks also to Columbus police sergeant Rich Weiner for helping me understand how a fatal arson investigation like this might unfold. Similarly, I'm appreciative of the information our friend Scott Mackey, an emergency room doctor and, like Andy, a German Village dweller, provided about injuries suffered by smoke-inhalation victims and victims of head trauma.

I'm indebted to Gillian Berchowitz, director of the Ohio University Press, for her long-time support, and where *Slow Burn* is concerned, for her valuable recommendations after reading a first draft. The press's managing editor, Nancy Basmajian, shepherded the manuscript with her usual finesse. Press production manager Beth Pratt has produced another fine cover, while marketing pros Jeff Kallet and Samara Rafert are peerless in their efforts promoting my work. I'm grateful as always to copy editor John Morris and his suggestions, corrections, and good humor. Finally, a fist bump to my friend Pete Brown, who reminded me that Keanu Reeves had a second career playing ex–Ohio State quarterbacks.

I read a bunch of Erle Stanley Gardner's Perry Mason mysteries as a kid, thanks to my mother, Mary Anne Huggins, who kept them around from her beach reading days. My late father, Richard Huggins, leaned toward thrillers, historical fiction, and those saber-toothed-tigerskin rippers, the Clan of the Cave Bear books. I owe so much to their support and inspiration.

Slow Burn involved a lot of early morning and weekend stints at the computer. My wife, Pam, encouraged and instructed me along the way, both when it was going well and when it was going not so well. She was a cheerleader for a day decades ago, but she has been my chief booster in every way since. I'm continually grateful for her support.